D1012728

AL DENTE'S INFERNO

AL DENTE'S INFERNO

STEPHANIE COLE

BERKLEY PRIME CRIME
New York

BERKLEY PRIME CRIME
Published by Berkley
An imprint of Penguin Random House LLC
penguinrandomhouse.com

Copyright © 2020 by Shelley C. Bloomfield
Recipe copyright © 2020 by Shelley C. Bloomfield
Penguin Random House supports copyright. Copyright fuels creativity, encourages
diverse voices, promotes free speech, and creates a vibrant culture. Thank you for buying
an authorized edition of this book and for complying with copyright laws by not
reproducing, scanning, or distributing any part of it in any form without permission.
You are supporting writers and allowing Penguin Random House to continue to
publish books for every reader.

BERKLEY and the BERKLEY & B colophon are registered trademarks and
BERKLEY PRIME CRIME is a trademark of Penguin Random House LLC.

ISBN: 9780593097793

First Edition: February 2020

Printed in the United States of America
1   3   5   7   9   10   8   6   4   2

Cover art by Brandon Dorman
Cover design by Judith Lagerman
Book design by George Towne

*For Walker, Evie, and Barrett,
with great love*

1

Twenty minutes after the train deposited me on a warm, deserted platform in Camucia-Cortona, Italy, I was still waiting for my ride. The small station building was made out of brick that looked like it had been swiped from a time when Elvis was still alive and, better yet, sexy. Overhead a plexiglass awning was cloudy with age, and the clock mounted high on the brick wall, which was missing its minute hand, said it was noon. Maybe the guidebooks were right: In beautiful Tuscany, time stops.

Here in this corner of Italy, where bestsellers would lead you to believe that the sun always shone on colorful lizards and clever you, why did I feel like I was back in Weehawken, New Jersey, where I'd lived for a year after college just to get away from my parents for a while? Seven years later, not much had changed. I was still living, on and off, in Weehawken. And I was still trying to get away from my parents.

Maybe, I thought as my eyes swept this place, I had finally managed it.

For one quick moment I caught sight of a slim man dressed in jeans, wraparound sunglasses, and a black T-shirt leaning against a boxy old gray Fiat. With his arms crossed, he seemed to be looking my way, but when he didn't make a move, I figured he wasn't my ride. Still, I was the only one at the station, and it was several hours until the next train. Suddenly nervous, I patted the theft-proof shoulder bag I had bought at a paranoid traveler shop back home.

With a quick zip, I groped my way through my passport, wallet, phone, lipstick, travel-sized mouthwash, earbuds, and cheesy book for the flight—had I actually forgotten to pack a photocopy of my passport in my suitcase? Squatting, I fumbled with the suitcase, flung it open, and jammed my hand inside my chef's toque, my fingers ruffling the photocopied papers. This was good news. Maybe, after all, I had the packing skills of a true adult.

When I locked my suitcase back up, and pulled it—and my Coach Metropolitan Briefcase that had cost me more than a month's rent—closer to my leg in some kind of crazy safety move, I realized the slim man in jeans and wraparounds was gone. So was the boxy old Fiat. Maybe he'd been waiting for a traveler who had never arrived. I stretched and indulged myself in the thrill of the days and weeks ahead. I was meeting my culinary hero, Chef Claudio Orlandini—no, more than that, I was going to work for him. That day in mid-September, when I arrived to take up my new job, was momentous.

So what if the sky in Tuscany was a white gloom and even the soft rain seemed to question its reason for being? So what if almost as far as I could see there were no people, no stray dogs, no tourist information kiosks? For that matter, it seemed to me, as I whirled to check out the landscape and tripped over my own suitcase, this Camucia-Cortona train station had been set down in a field erupting with weeds, a field too small to pave, too big to maintain.

Who knew an hour and a half southeast of Florence, by train, could be so totally . . . anywhere?

Just then a harsh, steady sputtering caught my ear and I watched what looked like a souped-up Vespa approach the station. When it swung around and came to a stop on the edge of the grassy lot, I could see it wasn't much bigger than a Smart car, but had a flatbed attached. With one wheel in the front and two in the back, this little vehicle looked like a motorized tricycle. It had round headlamps that give it a cheerful, can-do look, and it gleamed at me in baby blue soft lines.

The man who stepped out of this contraption lost no time striding across the field toward me, scowling. Considering he was wearing tan work pants and a dazzling white shirt open at the collar, he looked official, like he had every intention of finding out just what I had done with all the dogs in Cortona.

"Ornella Valenti?" he hollered.

"Sì, sì," I hollered back. Feeling braver, I launched into one of my *Italian for Idiots* handy phrases. *"Mi chiamo Nell Valenti."* I gave myself a B+ for inflection. In Italian, every phrase needs to sound as though you're announcing the week's Powerball winner.

The man stopped just short of the platform and swept a look over me—not so brief as to be insulting, but not so leisurely as to be interesting. His black hair was cut short, and his long cheeks could use a shave, getting on toward five o'clock. If you were back in high school, his dark eyes were the sort where you could debate forever whether they were hazel or brown. But I wasn't back in high school. They were hazel.

Looking past me at the deserted platform, he tipped his head this way and that as though he was deciding against his better judgment to give me a try. Sighing soundlessly, he thrust out a hand. "Pierfranco Orlandini," he said with a little lift of his chin.

I shook his hand and was about to launch into some well-rehearsed Italian small talk about how much the red skirt costs when he added in excellent English, "Call me Pete." At my look of surprise, he smiled. "Four years at Cornell."

"Ah," I said winningly. Sometimes my English is second only to my Italian.

"Plus another four knocking around Chicago and L.A." He added: "Chef is my pop."

With that, the man scowled at a crumpled candy wrapper on the train tracks, and I shot a pensive look at a cloud that looked very much like a lopsided vase I had made in pottery class two years ago. All of a sudden Pete Orlandini swiped my suitcase and took off.

For one bad moment, I thought he was stealing it. *"Aspetti!"* I cried, springing after him through the tall grass, remembering all the Tuscan vipers, adders, and asps one travel writer cheerily noted "probably won't kill you." Call Me Pete reached the baby blue vehicle just ahead of me and, with great attention, was securing my suitcase among the crates in the flatbed. "I'm sorry I was late fetching you."

"Fetching me?"

"Three years in London." He tugged at the bungee cords slung across my suitcase. "Our local vintner"—he shot me a quick look—"is a talker." He said it affectionately.

I smiled. "And after London?"

He smiled back. "Three years in New York."

"More knocking around?"

"Culinary school, restaurant jobs. You know the life."

Nodding, I turned slowly in the light rain, catching my breath, suddenly smelling the wild flowers I had trampled. It was the sharp scent of what I think of as edible pine tar—my good kitchen friend rosemary, with its silvery spears and pale blue violet flowers. There was hardly anything I got the notion to cook that wasn't improved by rosemary.

I pinched a sprig, nibbling it lightly between my front teeth, and felt like the Connecticut I had left behind wasn't really four thousand miles away. In both places, the sound of raindrops pecking the tall grass settled my heart. This place wasn't home, but if I closed my eyes I could be back in Gristmill Falls, hidden in the gentle Berkshires, where, back in the spring, I had turned a commercial kitchen into a farm-to-table cooking school at the Prajna Retreat Center and fallen into an ill-fated six-month relationship.

Pete Orlandini pulled a rustling tarp over my suitcase and tucked it in like a father putting a child to bed. *"Grazie,"* I said, taking in his tan work pants that looked soft from use. His cuffs were tucked loosely into a battered old pair of muck boots, the kind I used to wear back in Connecticut while I developed the cooking school that had somehow gotten the Orlandinis' attention.

As he leaned toward me, his arm swept over the baby blue truck. "As you would say"—he shot me a tight-lipped smile—*"andiamo."*

I climbed into the passenger's side of the little two-seater and noted, when Pete slid in, that there was very little real estate between the passenger's side and the driver's side. Forget bucket seats. Forget seat belts. Jammed against each other as we were, if he had a sudden heart attack, I could drive us to safety without climbing over him. Baby Blue blurted, lurched, sprang, and off we went, one of my hands gripping what passed for a dashboard, the other gripping his shoulder. "You run the villa on this"—I couldn't find an accurate word—"tricycle?"

Pete gave me a wounded look. "This is the Ape." He pronounced it *Ah-pay*. For a brief moment, his hands left the steering wheel to make one of those large, sweeping Italian gestures that leave no room for discussion. My heart stopped. Then his eyes got dreamy. "In many ways," he murmured, his hands stroking the steering wheel again, "the Ape *is* the Villa Orlandini." This little souped-up Vespa? The villa? What about the world-renowned chef who made a *pomodoro* sauce so exquisite you never had to make dinner reservations in Rome?

Just shy of joining the traffic, we hit a pothole too fast, and I was flung across Pete in a manner I was proud to say had never entered my dating life. Not in cars, at any rate. *"Scusi,"* I choked at him, trying to push myself off the man. *"Eccomi."* I gurgled, regaining my half of the seat and spreading my hands. "Behold me," I thought I had said, with the subtext going something along the lines of *Look at yourself, Nell, you silly jackass,* not caring whether Pete asked me what in the name of his pop's holy *vitello all'Orlandini* I was talking about.

"Scusi," he flung over his shoulder at me—his head out the window like a big, friendly dog sniffing the air on the way to the Grand Canyon—then swerved to get us into traffic. There was some honking of horns, which Pete seemed to interpret as *Cool car, man!* Sure enough, as an old red Alfa Romeo passed us, the driver kissed all five of his fingers grouped like a rosebud, then pointed at the Ape that was apparently the heart of the operations at Villa Or-

landini. Pete and the other guy shared a moment of automotive joy, and then the Alfa Romeo sleeked ahead.

He settled back into our seat, savoring. I stared straight ahead, waiting for him to light up. Then: "For as long as you're here, Nell Valenti"—he slipped me a veiled look—"I'll share her with you." With true horror, I realized he meant the Ape. At that moment, as the roadway opened up and we drove into the Tuscan hillside, I had two unsettling thoughts. For one, the beltless little Ape as my sole means of transportation. For the other, what exactly Pete Orlandini had meant when he had said *For as long as you're here.*

*I*t was the light.

And that was something I understood in my first hour in Cortona. As Pete drove in silence, I studied the landscape as the little Ape rose in my estimation. It took the swerves without side-sliding, although I had a few bad moments as I heard crates of local wine jostling in the back, and it took the hills without a sputter.

We passed olive groves and vineyards, then a plain white sign with CORTONA lettered in no-nonsense black, and slowed as we approached a grand archway in a high stone wall lavishly covered with vines. Cortona was a walled city from a time when stonework was your first line of defense against invaders. There was nothing angular about this one, and nothing predictable about the layout of the streets in this small Tuscan hillside city. Walls can wend, and streets can lead us astray. Like strangers. Like friends. And, as I'd later discover, like murder.

In the late-afternoon sunlight, I could tell the city wall sank and rose and turned in harmony with the natural landscape. When Pete mentioned it had been built in 1259, I wondered if it had done its job against invaders. Was I, in fact, just one more invader? Hired to take Chef Orlandini's small operation at his villa into a major, premier cooking school? *For as long as you're here.* What would it take? Six months, tops? Order another commercial stove or two, order another Sub-Zero refrigerator—or expand the walk-in freezer—hang more pots and pans, dedicate a couple more rooms in the way of accommodations, design a new website . . .

In my talks with the Orlandinis' lawyer in Florence, I learned that I'd be earning double what I had made from the Prajna job in Connecticut, "all" I needed to do was beef up ("biff opp") what was already in place, design a curriculum with American gastrotourists in mind, and "get the word out"—he sounded so vague on that score that I realized he had to be over fifty and had no expertise in strategic communications, the job formerly known as marketing. Twice he mentioned how I was the personal pick of Chef Claudio Orlandini to undertake this project. He would have nothing less than Nell Valenti. So I had some concerns about my culinary hero's mental health.

I gazed at the sight of sunlit Cortona, picking out the dome of the basilica, church spires, stone buildings in sand and ocher colors, slate roofs—all clustered in the smaller hills that rose higher and higher to the four-hundred-year-old fortress at the very top. We made our gentle way up winding streets through the heart of Cortona.

It was then as Pete shifted into second that I understood the Tuscan light. It was original light, when everything quietly shone. Not in a harsh brightness, but in a simple clarity. Almost as if each tree and creature and rock was the source of light itself. Before fire, smog, imperfect lanterns, and evil. And it truly took my breath away.

"It's the light," I said softly, turning to Pete Orlandini. He widened his eyes and waited. My shoulders hunched. "It's like the light before there were any shadows."

It was just the angle, I was sure, but his cheek looked like the light. And I could swear his hands on the steering wheel of the Ape were a little bit ocher. "Is that what you think?" he said softly. My eyes studied blue shutters at a window in the distance. I gave a tiny nod. At that, he sighed. "It's early days," was all he said.

T o my surprise, we headed out through a slightly less grand archway at the rear of the city wall, which seemed to disappear behind vines and housing and swells in the terrain. In other places it disappeared altogether, where it had fallen to age and force. The road just beyond the urban limits of Cortona wended sharply left, and in about two hundred yards the Ape turned into a private drive overhung with leafy boughs.

On either side of this shady entrance were dry stone gateposts bordered by pink and purple bearded irises. The flowers nearly covered a modest brass plaque mounted on the gatepost on my side of the Ape: VILLA ORLANDINI. No date of ownership, no street address. Nothing needed. And the practical, on-the-job side of me noted with relief that the entrance to the villa property was wide enough for a small tour bus.

Once we passed through the shaded entrance to the property I was surprised to see that the drive opened up pretty quickly into a kind of courtyard. Pete pulled Baby Blue over to the left of the courtyard and parked alongside a two-story stone building that was dotted with open case-

ment windows sporting a line of burnished copper window
boxes overflowing with blue verbena.

I sprang from the can-do little farm truck and took a
look around. This building connected at the rear of the
courtyard with what looked like a cloister—but open all
along the back—to the taller, grander stone building on the
right side. There the windows were long, and the center two
were stained glass barely in the path of the late-afternoon
sun. On the far side of the cloister were two or three smaller,
plainer buildings.

At the back of the courtyard were two women lounging
on a broad stone staircase scaling the side of the two-story
building with the window boxes. The older of the two, who
was sitting and snapping beans into a metal bowl, was what
we call handsome—salt-and-pepper hair pinned with practiced artlessness, a strong mouth and elegant nose, and a
chef's apron over a rose-colored dress. The younger woman,
who was leaning against the low wall of the staircase, was
lanky and boyish, dressed for farmwork in durable work
pants and a T-shirt, a floppy, broad-brimmed hat crushed in
her hand. Her short hair had green highlights, and her skin
looked weathered from the Tuscan wind and sun.

As Pete lifted my suitcase out of the Ape's flatbed, I
waited—although I wasn't sure for what exactly—against
the side of the little truck, where I picked up on the smell
of what couldn't possibly be beef stew. I stifled a laugh at
the thought of something quite so plebeian as beef stew
from the world-class kitchen of Chef Claudio Orlandini.
Something else, then, something ingenious with flank
steak, possibly, instead of chuck, and a fresh bay leaf. Like
what? When I had no answer, I cursed my lack of imagination. Staring at a beautiful cascade of nasturtiums in the

window box closest to me, I felt even sadder. Did I really think I was up to the job in this gorgeous place?

"Benvenuto alla Villa Orlandini," said a voice at my elbow. Then, in careful English, "You have arrived." It was the woman in the apron. But, close up, I could tell it was totally inadequate to call this particular person "a woman in an apron." It would be akin to calling the source of the mouthwatering smell "beef stew."

Pete weighed in. "Nell, this is Annamaria Bari, Pop's—" When he hesitated, I wondered why.

Something pained her—maybe it was the "Pop"—but then she held out a hand. "Sous-chef," she said, blinking several times. Around her ageless neck hung a small silver crucifix. Behind her, the younger woman in work pants pushed herself off the wall and started over.

I took Annamaria Bari's hand, but felt myself sliding into one of those awkward states that usually end in my saying something notable like "jeepers" or "shucks." So I fought it. Looking the Orlandini sous-chef right in her smoke-colored eyes, I said with Tarn-X brightness, "Nell Valenti. I look forward to working with you." Suddenly it felt very unclear to me where I'd land in the organizational chart. In their secret little hearts, kitchens are Camp Lejeunes, authoritarian down to their toothpicks. But technically I was developing the cooking school, taking it to what the Italian lawyer called an *"ire leffel,"* "upper floor," by which I believe he meant a higher level, so I wasn't going to be involved in the day-to-day operations of Chef's kitchen. As a chef trained at the International Culinary Center, I could pinch-hit, but Chef was the draw.

"Macy Garner." The young woman thrust out her hand, saw some dirt, shook it off, and apologized that it didn't make much of a difference, and I grinned at her sheer familiarity. "New York?" she asked me.

"Mostly Jersey, some Connecticut. You?"

"Upstate. Then, around." She opened her arms wide and beamed. "I got assigned here by Global Farm Friends about a year and a half ago and never left."

"One day we'll kick you out," said Pete, who was heading toward the cloister with my suitcase. The man always seemed to be making off with my stuff. "Whenever I give up on the olives."

"Ha!" Macy barked at him. Then she turned to me. "Which means never."

Over his shoulder Pete rattled off some Italian to the patient Annamaria, who waved him off. I smiled at the women and tried not to stumble on the flagstones. In a gesture of trust I really didn't feel, I stopped clutching my shoulder bag and darted after Pete. Annamaria cupped her hands around her mouth. "At seven is a simple meal."

A simple meal. False modesty? I stopped short. *"Grazie,"* I called back extravagantly—something just shy of "jeepers." "What will it be?" Whatever Chef was preparing, they didn't know me well enough to offer many details, but—

"Biff stoo," called Annamaria, with a tired smile.

P ast the cloister walk, I slowed at the sight of a panoramic view of a valley. In every direction, I saw miles and miles of graceful rivers cutting through green and brown hummocks of Tuscan earth. Villages and farms and roadways. Overhead, a sky of modest blue. Sometime during the ride from the train station, the drizzle had stopped and the gloom lifted. I squinted at the clouds that, like clouds everywhere, seemed motionless, but slipped boldly sideways in a wind so far aboveground we can never feel it or see it at work.

This felt like more than Tuscany to me, as Pete waited for me on the gravel path ahead. This felt like life. *For as long as you're here,* he had said. I was gazing around me at a life in these olive groves and vineyards and brilliant kitchens where I couldn't picture a big bald man, my former boyfriend Bu. Where I couldn't picture my powerful and hovering parents with their precious cable TV commodity of shrinkage for sale, my father's weekly Dr. Val Valenti brand: *My couch is your couch.*

Pete stood in the extra-wide doorway of the closest of the adjoining one-story buildings. The door itself and the wooden frame were a lovely faded red. "I've given you the Abbess's room," he said, stepping aside so I could pass him.

Inside, the air was cool, and the stuccoed walls were off-white. There was a gleaming iron headboard to a double bed with a buoyant white comforter. An armoire in a richly grained hardwood. Framed posters of the famous blues and golds of Gustav Klimt. A chaise in worn violet velvet. Glorious white pots of succulents. A piano. A hanging Victorian gilded birdcage. A vintage black Victrola on a stand. The arm had been raised from a 78 of *Rhapsody in Blue.*

"The Abbess? Was this a girls' school?"

Pete set down the suitcase. "It was built in 1587 for a small order of nuns."

"It was a convent?" I was amazed.

"Convento di Santa Veronica del Velo. Saint Veronica of the Veil."

I indicated the sensuous Klimt posters. "Not a monastic order?"

He smiled. "More recently," he went on, slipping his hands

into his pockets, "this was my mother's room. By the time she needed to be on the ground level because of the wheelchair, we had made a few modifications." He spoke simply.

Overwhelmed, I walked over to the gilded birdcage in the corner, where I fingered the thin, decorative bars. The door stood open. I liked it already. No bird. Inside, the bottom of the cage was littered with feathers of all sorts. Plain, small gray ones. Tiny iridescent blue ones. Large black quills. Bright yellows. Soft reds. Pete explained, "My mother's hobby. Whenever any of us found a feather, we'd bring it to her, and she'd set it inside. She said it was what the bird left behind when it flew off *per sempre*, for good." His fingers, sifting through the feathers, pulled out a chain with a single silver feather pendant engraved with the name Caterina. Turning it toward me, he explained, "This was hers, and we set it inside when she died." He slipped the pendant back into the birdcage.

"I'm sorry," I told him.

Pete opened his hands in a gesture that said it was what it was. *"Grazie."*

At the sound of someone calling his name, he disappeared through the open doorway.

Tossing my shoulder bag and briefcase onto the bed, I stepped outside, where Pete was pinching a few dead blooms from a large patio pot of geraniums, nodding at an old man who stood in a sleeveless undershirt about ten feet away.

He was wearing long black spandex pants and what looked like soccer shoes. White chest hairs sprang over the low neck of the undershirt. The man had skinny legs, narrow shoulders, and hairy arms. His gray hair was cut close to his head. He was tanned and was carrying what looked like a bowling bag. Pete seemed serene as the man delivered a lively one-sided account in rapid-fire Italian of something that had happened while gesturing lavishly with his arms. Some freeloading distant cousin? When he finally noticed me, his great, pale eyes narrowed and he took a step closer. "You!" he barked. Then he took a wide, challenging stance in his revealing black spandex and lowered his voice. "Are you here about the body?"

2

No!" I proclaimed my innocence on the matter of whatever body this demented soccer coach had stumbled over. "I'm here about the cooking school."

Perplexed, the man in the sweaty undershirt tried to understand me by tapping molecules of air into some familiar shape, gave up, then turned to Pete to elucidate. "Pop," he said, brushing dead petals from his hands, "this is Nell Valenti. You remember." When the other man narrowed his eyes at him, Pete went on as I stood there, stunned. "Valenti. Nell. From New York." Nothing seemed to be helping. "The cooking school. Not the body."

Grunting, the other man dug reflectively at his ear with a knuckle. "Yes, of course," he said suavely, then pointed roguishly at me. "Not the body."

"No, Chef." And since the conversation deflated right before our very eyes, I jumped in. "Jeepers, has someone—?"

"Died?" filled in Pete.

This led to some expostulations from Chef, for this was Pete's Pop, this was my brand-new employer, this was my culinary hero, my culinary crush, this middle-aged has-been ruffian, who couldn't help shouting some dramatic Italian epithets at the mere mention of death, pushing away the *malocchio*, which I didn't need *Italian for Idiots* to tell me was the evil eye.

He picked up fast on how aghast I must have been looking, so he switched to almost gaily singing "no, no, no, no, no, no, no" and punctuating these assurances with casual shakes of his sweaty head. *"Una mucca, niente di più, capisce?"* At that, he tried a smile. The right bicuspid was missing.

"A cow," Pete translated.

"You have cows?" Just how much of this farm-to-table gig was I expected to handle?

"No, but our neighbor does," said Pete. "This one died in my olive grove."

Chef Claudio Orlandini held my hand in a courtly fashion. For my part, I tried to keep from staggering. The last photo I had seen of him was in *Global Kitchen*, the premier industry periodical, but the issue must have been ten years old. At least. At that time he had leonine graying locks and actual clothing and all his teeth, and he certainly hadn't looked like a runaway from Easter Island. What had happened to this man?

"Nell Valenti," he announced for no particular reason. "Yes." Then his other hand patted our tangled fingers while he scrutinized me. "You will make my cooking school, *sì*?"

I wanted to be clear, but I managed a little smile. "I will develop your existing cooking school, Chef."

"Existing?"

"Yes," I repeated, "I will develop it."

"Not . . . make it?"

"Develop." I was still smiling.

There was a fugue-like moment between us, then he got philosophical. "Make, develop, *qualsiasi cosa, eh?*" It sounded like Italian for *po-TAY-to, po-TAH-to.* Suddenly: "You will join us in the *cappella* for a meal?" He raised my hand so slowly to his lips that I discovered what Italians consider to be suspense. A kiss like little insect feet landing. A brush, a tickle. "Annamaria I am sure will outdo herself by way of welcome—" From Chef's lips, it sounded like pillow talk.

"Pop," said Pete good-naturedly, "it's beef stew."

With a sharp inhale, Chef pressed his eyes shut. His studious expression looked like he was trying to figure out just how close to his heart this dagger had come. "That woman," he murmured. Then suddenly he sprang away from us both, his arms spread wide, little droplets of sweat seizing their chance of escape. *"Fino a cena, tutti i miei cari."* I could tell he was spinning a movie scene filled with robust life and goodness, waiting fruitlessly for the swelling music. With a shrug, he gave a joyful *"Alle docce!"* At that, he mimed scrubbing his body and I shot him a wan smile by way of encouragement. Retrieving his bowling ball bag in a manly swipe, Chef headed off down the gravel path, his body a proud jangle of uncoordinated limbs.

Pete watched him go fondly. "Today's loss was tough," he said. "He's the captain."

"Captain of what?"

"His bocce team."

I had a vision of old Italian men in baggy pants in city parks. On the one hand, it seemed a strange outlet for the world-renowned Chef Claudio Orlandini. On the other hand, maybe it gave him a bit of fresh air free from the kitchen, let him show his face around Cortona every so often to reassure the townspeople he still had the common touch. Perhaps the occasional game of bocce was a healthy thing for a chef about to rocket into the culinary stratosphere with the expansion of his cooking school into the American market. I felt indulgent. "How often does he play?" I asked Pete as Chef disappeared through the cloister.

"Oh," he told me, "pretty much full-time." With a cheery *"Ciao!"* he headed off in the other direction, calling back something about picking me up at six for a tour, then leaving me in stunned silence.

My internal organs felt like they had landed down around my ankles.

The dead cow had it good.

For an hour I tried to look at the bright side. I sat on the edge of the bed, my legs uncrossed, my hands set palms-down on my thighs in a yoga mudra I had learned at the Prajna Retreat Center during my most recent project. Bu, formally Buford Kaplan of the Albany Kaplans—which is how he put it, as if he was talking about the Newport Vanderbilts—had taught me the joys of mudras as a way of decompressing in tense situations. He joined me almost nightly in my room, where, in all honesty, I could only call his approach to sex meditative. Although the chanting brought some life to it. Not even the serene, searching Bu Kaplan could help me now. There was no mudra I could do with my floppy hands that would enlighten me about this predicament.

It appeared I had to build (make, develop, *qualsiasi cosa*) a high-end, class-and-flash cooking palazzo with a man who was rarely in his own kitchen anymore. Chef Claudio Orlandini was the brand. His brilliance, his dash, his spontaneity, his—I choked out a little sob—good looks. *Tell yourself the brutal truth, Nell:* Right now the brand smelled like a dead cow. I had set up the Prajna cooking school in six months. Here, it would take at least three months just to get his dental work done. A whole cooking school in six months? I knew it couldn't be done, so I was going to have to reason with the Orlandinis. They'd be lucky to open up for the first busload of American gastro-tourists in a year.

I clicked my tongue a few times.

I even tutted.

Somehow I had neglected to account for the human factor. I myself, who should have known better, had been seduced by the image. I, who had seduced plenty with images in this farm-to-table cooking school setup career that was growing shorter by the minute—chickens borrowed from nearby farmers, authentic big sexy farmhouse dining tables delivered by Arhaus, "local wines" about as local as the nearest Trader Joe's—I hadn't seen it coming. It was ironic. To fully understand this cosmic payback, I would need a good two glasses of wine. Did I have to wait for dinner in the *cappella*, whatever that was, or could I swipe one of the crates from the back of the Ape?

As I splashed water on my face in the adjoining bathroom and swept some color across my lips and then my cheeks, it struck me how low the sink was—the proper height for Pete's mother, in a chair. Had her death unhinged Chef? To bring him even halfway back from whatever bocce-playing, tooth-decayed wilderness he was in, I might have to find out. I had just finished changing into a pretty gold sleeveless top I had paired with a brown jersey skirt and gold sandals when a gentle rap came at my closed red door.

It was Pete. He looked nice in a short-sleeve white shirt with a small pattern of faded blue petroglyphs, worn over a pair of light drawstring pants that flowed toward his ankles. He had even shaved. "How's the cow?" I asked.

"Still dead."

"Old age? Mad cow? Some other bovine ailment?"

"Hard to tell." We went through an arbor that had been added in the last century. In the distance I heard a chainsaw ripping away at wood. "That's Macy—she's clearing away some brush."

"Big job."

"Cortona's got a summer ban on bonfires. But the ban gets lifted for the season in two days." He laughed. "Macy plans to be ready for it." Then he added, "Bring marshmallows."

We reached a very old stone courtyard, smaller than the one where we had parked the Ape, with what remained of a fountain. Even the water was gone. Pete told me that in the round base, which had a diameter of about eight feet, the bricks used to enlarge the pool in the eighteen hundreds lay untouched where they had broken. Two cherubs were doing the best they could, what with a total of half a wing, a missing arm, and toeless feet. At the center was a statue of the convent's patron saint, Veronica—from an original, Pete told me, by a Tuscan sculptor named Mochi, who made her big and brawny and active, brandishing a veil like a matador's cape. The eight-foot original Veronica was in a niche in St. Peter's Crossing in the Vatican.

He pointed to a small building with blue shutters at the windows. "The old carriage house," he told me, "where I live. An eighteenth-century addition." Then he opened his hands and gathered in all we could see.

"Some backyard," I said with a smile.

"This was the original entrance to the convent, facing away from the worldly bustle of the town." It made sense.

Beyond the carriage house I could see a graceful wrought-iron gated archway in a split-rail fence that ran in both directions, partly obscured by ornamental grasses and cypress trees. An earthy wooden sign strapped to the wrought iron was too far for me to read. Pete said casually, "My olives. We'll save them for tomorrow. Also," he went on, "there's the cow. The local vet is having the remains removed."

Turning back toward the main buildings of the villa, we picked up the pace in the fading light of the day. "What can I show you?" He clapped his hands together and gave me an expectant look.

I took a breath. What did I need to see first in Chef's current operations so I could better figure out how long this project would take, given the shock of Chef himself? "The kitchen, any classrooms, administrative office space, student accommodations, any common areas shared by students and staff—"

"Hold on." Pete raised a hand. "Too much, too fast. I'll show you what we've got."

My sandals pattered across the tiles of the cloister, we crossed a walkway, and Pete showed me through a door that led into what he'd called the old clerestory. The smell of mildew hit me right away. It was a high-ceilinged room, filled with angles of western sun, with stuccoed walls painted indigo and woodwork painted a soft white. A wall of bulging books framed a cavernous fireplace that looked like it hadn't sported a fire for a good couple of centuries.

The other walls had framed oil paintings of birds of paradise, an Annunciation or two, at least half a dozen watercolors of clowns, by different artists. Pierrot, Emmett Kelly, Bozo—because a sixteenth-century Tuscan villa simply cannot have too many clowns. Panic gripped me right around the ribs and squeezed. Across the outer wall was rippling wallpaper sporting fruits and their Latin names. It was also sporting a lot of 3-D greenery that, when

I got close, turned out to be moss. Actual moss. I touched the ripples and sniffed, finding the source of the mildew.

"This is our parlor," said Pete, "where we hang out." Macy Garner, still in work pants, raised a hand at us from where she was sprawled on an Art Deco–style sofa with white cushions and black piano lacquer arms. Pete had a bright idea. "This would be fine as a common area for the farm-to-table cooking school, Nell, don't you think?" *Farm-to-table?* The farm just got a whole lot closer to the table in this genial disaster of a common room.

Aside from the unwashed Macy, there was a fifty-five-inch flat-screen TV on a stand that could only be the equivalent of IKEA-goes-Italian. Two sagging, overstuffed easy chairs that looked like the eight-foot marble Veronica might have spent some time in them were, oddly, back-to-back in the center of the room. Nearby was a Formica-topped kitchen table straight out of the fifties that someone was using, judging by the clutter, as a desk. The rug, in faded reds and golds, was quite old and quite worm-eaten. In fact, I didn't look too closely, but I thought we were interrupting the present generation at their evening meal.

I nodded noncommittally and raised my eyebrows at Pete. "Next?"

I followed him outside, heading back along the cloister, and through the final archway at the far end that led into the first floor of what Pete said was the convent's dormitory. For a second I squeezed my eyes shut, hoping for some tasteful remodeling from, oh, the 1990s. The hardwood flooring of the corridor had been repaired and replaced through the ages, and on both sides were a few of the simple black doors to the Veronicans' cells, some of which stood open. One room had a bed but no mattress. Another had a washstand and a mattress, but no bed. Another had a folded wheelchair, three canes, a walker missing one leg, and a bedside commode. All of them had crucifixes. One of them had a porcupine.

But just a porcupine, I told myself, and a window with broken glass.

It eyed me uncertainly, and the quills started to move forward.

Bring it on, I willed the creature.

It would solve all of my problems. All of them.

I turned to Pete mutely.

Pete stepped in front of me and gently drew the door shut.

"She comes and goes."

"Maybe it's the broken window." I widened my eyes at him.

He nodded, in complete agreement.

Would he be in complete agreement when I told him in the morning that I quit?

"This is Pop's place," Pete went on helpfully, in an apparent attempt to explain why I shouldn't worry my head about shambles and porcupines. We stood facing a door sponge-painted in swirls of red, orange, and yellow at the end of the short corridor. "The team colors," said Pete. I could tell the rest of the floor had been redesigned as an apartment for Chef. A bronze knocker was mounted directly below a framed photo of grinning, mugging middle-aged bocce players. From inside came a lively one-sided phone conversation in boisterous Italian. "We'll see him at dinner," Pete said decisively, and we turned away.

I was almost afraid to enter the kitchen, since that space was key to the project. Surely, not even Captain Claudio would allow a woodland creature into his kitchen. Somewhere deep, deep inside him there still had to be an un-

crossable line in the sand. On that score, I was correct. The
kitchen, which was the final destination in a warren of
rooms in the building across from the dormitory, was really
lovely.

As I entered, with Pete behind me, Annamaria turned
with great dignity. A queen in her throne room. The appli-
ances were old but, I could tell, used, cleaned, and cared for
with love. I understood this proud and handsome woman a
little better. Annamaria could see the respect in my eyes,
and she let a small smile escape. Gesturing grandly with a
long-handled wooden spoon, she indicated another woman,
a smaller, younger version of herself, who was breaking let-
tuce with quick fingers. *"La mia sorella Rosa."* Her sister.

I liked the kitchen personnel, and the hardware was
grand, and the pale yellow walls and the terra-cotta tiled
floor were lovely. But the kitchen itself was about a third of
the size it needed to be for the kind of cooking school for
Americans that I had been told the Orlandinis wanted. The
bedroom I'd been assigned at the Prajna Retreat Center was
bigger. With a quick, practiced scan of the space, I saw that
I would have to look into expanding into the next room—or
two—and adding about three skylights. This was going to
be expensive news for Pete and Pop. What kind of money
were they willing to spend?

I raised a friendly hand toward Annamaria, asking if I
could help.

"No!" She stiffened visibly. "You are our guest."

"In that case," I said, hoping I was getting it right, *"fino
a cena."* Until dinner.

Pete led me down a dimly lit hall and through a beautiful mosaic archway. *"La cappella*—the Veronicans' chapel."
As soon as I stepped inside, I gasped at the beauty of the
chapel, and it instantly became my favorite place at the

villa. What had been the site of the Veronicans' devotions over four hundred years ago was now the Orlandinis' dining room. And it was completely secular. No pews, no altar, no holy water fonts—all that still remained of the religious life in this chapel were four original stained glass windows depicting scenes from Jesus' childhood, two on each side of the nave.

From the vaulted ceiling hung pendant bronze electric chandeliers that lit the room's centerpiece, a gleaming walnut table that looked like it was about a hundred years old and seated eighteen. Finally, some good news. A proper dining table for the premier Tuscan cooking school I was hired to make, develop, *qualsiasi cosa*. Pete moved toward a sideboard along the far wall, where he poured two glasses of wine.

The more I looked, the more I saw the smart modernizations—unobtrusive track lighting, electric baseboard heat, and triple-paned casement windows flanking the stained glass. I met him halfway and took my glass. In a little gesture, he lifted his glass—"To your joining our little villa family"—and we clinked. I felt sad, for a moment, knowing my stay with this "little villa family" would come crashing to the terra-cotta tiles in the morning.

Was the vision of a Villa Orlandini cooking school impossible or just crazy? I looked into my wine, which offered up no answers. Maybe the job was just too big for one person. Maybe I could do a little sleuthing and come up with a small kitchen design outfit that could do it better, faster, than I could, at no cost to their mental health. The wine was exquisite, a ruby red. I studied it. "Montepulciano," he told me. "We're known for it in this corner of Tuscany."

The table had been set for six, all of us clustered at the near end. Pewter dinner plates, Bakelite cutlery, rough-woven place mats in ocher and gold. Annamaria had set out crystal goblets. Pete leaned into me. "Sit wherever you like, Nell. Nobody cares." I sat to the right of what would be the head. In everyone came, Macy bounding over and setting down a covered tureen of beef stew. Rosa, silently, her shoes somehow not scraping on the stone, setting down a bowl teeming with greens and what Pete mentioned with a wink were "very local olives." Annamaria carried in a breadboard that held a serrated knife and a warm, hard-crusted loaf. I saw Rosa fold her hands in a silent grace and stab a furtive sign of the cross. We were all unfolding our cloth napkins when in came Chef himself, who boomed *"Buona sera, tutti"* and slung down a brightly painted ceramic pot of forget-me-nots right in the middle of the dinner party.

At the sight, Annamaria caught her breath and nearly wept.

She had chosen the head of the table, so Chef pulled out the chair across the table from me with a flourish. I stared at him. He was showered, groomed, lightly scented, shaved, and dressed in clothing that had nothing to do with bocce. When he asked Pete to pass the stew—here he smiled and glanced appreciatively at Annamaria, who acted as though it was inconsequential and set her curled fingers at her collarbone—I noticed he had all his teeth. A bridge! Suddenly, my relief was enormous.

Without too much squinting, I could see the Chef Claudio Orlandini of yore—or, if not quite of yore, of ten years ago, on the cover of *Global Kitchen*. All his wits, his teeth, his fire, and his brilliance intact and in play. The Orlandini brand was alive.

And so, maybe, was I.

I eyed my companions, the secretive and mercurial

bunch of Orlandinis—although Pete seemed reassuringly sane—and had a flicker of an idea that if I could single-handedly develop this Tuscan cooking school for American gastrotourists, it could be my youthful masterpiece, what in cooking circles would always be referred to as the singular achievement that anchored my career. The chatter around me turned suddenly to the story of the dead cow in the olive grove, and Pete sat nodding contemplatively as he trimmed a little piece of fat from a piece of stew meat on his plate. Watching, Annamaria winced as though she held herself responsible for all fat everywhere.

Reaching for another slice of bread, Macy frowned. "I wonder who shot her?"

"Oh," said Pete, looking up at her. "I did."

I dropped my fork. Only Pete noticed. Frozen in my seat, I felt like there was less life in me than in the marble Veronica out back. His voice dropped. "She was suffering," he said. "Natural causes, or something she ate. Either way"—he sighed, reaching for more bread—"there was nothing to do but put her out of her misery."

After half a minute of silent chewing around the table, everyone turned to going over the plans for tomorrow night's meal. Chef had invited five dignitaries to dinner. He swerved toward Annamaria. "We will prepare *il nostro osso buco, sì*?" She murmured *"sì"* as though she was letting Chef into her boudoir. In less than twenty-four hours, the director of the chamber of commerce of Cortona, an international food critic, a wealthy Roman socialite, and an American filmmaker and his assistant would be on hand to launch the new Villa Orlandini premier cooking school.

I thought I had uttered the words "A bit premature—" while I edged my chair away from the pistol-packing Pete, but no one appeared to have heard them.

"The filmmaker will be working, naturally—"

"Naturally," said Rosa in a tiny voice.

"But"—Chef brandished a potato—"we will still feed him."
General laughter.

Annamaria sat up straighter. "This film person is *ben rispettato*?"

"Well respected," Pete translated for me, then chimed in. "This guy has great credentials. He has several other Netflix documentaries to his credit."

"What's his name?"

"Buford Kaplan," said Chef.

It was Bu.

I dropped my knife.

3

The Buddhists—or so I was told during my six months at the Prajna Center—have a teaching that goes *Don't ponder others*. I can argue this both ways. Certainly, the Not Pondering Others leads to the kind of quick and cheesy complacency that frees you up to attend family gatherings with enviable sangfroid. But if you're a student of human nature, pondering is irresistible, because the payoff is that it's just a matter of time until you gain insight and understanding, and just a matter of a little more time before you weaponize them.

As I sat at the Orlandini dinner table at seven fifteen on the evening of my arrival, I had nothing. Pondering why Pete would shoot a stray cow or Bu would have so much going on, after all, that he would be turning up the next day with a film crew was getting me nowhere. If I tried not pondering why Chef appeared so supremely bland about any of this direness, I got nowhere. Worst of all, I had no beef stew now, because all my utensils were somewhere in the dark on the floor—and nobody was noticing me enough to offer to replace them. I felt myself ossifying from sheer panic.

Suddenly ripping a page from Annamaria's playbook, I stood regally and pounded the table with my fist. Gristmill Falls felt very far away. "I am calling a meeting," I announced to them, "for eight o'clock sharp. In the common room—"

"In the morning?"

"So soon? What about the *panna cotta*?"

"And the *caffè* . . ." Rosa looked ready to cry, and *"caffè"* sounded like "wounded fawn."

"Common room?" Chef peered at the others. "What is this common room?"

"The one with the moss," I clarified, noting a tic starting in my right eyelid.

Pete launched into a murmur of translation. "*Il muschio*, Pop."

"Ah." Chef nodded, fondly. "*Sì, sì.*"

As I glowered around the table, looking for dissenters, I caught a spark of respect in the eyes of Annamaria. "I don't mean tomorrow morning," I said, pressing the palm of my hand against my eyelid. Now I had their attention. They were—well, in a word—pondering me. "I mean in forty minutes." Generalized protest. I held up my free hand. "For what is about to happen to us all tomorrow, we need to plan. Do you understand?" Macy squinted at nothing, Pete pushed around his place setting, and Chef sucked on his false teeth. The mousy Rosa fixed her stately sister with pleading eyes.

Annamaria turned to me with her chin raised slightly. "May I serve the *panna cotta* in the . . . how you say . . . moss room?"

I tilted my head, daring to sweep my hand from my twitching eyelid. "You may."

With that, I gently pushed in my chair and announced,

"Eight o'clock—*a punto!*" As I breezed past my new ally Annamaria, not at all sure where I was heading or, for that matter, why, only that I pretty much knew an exit line when I heard one, she whispered, "Your stew will be waiting for you in the *frigorifero.*"

"*Grazie.*"

"*Prego.*"

Italian for Conspirators.

*W*ith nothing better to do, I built a fire against the revolting mustiness in the common room. There were actual fatwood fire starter sticks crammed—unused—in a box shipped from Amazon, and a settle full of chopped wood that looked like it had been there since the nuns moved out almost five hundred years ago. Yanking open a couple of drawers in this room for disabled furnishings, I came across everything I needed—some curling pads of paper, some dried-up ballpoint pens, a couple of pencil halves I guessed the porcupine had enjoyed, and matchsticks.

My fire-building skills are negligible, despite some camping trips with my wilderness-crazed parents. But that first evening with the Orlandinis gave me a competence I was appalled to discover. Stuff the starter sticks, top with a shaky tepee of logs (accompanied by abandoned mouse nesting), light, light, and light with many matches. It started.

Then I pulled six chairs in varying states of disrepair close to the hearth and wrestled what would work as a coffee table into the middle of the grouping. As eight o'clock approached, I had only enough time to scribble in pencil four major disaster areas that demanded our immediate attention—*everything, the whole place, whatever the eye can see*, and *porcupine*—and then, with a sigh, crossed them out as too general and not at all helpful. My second shot at an agenda seemed more useful—*broken window, porcupine, mossy wall*—although possibly too focused. To the sound of my rumbling stomach, I closed my eyes for a minute and began to feel the fire at my back.

Got it. *Porcupine, common room, Chef.*

I was ready for them.

The fact that Annamaria entered first, pushing a well-oiled and shining tea cart, laden with coffee and custard, helped my mood considerably. I felt like blubbering on her shoulder. From the look of her, I gathered she felt like blubbering on mine. Too old softie-steelies sharing an emotional moment. Close on her soft black leather heels came Rosa, followed by Pete, Chef, and Macy, who was thumbing her phone with one hand and munching a heel of bread with the other.

Chef oohed and aahed at the fire, somehow demonstrating it like a model at the auto show, then turning to me with an obsequious little bow. I indicated a chair. He sat. Along with the others. *Panna cotta* was passed. I waited. Coffee was passed. I waited some more, noting how the room was not only warming up, but also drying out. I caught Pete pondering me with his eyes narrowed. At least he was smiling. Slowly, he looked away, and the firelight caught a lovely spot between his jaw and neck.

I checked my watch and spent a happy minute cramming *panna cotta* into my face. Then I blotted my lips daintily, checked my watch again, and spoke. "Thank you all for coming on time." To everyone's credit, they didn't launch into any mockery about the *americana*'s passion for promptness. "It's battle stations, folks," I announced. Pete translated for Chef, who thrust out his manly bocce-playing chest. "I won't belabor the fact that tomorrow's launch of a nonexistent cooking school is premature—" At the last possible moment I decided on "premature" instead of "harebrained."

"Eh? Eh?" Chef was mystified. Pete ramped up the translation.

I went on. "I have identified three"—quick, quick, Nell, euphemism for "disaster areas," considering one is Chef and he's patting your arm avuncularly—"attention zones"—here, at Rosa's shy gestures at my chest, I flicked a stray piece of *panna cotta* off my shirt—"places where we will concentrate our efforts for the biggest bang for the buck." However Pete translated "biggest bang for the buck," all I knew was that it resulted in ribald laughter. "First," I hollered, holding up one finger, "the common room. This room. A key place for tomorrow's dinner guests, although key to our success is keeping them out of here as much as possible, and"—I scanned the room—"removing a few lightbulbs."

They agreed, but without much enthusiasm.

Pete continued to translate.

"We don't have enough time to remodel, obviously, but we can make a few—well, key"—in my head, I was stuck on whether I was using "key" too much—"improvements. Although we do not have time to scrape the fruit wallpaper off that wall, we can scrape off the moss, dry out the room, and hide the worst of it with a decorative screen. I want every stick of furniture in this room removed, including the TV and—I use the term loosely—rug. And I want rental furniture delivered. I want the fire continually stoked. I want the clowns removed."

I waited while five sets of eyes cleared. Then came the bellows of protest, split among various things, clamoring for reprieves of the Emmett Kelly clown and the TV.

"Next," I just about shouted, holding up another finger, "I

want the porcupine relocated, the window fixed, and the entire dormitory"—here I made a bold, sweeping gesture— "off-limits." Three of the listeners were studying their fingernails as though "off-limits" couldn't possibly apply to them.

Annamaria sputtered, "I liff there." Her "you idiot" went unspoken.

Pete put in quietly, "Pop, too."

I was serene and implacable. "Off-limits to the guests."

Finally, they settled down, hunkering low in their seats, whispering like assassins.

I decided to leave the third attention zone, Chef himself, as a covert op.

"Pete," I said, turning to him slowly, "I want the piano, the birdcage, and the Victrola from your mother's room moved in here"—a quick shocked look from him, which passed—"just for tomorrow." Wobbling a little, Annamaria refilled coffee cups. "Annamaria and Chef are responsible only, only, only for the meal. That's their domain. Are we clear?"

Chef and Annamaria exchanged shrugs. No biggie? Which made me wonder if they were seriously planning on serving biff stoo leftovers to the important dignitaries and filmmakers. "Please let me hear the menu." Then I added, "At your earliest convenience."

"Of course, of course," Chef said with a laugh.

Which did not reassure me.

I plunged back in. "Clearly, Macy, Rosa, Pete, and I cannot accomplish all these things alone. We need more help. Who can we . . ." My hands were circling kind of weakly, because I had no ideas on this score, having just arrived in town.

Now it was Annamaria's turn to be serene and implacable. She folded her hands across her apron. *"Le mie sorelle."*

Sisters? More sisters?

At that moment, Annamaria looked like something out of one or more of the Annunciations. She ticked them off on her slender fingers. "Lisa, Laura, Sofia, Giada."

Rosa was beatific. "Our . . . what you say . . . team!"

This plan met with hearty approval, plus the adding of bourbon to the coffee cups by all. Apparently, the sisters—including Rosa—were all Poor Veronicans at a nearby convent, whose mission was the Doing of Good Works. The definition of Good Works being subjective in the Italian way of things, blitzing the villa in the morning seemed an acceptable use of their skills. Stories about the absent Sister sisters, none of which I understood, abounded affectionately. But I got the idea from Macy that one of them was "bossy," one was "underbaked," one was "having trouble with the celibacy thing," and all were hard workers.

By this time in the Situation Room at Villa Orlandini, Chef was staring at the ceiling, Macy was whistling "Climb Ev'ry Mountain" through her white, even teeth, and Pete was tired from grasping the full extent of the villa's neediness, looking frustrated that none of it seemed like anything that could be solved with a .45. In a sudden spurt of energy, he offered to stay up half the night to keep the fire going. I thanked him, but pointed out we all needed as much rest as possible to face the morrow (when I'm dead tired, I get quaint). The others expressed agreement with various combinations of mutterings and eye rolls. So I proposed having Chef take the first shift (I figured he was already awake, and while I helped the sisters clean up the kitchen, I could keep an eye on him), followed by, in order, Annamaria, Rosa, Macy, Pete, and me.

"Buona notte," I said with some spirit. More mutterings and eye rolls. Then I gave them the bad news: "Our day begins tomorrow at six." Then I made a hasty getaway and, in

the wan light from the wall sconces in the corridor, found my way outside. In complete darkness. A hand squeezed my elbow. It was Pete.

"I'll point you in the right direction. I have to bring in some firewood, so . . ."

Stumbling, I let him take my arm. "Look, I'm sorry all this seems like a mess right now."

"Step up right here," he said, and I realized we were crossing the cloister. My eyes started to adjust to the deep Tuscan night. He heaved a sigh. "I feel bad about the villa." When I tried to say something encouraging—*There, there, we'll get it done!*—he shook his head. "We've always been pretty private here, Nell, and I just never really saw all the—"

"Decrepitude?" I said gently.

He looked pained. "I was going for 'disrepair.'" At that moment, I tripped over the tumbled bricks around the old fountain that had been out of order for who knows how long. Grabbing my arm before I hit the ground, Pete pointed out a pale red Mars in the night sky with his other hand. I felt a liability chill sweep through me.

I had read online about the odd, dark places in Tuscany that made stargazing particularly easy, but broken bones wouldn't play well on Yelp. "We need everyone to sign a liability waiver," I told him.

"For tomorrow?" He managed a small laugh. "It's dinner, Nell," he went on, "not river rafting. Assuming Pop doesn't leave the ricotta out too long, the guests will be fine."

When I protested, he shook his head. "No, no. I can understand the sense of it with students. It's a business. But these are our guests. I know some of these people, and believe me, it will not play well with the hospitality and fine dining they'll be expecting if we make them sign a legal document before we pass around the shrimp and rosemary crostini."

When I started to argue, he touched my lips with two fingers. Just as I found myself wondering whether it was going to get any more interesting than that, my phone trilled at me. As I fumbled it out of my pocket, Pete wished me *"Dolci sogni"*—either "sweet dreams" or "I dream of candy"—and disappeared in the direction of his cottage. Squinting at the phone, I saw it was 9:53, dark, late, and far from home. Then my shoulders drooped when I saw who was calling. No point in evasive maneuvers. Never any point. I took the call.

"Dad?" I said, sounding the way I always did with this parent—like whoever's on the other end is some kind of imposter. Which, of course—I let myself into the room with the red door—he was.

"Buongiorno, Sugar Pie Honey Bunch," he bellowed transatlantically. So today he was doing Motown, the voice he chose whenever he wanted to be considered affable and cool. For a man who spent his absurdly well-paid professional life on TV trying to coax personal identities out of sad people as though he was housebreaking puppies, Dr. Val Valenti had also spent thirty years undecided about a pet name for his only child, me. For as long as I could remember, for reasons I figured had something to do with the fact that he could neither sing nor play a musical instrument, he had subscribed to *Billboard* magazine. From those charts he pulled every single pet name for me he ever used: I, Ornella Valenti, had been Teen Angel, Long Tall Sally, Sweet Caroline, and Little Red Corvette.

I began in the usual way. "I'm not coming to work for you, Dad."

"Tootootoo," he said affably. "Have I asked?" To be fair,

he had not, but we were just thirty seconds into the phone call. The night was still young.

"You're well? And Mom?" These were the only questions I really wanted answered.

"Certo!" It was the one Italian word he knew for sure. *Of course!* The King of Pep. The Swami of Smooth. "Your fine mother has been promoted to CEO of the LLC."

"Who died?"

"Arthur Bendix."

I remembered the testy Arthur. "Natural causes?"

"Certo!"

My mother, Ardis Valenti, had made her way to what any reasonable person would assume was the tippy top of the DVV LLC—Dr. Val Valenti Limited Liability Corporation. But nobody knew these two better than their daughter Nell, and I was never quite sure which of the two of them was the more artful player. Once I hit adulthood, I had worked hard to keep a healthy distance without insulting them. They were oddly dear to me.

"Then what's up, Dad?" I turned on another lamp, a kitschy glass affair shaped like an angel.

"Just wanted to hear your voice, Sugar Pie Honey Bunch. So what's it like?"

"Early days, Dad," I temporized, "early days." I didn't want to convey anything about the crumbling villa or resident porcupine, not to mention anything about the nightmare launch dinner in the making. But I could give my father a little something. "Chef seems—"

"Gotta push off, honey," he broke in. "Wanted in Makeup."

"Say hi to Mom."

"Will do. Your Moomie misses you." His use of Moomie, what I first called my mother when I was a baby—apparently—was always his default when he wanted to seem nostalgic . . . and was pretty much done talking. I had a suspicion he always timed his calls to five minutes before he knew he had to beg off and head somewhere else. Makeup, rehearsal, the set, the astrologer, the chiropractor. "Everything good? You handling everything okay?"

There was only ever one answer to that question—otherwise he was out of his depth. *"Certo!"*

In the next ten minutes, I set the alarm on my phone for five thirty a.m. to show up for my fire-tending shift, plugged it in, pushed open the casement window that was propped open with a dowel, and crawled into bed. There on my back in the dark, I tugged a light comforter up to my nose, hoping I'd take Pete's advice and dream of candy. Through the window wafted the smell of the fire burning in the common room's fireplace—either that, I thought placidly, or Chef was managing to burn the whole place down, which might not be a bad thing—and I listened to a nightjar making its quick, hollow call, more busy and optimistic than I felt. The bird suddenly reminded me of the woodpeckers back home, and feeling more lonesome than I could ever recall, I finally drifted off.

4

I sat straight up in bed. Had the nightjar gotten into my room?

It was daylight. No bird. Swiping my phone off of the nightstand, I read the display—6:30.

And there was an insistent tapping on the door. I was doomed.

Not to mention embarrassed. A fine thing, Nell, Sugar Pie Honey Bunch, to get all bossy with these Italians about starting their day at six, but you lose credibility by oversleeping and leaving wetlands of drool across the late Caterina Orlandini's pillow. "Coming!" I croaked, misjudging the tangle of sheets and landing on my hands and knees. I manhandled myself into my wraparound travel robe and wrenched open the door, but just a crack.

It was Rosa, her straight brown hair brushed back into a low ponytail, her face concerned. Close up, I noticed the fine lines. The cheerful little Rosa Bari was a good ten or fifteen years older than I had thought. What followed from her was a cascade of Italian, something about cheese and

Pierfranco. Then she mimed sipping and pointed in the direction of the rest of the villa. In response, I held up both my palms and twiddled all ten of my fingers at her. *"Dieci minuti, Rosa, sta bene?"*

She seemed encouraged, and bounded away, off to report to the breakfast club that I was indeed not dead. I wondered just how many of them would be pleased. After a quick clanging and spurting shower, I towel-dried my hair in a frenzy and wiggled into jeans and a light jersey top. Unlike Dr. Val Valenti, I could leave the makeup until later, before culinary showtime in the chapel, so I slid into my slip-on shoes and headed out with as much grace as possible, patting my hair down to keep the whole Medusa thing at bay.

All around me were more people than I had seen since leaving Florence a day ago. Chattering workers were toting a sheet of window glass, buckets of tools, cans of paint, lumber, a decorative screen, and what looked like a caged porcupine. I didn't recognize a single soul, and I nearly backed into the sheet of glass, which led to a screech of *"Idiota!"* and rude gestures. And this a convent . . .

The early-morning light spilled through the cloister, and I watched a large white van pull to a stop close to where Pete had parked the Ape yesterday. A platoon of nuns—Annamaria's *sorelle*, no doubt—swarmed out, wearing plain identical street-length dresses and what could only be called sensible shoes. They bore aprons and kerchiefs of assorted colors. One carried a box of silicone gloves. One had a boom box that looked very state-of-the-art. Another swung a foam cooler at her side. From the straight-backed Annamaria they apparently received urgent orders and headed into the kitchen wing. Nobody paid me a bit of attention. I felt right at home.

Slinking inside after them, I heard them setting up shop in the terrarium we hoped to turn miraculously into a common room in twelve hours. From the boom box came Billy Joel's "The Longest Time" and a raucous chorus of Sisters snapping fingers and singing "whoa—oh—oh—oh." I decided to check on their progress later, and made my way into the kitchen, where I discovered Pete, looking freshly showered, shaved, fed, and on task—at least one of us had been up since five thirty.

Lounging alongside a stainless steel worktable, he glanced up at me with a warm smile, shaved morsels from three different blocks of cheese, and set them on a plate. This he pushed across the table in my direction. "Sleep well?"

"Fine, thanks. You?"

At which he and Annamaria exchanged amused looks. "Well, there was my shift tending the fire."

"Oh. Right. How did it go?" Then my heart sank. "Oh, no, no, don't tell me you had to—" Cover for me while I overslept went unsaid.

He held up a hand with more graciousness than I could have mustered if the tables had been turned. "When you didn't show up, I figured you were out cold, so—" He shrugged.

Not content to let it lie, Annamaria stated the obvious. "Pierfranco took your shift."

"I'm sorry," I said to him. "And thank you."

When his phone rang, Pete snagged it. *"Pronto,"* he said, listened, and left the kitchen in a cloud of murmurs.

Wordlessly, Annamaria poured me a cup of fresh brewed coffee. My field marshal thinks of everything. Her eyes kept slipping to the far corner, where Chef stood huddled over the day's newspaper, chewing his lower lip, swearing at soccer scores. He shot a look at me that made me feel like he suspected I played for the opposition. Had I let him down? I think he growled. "I'm sorry I'm late, Chef." I nodded to him. "Annamaria." I nodded to her. Both waved me off.

"Ah," she said, meaning to reassure me, "nobody believed."

"Sei a punto?" Chef sneered. "Six?" He was clearly tempted to do the bocce equivalent of trash talk, only Annamaria flashed him a warning look. *"Cha cha cha,"* he temporized generously. Then, with the backs of his pasta-producing hands, he indicated my cheese plate and coffee. I took a hint and lifted what turned out to be a square of local pecorino—"Ship chiss" Annamaria declared proudly, and I pretended I understood whatever she was trying to convey. At that she gave me a suspicious glance.

Holding the square gingerly between my thumb and index finger, I repeated, "Ship?"

She nodded at me, then, with a fond, patient look as though I was the underbaked sister, said, "Baaa. Ship. Baaa. Ship!"

I stared at the item I held. I was far from a cow snob, you understand, and really only half believe that I'm lactose intolerant, although I draw the line at bovine murder in olive groves. But I eschew lamb dishes as fatty and indigestible. Mutton holds no appeal, and let's not even get into haggis. But chiss made from ship's milk? It gave me pause. I made myself appear interested. *"Tutti il pecorino?"* I inquired with as much of an open expression as I could manage. "All pecorino cheese everywhere?" I hoped I was asking.

"Sì." Annamaria pushed out her lips, which I translated as a version of "Of course, you ninny."

By way of reply, I pushed out my own lips and topped her with an expression I hoped signified, *That may be all fine, well, and good, but it's not how we do things in New*

York, hoping she wouldn't know otherwise. Then I sampled the square of pecorino boldly because I sensed that, what with two sets of eyes narrowed at me—ship chiss apparently topped soccer scores—I was running out of time to pull off "normal." No sooner had I given them a sincere *"Molto bene"*—and we had exchanged grudging looks— than Macy sprang across the threshold.

She was flush with news and questions. "Snagged a guy riding by on a bicycle to help move the piano—all right with you, you out of your room for a while?"

I told her yes but wasn't entirely sure what I was agreeing to.

Her blue eyes widened. "Birdcage, Victrola, the works?" She already had a leg out of the room and stood jiggling. "The works?" She snapped her fingers as though to speed up my response times.

"Now?" I felt agitated. "Now?" What did she mean by *the works*?

Macy snorted. "Look, I snagged this guy. I can't keep him forever—"

"Leave me a bed."

She was already out of sight. "—arrange it later."

"Be careful with the piano!" I yelled after her. I was so rattled I felt like I was speaking from my subconscious, where connections were left undone. Was the whole day going to go like this? Could I hide out in the kitchen with my unpredictable Chef and the serene and martyred Annamaria?

Macy yelled back at me, something reassuring, I thought.

I stared at my cheese plate, where I recognized a small wedge of Gorgonzola, plus a couple of squares of something other than pecorino. These I wolfed down shamelessly— followed by a slug of mineral water—and watched a strange dance begin between Chef and Annamaria. She confronted him with a lopsided two-step and a declaration of *"Osso buco."* The dinner menu negotiations had begun, and I could tell she anticipated resistance. She got it. Chef swatted playfully at her—she made evasive maneuvers—with the sports section. *"Cara mia,"* he parried smarmily, *"pappardelle con tartufo bianco."*

"Tartufi!" Annamaria stood her ground. *"Pfah!"* I believe she then called him nuts in conversational Italian.

Blowing her a kiss, he either called her a small thinker or wondered where his piccolo was.

At that she launched into a lively argument that seemed to dwell—if I read her gestures correctly—on plucking *tartufi* from the skies.

Looking away from Annamaria, who seemed oddly turned on by all this talk about *osso buco* versus *tartufi*, Chef delicately fingered through the rest of the newspaper, then set aside the sports section. "Stella"—here he slid her a fake bland look—*"ha trovato due tartufi."*

When Annamaria's hand flew to her mouth, I wondered if Stella was a rival.

Chef tilted his hairless head and seemed interested in a newspaper picture of a bocce player.

"Quando?" she whispered.

"Ieri," he whispered back. *Yesterday.* Then, to me: *"Tartufi,"* he explained, his fingers curling gently around nothing at all, "what you call truffles."

I was lost. "And . . . Stella? She, what, cooks them?" More help always welcome, especially today. Let's sign her up.

At that, Chef and Annamaria both fixed me with one of those looks I was getting used to—Italian disbelief was a grand affair, full of facial features that suddenly go slantwise in several directions. "Stella"—their shoulders lifted dramatically—"è un cane," Annamaria said. When I didn't react, they slumped, then leaned toward me, clearing it up at the same moment: "A dog!" This they made into a two-syllable word, and at that moment I could have sworn I was back in New Jersey.

While one of them mimed sniffing and the other mimed digging, I nodded, and stuck a plum cake in my pocket, unwrapped. For some reason, Annamaria was deeply scornful of the idea of truffles for the evening's dignitaries—she kept repeating *"Non c'è tempo, non c'è tempo, capisce?"* which I took for "No time," but Chef waved her away with an Olympian "Budda budda budda." I ducked out, leaving them to figure out the dinner menu. Personally, I was voting for *osso buco*, one of Chef's signature dishes from the old days, when he had teeth.

When I stuck my head into the chapel, all was silent, empty, perfect. The Tuscan morning light was just hitting the stained glass, and sometime later on Annamaria would set the table. I nearly wept at the beautiful no-maintenance of this room in the villa. Then I skirted the common room, where the Sisters were booming Billy Joel's "Piano Man," and stepped outside.

The scene in the courtyard looked like a pileup on the Jersey Turnpike. The little blue can-do Ape was whimpering over by the far wall where Pete had left it yesterday, when life was simple. In addition, there were the Sister-toting van, an old red pickup truck, a modest little gray Fiat, an older pickup truck of indeterminate color, a swank gold delivery truck labeled CASSINA with a Firenze phone number, and a couple of SUVs.

Clearly someone at the Villa Orlandini had some stealth competency skills.

I suspected Pete, who later admitted he had arranged for the Cassina furniture rental.

Burly women in jeans and T-shirts—GRAB YOUR BALLS, IT'S BOCCE TIME—emerged from the main building toting the Art Deco–style sofa, which they slid into the back of the red pickup truck, then went back for more. Pete appeared from the dormitory, still on his phone, and started over to where I stood. Suddenly he was assailed by a small, wizened man in baggy pants and a plaid work shirt, who climbed out of the other pickup truck, followed by a dog that resembled a tawny poodle. He hailed Pete with a high, hoarse voice, and I noticed one sleeve was pinned up behind him, empty.

"Vincenzo!" Pete called, quickly handing me a list. Then he bent to the dog, ruffled her wavy curls, and led the old man in the direction of the olive grove. "Nell," he called back to me, "we got a call from the Netflix guy, who caught an earlier flight. He'll be here at three p.m. and will need a day or two of footage. He says he enjoys sunrises, so he would appreciate an east-facing room."

O nce I digested this annoying piece of news, I turned on my heel and took off toward the olive grove, where Pete had steered the wiry old fellow and tawny poodle.

Passing his cottage, I picked up the pace over the next hundred feet to the graceful wrought-iron gated archway in a split-rail fence hedged by ornamental grasses. Today I was able to read the rough wooden sign strapped across the top with leather ties. VENTO D'ARGENTO. Silver wind. Stepping through the open gate into Pete Orlandini's olive grove, I felt like I was leaving the weight of five-hundred-year-old villas behind, and I peered through the light canopy of mature olive trees that moved in a faint rustle as far as I could see.

I would always think of Tuscany as a place of gentle slopes and delicate scents and a kind of blessed light. If I broke my contract and left the Orlandinis the very next day—once I saw them through their ambitious dinner party that evening—I was at least very glad to see the olives. In some ways, I like speechless lessons the best. From the olives I saw right away that man's plans don't amount to terribly much, and that generations of trees will humbly outlast a five-hundred-year-old villa any day.

In the distance, only partly visible over a slope, were Pete and Vincenzo. There were no trails through the grove, just hardened soil and trimmed and flattened grass. When I reached the men, I saw that Vincenzo had tightly leashed his dog. Pete lifted a hand to me, drawing me closer, and in Italian and English as simple as he could make it, he introduced me to the wiry old fellow, who had sharp, friendly eyes and a wide grin. "I'm showing him where his poor cow died."

"Did you mention she ate some . . . bad grass?"

At that, Vincenzo lowered his bristly head and muttered a quick prayer. When the dog tried to sniff the ground, the old man tugged at the leash to keep her clamped to his leg. Pete explained that the lab results should be along soon. When Vincenzo shot him a quizzical look, Pete raised his voice. *"Presto."* He turned back to me. "Vincenzo has just a small herd, and Mathilde's death has hit him hard." At the name Mathilde, the old man's jaw quivered, and he looked away. "We're working out fair compensation for her loss, although we agree that the fencing on both our properties needs to be better. We have yet to agree on a dollar value, but we will."

The two men shook hands.

"Ciao, tutti." At that, the old farmer crooned to his dog, and they headed off across the field toward the horizon. When they were safely away from the grove where poor unsuspecting cows die, Vincenzo snapped the leash and the dog bounded ahead of him, her long ears flapping as she went. As Pete rolled up his sleeves and watched them thoughtfully, my eyes looked over this section of his olive grove, where a blight was affecting maybe a dozen trees. How had it gotten here, to these few trees in Pete's grove? How widespread was it? Most importantly, was it accidental? Or not? If not, Pete Orlandini may very well have an enemy.

"We need more information, Pete," I said quietly. "There's no sense in speculating."

He gave me a sharp look. "Are you offering to help?"

"Well, yes."

He seemed interested. "Why?"

I shrugged and smiled. "Because we can figure it out."

"I wish I could be so sure." Putting a hand lightly on my shoulder, he steered me toward a section of healthy trees. Where the sunlight was particularly strong, he gently pulled an olive branch closer to my face. One hundred fifty trees, nearly all Moraiolo variety, which produce less—he shrugged philosophically—but according to him, the best. As I studied the olive branch, I understood the grove's commercial name, Silver Wind. Olive leaves are silver-green spears with a bit of crackle to them, clustered along thin silver branches. The Moraiolo olives themselves are dark and round, sweeter than other varieties. "Still peppery," added Pete. "After all, it's Tuscany. Any day now we harvest by hand. Care to help?"

He asked me with a radiant smile, and I didn't have the

heart to tell him I would probably be back in the metro New York area by then. He let the branch spring back from his hand, and we headed through the grove as he explained that they harvest the olives before they're fully ripe, which keeps the level of acidity lower.

"And the oil?" I asked.

A rueful smile. "I can't afford the oil production setup yet," he said, scratching his cheek. "So for now I sell my olives to a producer in Siena, and I press enough just for us here. So far, I'm a small operation, Nell. Besides," he added, as we arrived at the gate to Vento d'Argento, "first we'll get the cooking school up and running, right?"

"Right." Might still be a good idea, but in somebody else's hands. He seemed so tickled at the thought of giving Chef Claudio Orlandini something more to do with his time than pitch a bocce ball that what passed between us was one of those moments of pure hum—when the music of the spheres is just a fancy term for friendship. Two people with a single vision. Pete Orlandini actually believed I could come through. It's bad enough to mope after a failure, but I felt I was stocking up on a good supply of mope in advance of the failure, like clearing the supermarket's shelves of bottled water before the hurricane hits.

*A*t noon I made my rounds, checking on everyone's progress.

Chef was humming, hunched over what looked like a beaker on a Bunsen burner. Daintily adding droplets of carmine-colored liquid, he looked serene. Annamaria was extruding pappardelle noodles from a crank machine, her serious, lovely face looking as stormy as it possibly could through dabs of flour. From what I could tell, they had decided on most of the dinner menu, and as I softly drew the kitchen door shut, they were now arguing over the dessert for the evening's crescendo. It was going to be a galette, a rustic tart, oh yes, it was all decided, but Chef pushed for fig and pear, and Annamaria countered with plum and toasted almond.

And then I stood still on the threshold of the common room.

I crossed my arms, amazed at the changes. Luscious rugs in geometric whites and golds, a rococo decorative screen sporting a bunch of round, pink cherubs, a sleek sofa in luxurious saddle brown leather, two black back-wing armchairs, and a stainless steel worktable doubling as a desk and glinting in the daylight. For a moment, my heart picked up a beat, and I thought the Villa Orlandini Cooking School might really stand a chance.

I loped back to the Abbess's room to change into a light-weight top, when there was a knock at my door. It was Pete. I grabbed his arms. "The common room is gorgeous. How did you do it?"

"How do you know it was me?"

"There's something about those pink cherubs."

"They just scream secure forty-year-old male?"

"They would have to." By now I was laughing. "I figure you must handle the villa books—no one else I've met here shows much interest in the practical side of things—so when it comes to expenditures, you're the go-to guy."

He was nodding. "I made some calls. Plus a few threats." Then he sucked in a big Italian breath. "I have some news."

"Go on." I narrowed my eyes at him.

"It's about bathrooms."

I was liking it less and less, and I didn't even know what it was. "Go on."

"Aside from Pop's apartment, there's only one other bathroom in the dormitory."

"What!" Then: "You just remembered this?"

"Yes," he said reasonably. "We can put Mr. Kaplan and his assistant, Ember, in my cottage and I could bunk anywhere."

"That could be awkward."

"Or we can put Mr. Kaplan and his assistant in the Abbess's room and you can have my guest room."

"That could be even more awkward."

His voice rose. "Well, something's just going to have to be awkward, Nell."

I burst out, "Why isn't Bu staying in Cortona?"

He was truly lost. "Bu?"

Now I'd gone and done it . . .

"I mean Mr. Kaplan. Aren't there charming inns or Airbnbs?" I waved my arms. "This is Tuscany, for the love of Pete." When I found myself blushing, I threw in a well-timed "Jeez!"

"What's the matter with you?"

"Where's the other one?" At his quizzical look, I explained, "The other bathroom. In the dormitory. Aside from Chef's."

"Next to Annamaria's room."

I was filled with sudden hope. "Well, there you are."

"What are you talking about?"

"We can put Mr. Kaplan in Annamaria's room."

"That could be awkward," said Pete, and then could barely get out, "What do you propose doing with Annamaria?" By then he was staggering away from me, laughing so hard it made me realize how tired he was, what with making all the crazy arrangements I had delegated, double shifting the fire-tending duty . . . When I caught up with him, he half turned to me. "That woman is key to this whole operation, Nell. It's not Pop, it's not me, and it's not you." When I started to object, he went on, "Nothing good happens around here—I know, I know, it all looks pretty poor to you right now—but believe me, nothing good happens around here unless Annamaria Bari is happy."

We were approaching the dormitory. "She doesn't seem particularly happy to me," I said.

He held up a hand. "Her version of happy."

"You're telling me she's happy with a version of happy."

We stepped inside the dormitory, where the air felt cool, and the brightness dimmed. I smelled cleaning supplies. "This dinner tonight won't come off well if at two thirty this afternoon we tell her she has to move, while she's rolling out pastry for the galette—"

I put in, "Fig or plum?"

"Plum. Pop always lets her win on dessert." We stopped in front of a door that looked like any of the others, only all it had was a brass push-plate instead of a doorknob. "It's how he tells her he's fond of her."

I digested this point, then stepped into a capacious bathroom that looked like something from my college days. Black-and-white honeycomb floor tile, two curtained shower stalls at the far end, three sinks and toilet stalls nearby. Big enough, certainly, for Bu and Ember the assistant to share with Annamaria. "It's just for two days," I said.

Pete stood there sighing, his brown eyes scanning the ceiling. "We promised her, Nell." With his arms outstretched as though he was about to shout his kingdom for a horse, and said softly, "Back when she came to live here, when I was just fifteen. Annamaria had known Pop since she was barely out of her teens, and she's been cooking longer than that. She took over my mother's job as pastry chef in his kitchen." In that painful slide so slow they could hardly see it while it was happening, as his mother deteriorated, it was Annamaria who stayed. She left the convent and moved into one of the dormitory rooms. "The least we could do was promise her a private bathroom. Who else lives here? We didn't need it."

"Pete," I said gently, "now you do. And not just for the Netflix guy"—I was proud of myself for not letting Bu's name slip again—"but for probably a dozen students, on average, when the cooking school is going full tilt." I had truth, sense, and reason on my side.

Stubbornly, he shook his head. "I won't do it, Nell. We have to think of something else."

I shouted something inarticulate and yanked open the door to the corridor. Plan B was, by me, a stinker. But: "Plan B it is, then, Pete." Out in the corridor I pushed open the doors to the two former nuns' rooms that neighbored Annamaria's bathroom. One had the stale smell of long disuse. Bed, crucifix, washstand. The other had the same furnishings, plus a brand-new window and an absence of porcupine. I jerked my head in the direction of the two. "Pick," I told Pete. "We give Annamaria a choice. She can have either you and me as bathroom buddies for the next two days"—he was about to state the obvious, I could tell, then thought better of it—"or Mr. Kaplan and his trusty assistant, Ember."

"She'll choose us."

I wanted to appear caring. Unfortunately, I couldn't help waving my arms about. "Will this make her some version of happy?"

He thought about it. "Some version, yes." He gave me a tight little smile. "Her sacrifice will make the galettes particularly sweet tonight. She might even throw in some fig."

I took off at a trot. "We'd better go get ourselves out of our real rooms, Pete—" I made the mistake of glancing at my watch, and groaned. It was 2:23. How much could we cram into the next half hour before the film crew arrived? Outside, we parted ways, Pete darting in the direction of the kitchen to offer Annamaria the choice, and I toward my precious haven of the Abbess's room. I burned, thinking of Bu or the unknown Ember tucked up inside my space. I didn't know her, but if she was willing to spend her waking hours working for Bu, I was ready to give her the stink eye.

Even a robust *malocchio* wouldn't be good enough for this twosome who'd arrive soon. The irony did not escape me that a mere month after I thought I had shed him and his Vedic scripture quotes, here he would be in my bed again. How in the name of anything other than karma did this happen?

As it turned out, I needn't have worried. Not about that.

5

Several things happened at once.

After a flurry of flinging my poor suitcase, briefcase, and shoulder bag into the room that had never sported a porcupine and looking around nervously, wondering what I had missed, I made up the iron twin-sized bed with a set of threadbare sheets Rosa had pushed into my arms, and I floated a thin old comforter over the works. In a graceless dash for some fresh air, I cranked open the old casement window and saw a red Range Rover whizz into the courtyard and come to a stop off to the side of the pileup. To announce his arrival, the driver sounded the shrill horn half a dozen times. I didn't need another clue. You can take the man out of the pantaloons (my first mistake) but you can't take the pantaloons out of the man.

I pounded on the wall. "They're here," I called to Pete.

Standing as far out of sight as possible, I watched as Bu Kaplan swung his legs to the ground, clutched the sides of the vehicle, and propelled himself from the Range Rover. Legs astride nothing at all, arms at the spot where he was pretty sure he used to have a waist, the man did the kind of side bends you see in people who think you can't tell they haven't been to the gym in about five years. Still bald, he was sporting thick-rimmed glasses, and over a pale pink T-shirt he wore a black bomber jacket and drawstring jogger pants. On his feet were a pair of gray Converse hightops. So much better than his hemp sandals from the Prajna Center.

As the door on the passenger's side swung open, I watched Laura, Lisa, Rosa, Giada, and Sofia hurry into the courtyard and automatically line up. In their workaday identical habits they reminded me of servants lined up outside Downton Abbey whenever marriageable men turned up for lunch. *Face the music*, Nell. Heaving a sigh, I sped out of the room, bumped into Pete, and followed him out to add to the reception committee. "Ah!" cried Bu Kaplan, every time someone new appeared, mixing it up with "Aha!" as though his benighted life was full of surprises.

There to welcome my former boyfriend was also now Chef himself, swaying with culinary importance, steadied unobtrusively by Annamaria, who smelled faintly of toasted almonds. Ember, the assistant, slammed the car door, walked around the back of the Range Rover, and came to a stop behind Bu, her tattooed arms crossed. She had asymmetrically cut bottle-red hair, and I couldn't decide whether the black eye smudges were runny mascara or badly applied kohl.

And then the big man from my recent and more absurd personal history ran his thumbs around the waistband of his drawstring pants in that way I knew so well. Next would come—there he went—an excruciating crack of his neck, in the three-part routine he had for sussing a situation. I stood there dying, waiting for the final bit of self-touching, the notorious crotch adjustment maneuver. And his hand was headed in that direction when we were all spared. Bu Kaplan noticed me.

He expressed his joy with several exclamations along the lines of *eff me, eff him, eff the whole lot of 'em.* "Nell!" Then, slapping his sizable knee, he went back through the litany of effs all over again. With quaint little jetés that were really more interesting somehow at Prajna, Bu leaped over to me as the others flowed away from us in every imaginable direction. Never fluent in body language, otherwise he'd have gotten the message that I was standing closed up tighter than the five nuns, he blared something inarticulate and wrapped me in a tight hug. Over his shoulder, I could see Annamaria's horror.

"Hello, Bu." My voice was muffled in his bomber jacket.

"Buford, baby, Buford." Then he added, his hands groping their way down my back, acting like they'd forgotten where anything interesting was, "Different gig, baby, different gig, know what I mean?" He murmured into my hair, making either his time at Prajna or his time at Villa Orlandini seem furtive. Undercover, even.

Pushing him away, I said primly, "Yes, I do," when in fact I hadn't a clue what he was talking about.

Chef was inserting himself into the space I had just managed to make between Buford Kaplan and me. A high-pitched, laughing string of Italian from Claudio Orlandini seemed to hinge on whether Signor Kah-plon and the Bella Nella knew each other already. This perfectly reasonable question he then followed up with a leer, a couple of well-placed elbow jabs, and "Eh? Eh?"

Crossing his meaty arms, Bu gazed heavenward. "They say I never forget a face," he announced proudly, "and that is true. Once seen, never forgotten." Then, with his tongue lolling, he let his hands grope the air. "Along with other choice parts, eh, eh?"

Chef howled appreciatively, although I was sure he didn't understand a word of it.

"Yes," I blared in plain English, my *Italian for Idiots* altogether disappearing in the moment. "I met Signor Kaplan at my last job, setting up the cooking school at the Prajna Center." I kept my face neutral while I handed them this explanation that left them all in the dust—everyone, I noticed, except for Pete. To him I flashed a sickly "Tell you later" smile.

Bu found Ember bumping up against his back and introduced her rather dismissively, tweaking his nose as though he was storing essential information on her up inside it. She seemed accustomed to his vagueness on the subject of herself, and she said to no one in particular, "Where will I be staying? I'd like to grab some B-roll before dinner."

At our blank looks, Bu explained, "Establishing shots." Then he leaned toward his assistant. "For the dinner, we'll need the diffusion panel."

"I'll get it from the bag. No worries."

"Did you grab the lights?"

"Not yet. They're still in—"

Looking for anything better to do than just stand there, I stepped toward the Range Rover, where Pete was reaching into the cargo area for the camera equipment. Clearly, it was heavy, so with a sweet smile, he handed one bag to me, adding quietly, "I sense there's a story here."

I whispered, "You can't possibly be that bored."

"If it's boring," he went on, looking me square in the eye, "so much the better."

I felt myself relax a little, shifting the bag's shoulder strap.

"Ah," shouted Chef, *"ecco Macy, la nostra contadina!"*

"Your what?" shouted Bu right back at him. Macy had indeed turned up, surveying the odd merriment in the courtyard, wearing roomy shorts and a gauzy red top. Bu looked her over.

"Contadina—"

Here Chef alternated between miming digging and throwing apologetic gestures at Annamaria, and I could swear he muttered something along the lines of "All these Americans know is pizza."

"How you say—" He caught the little word between his thumb and forefinger and enunciated, "Far-mare." Here he grabbed Macy and squeezed her shoulders. "Full of new ideas, eh?"

Planting his feet and crossing his arms, Bu studied Macy. "I'd like to hear what you have to say about the—crop."

"Tomorrow," called Ember with authority.

"Maybe tonight," countered Bu. Then to Macy, "I hear you're on the knife's edge of change here."

"You want her on-screen, it's got to be tomorrow." As Bu shrugged, Macy nodded slowly, looking like she'd have to find something in her closet for her close-up, and Chef went on to gloss over his introductions of the Sisters.

Ember came up nervously behind me. "That's my Red Weapon, Nell, my camera. It's the nearest I'll ever get to having a baby," she said, eyeing it. "So I'll carry it, but thanks."

Gently I passed the camera to her. "I'll get your stuff, Ember, and you can follow me." As Pete passed me her bulging beige Gregory backpack, all cross-strapped and strung, I asked him, suddenly hoping for a new answer, "Where will Ember be sleeping?"

In a flash of brilliance, he said with a lovely smile, "In the Abbess's room, Nell, wouldn't you say?"

"Yes," I said with conviction, "good choice." As I passed him, I mouthed, "Thank you," and he smiled.

"Mr. Kaplan," called Pete, and Bu turned, beaming. "I'll get your personal things and show you to the cottage where you'll be staying."

At that, Bu slung us all his jolly-good-fellow look. "Fine, fine. Only I carry the briefcase myself, capisce?" Then he brayed, "Too many bad experiences, know what I mean? Just a bit of harmless paranoia. But," he called magnanimously, "you can lug the rest of the crap, fine by me, hey?" Then he narrowed his eyes at an inscrutable Pete, as though he was deciding whether a tip would be appropriate.

Annamaria clucked sympathetically.

Rosa and Sofia hadn't understood a word of it.

As Pete and Ember Weston and I headed toward the Abbess's room, I knew that whatever the story about my brief and mistaken history with Bu Kaplan I would eventually share was, it meant a lot to me in the present not to have Bu using my room. Whether I was there, too, or not. Pete adjusted the backpack on my back, toying a little unnecessarily, I thought, but without complaining, and I realized with a tiny frisson of pleasure that the arrangements made us both happy.

So I didn't give it a thought when streams of sudden clouds passed in front of our Tuscan sun. If I had been paying attention, the day would have felt cooler and less trustworthy. If a cloud-crossed sun was saying something about being too happy, or something about the events to come, I didn't read into it as I showed Ember to the Abbess's room. No . . . I didn't read into it at all.

* * *

Within the hour, Pete caught me by the arm when I was heading for the kitchen.

I could take my pick of which crisis I wanted to tackle. One: Chef is still out in the woods somewhere with Vincenzo and Stella, nosing around for truffles—Stella, not the others—for Pop's *primo* course, his signature truffles with pappardelle? *Bring him home, with or without the edible fungus.* Two: Leo the local vintner has mistakenly sent a case of his Montepulciano, and Pop wants the Orvieto instead? *Make the exchange.* On the subject of Leo the vintner, I would call him and tell him he had to make the exchange—his mistake, his task.

That left me with the woods, never a favorite. Pete headed down toward the olive grove, where he mentioned he was running some chicken wire fencing to keep humans and livestock away from the patch of poisoned ground until he got the lab results and we could solve the problem. He lifted an arm in farewell, shaking his fine head as he went.

It took a distracted Rosa to point me toward the woods, which turned out to be east of the villa, in the direction of Vincenzo's property. As I traipsed across the low grass and gentle swells of the open countryside, I kept the woods—maybe half a mile away—in my sight. The closer I got, the more I could tell that calling that clump of trees "woods" was definitely being generous. I was pretty sure I had seen more trees on my street in Weehawken. I pulled up short where the woods began, and right away I appreciated how orderly it seemed. No treacherous undergrowth or shrubs, nothing like a dense canopy cutting out the lambent Tuscan sunlight, not the slightest bit of thicket. I could actually see clear through the woods to the open countryside. Forget dens and lairs. Nothing could lurk behind these tall, thin poplars. Even the bulkier oaks were set wide apart. Not even a porcupine could live here. All good news.

A victorious shout came from the other side of a slight slope, and I picked up the pace as I headed through the trees toward the voices. There they were. Chef and Vincenzo and the excited truffle-hunting Stella, who was wagging and doing a little two-step next to two particularly anemic-looking poplars, the kind you get rid of first when you're clearing land. I thought truffle dogs dug up the goods, but the sturdy Stella seemed to be delegating. The two men stood utterly still, nearly quivering, bent toward the pooch. What ensued was the sort of tense whispering that occurs at just that spot in a movie where all is about to be lost.

The wiry old Vincenzo raised a long-handled tool, just two feet long, with a squared-off blade. This he held in front of him like the holy grail. At that moment, Chef glanced at me, finger to his lips, an expression of intense concentration on his face. *"E ora,"* intoned Vincenzo, *"il vanghetto."* Stella was as still as a lawn ornament. With the tool, Vincenzo gently swept aside some twigs and fallen yellow leaves. Then he pushed tentatively into the soil, urging the blade with the toe of his boot. I moved closer.

Chef whispered warnings at Vincenzo, who muttered at him in reply, then crouched, jiggling the *vanghetto*, setting aside small clumps of earth. Stella lowered her head, waiting for the discovery, and there it was. A truffle. A gnarly thing the size of a handball, covered in dirt. *"Brava*, Stella," cried Chef, with a soft laugh and an affectionate rumple of her head.

First Vincenzo held out the truffle to Stella for a good sniff, then he and Chef took turns blowing at the cover of dirt. I took a turn, too, only mine turned out to involve some poorly timed spit. The men laughed, I looked contrite, and Stella shot me the kind of glance that wondered who had invited me along anyhow. With his hands on his knees, Chef bent closer to Vincenzo. *"Dimmi, Vincenzo"*—"Tell me," he asked—*"bianco?"*

Exhaling huffily while his fingers dusted the prize, Vincenzo turned slightly away from us, and he joyfully started naming a fair number of saints. Whirling toward Chef and me, he showed us what was cupped in his tough, sinewy hands. *"Ecco,"* he cried, *"il tartufo bianco."* A white truffle.

Chef actually tugged at where his hair used to be, and I thought he was about to weep. Then in a ritual act of friendship, or maybe just grandiose practical business, Vincenzo held out the truffle—still dirty, but unmistakably white—to Chef, with a stiff little bow. I believe he said something about great respect. This Chef insincerely pooh-poohed.

They bickered for all of ten seconds, and then Chef, who seemed to know the outcome in advance, slipped the truffle into a small soft leather bag, which he gave a pat as he slung the strap over his shoulder. The honors and respects all attended to, Chef now drew out a wad of bills and quickly counted out fifteen hundred euros with a rather bored expression. These he handed to Vincenzo, who in turn—and with moistened fingertips—counted them all again. Each man flipped a treat at the valuable Stella, who eyed me. All I could do was open my empty hands at her. *"Niente."* I shrugged. She gave me the sort of look that told me she had suspected as much, then averted her gaze.

I turned to Chef and tapped my watch. *"Andiamo, Chef,"* I said with just the right amount of starch in my voice. And then he treated me to a string of effervescent Italian, pats up and down my arms, and the sight of himself, world-famous Chef Claudio Orlandini, zigzagging through the stand of truffle trees, back toward the villa, gripping the prize underhanded like what he held was a bocce ball he was ready to bowl, and not the world's most expensive edible fungus, which he would shave over some pasta for tonight's guests.

Trust me: It is hard to get dolled up for a dinner with dignitaries when you're living in a five-hundred-year-old nun's cell. I was doubting all my choices. On the one hand, the life of poverty and contemplation, or, on the other, the pink lipstick? On the one hand, eschewing shoes and scrubbing tiles, or, on the other, the push-up bra? I finally decided on contemplation (best suited to dateless nights) and a lacy white bra. Plus something more neutral in the lipstick line. Jesus on the cross on the wall had his eyes rolled heavenward, which I tried very hard not to see as a criticism.

It struck me in the nick of time that I was attending the evening's event in my professional capacity. So I donned my navy sheath with the long sleeves and funnel neck—in the vicinity of the low-flying Bu, this was akin to a blackout during an air raid—and slipped into my abusive dress shoes, the slingback kitten-heel pumps in pale pink that my mother passed on to me recently when she had some edema.

Wearing those babies, the only thing I had in the way of dress shoes, even if they did sport decorations that looked a lot like little glass loofahs, I had to stick to the courtyard and chapel all night. I gave all of five seconds to the thought whether I could be called upon to go off any man-made paths over the course of the soirée, and decided "not likely." Which, it later occurred to me, was how blinded we can be by ugly footwear.

Slipping on my dangles and bangles, I stepped out of my cell.

At that moment, the clear, sweet sounds of Miles Davis penetrated from deep inside Chef's apartment, as did the scent of sandalwood incense. Chef, I hope, changing for the main act: him. The whole second floor of the dormitory had been roped off with a commercial sign on an easel proclaiming *Prossima Apertura! Opening Soon!*, rope, sign, and easel borrowed—so I was told—for the evening from a café in downtown Cortona.

Outside and just past the cloister walk, Bu and Ember were getting establishing shots of the villa grounds, Bu ordering around the hard-to-read Ember, who never seemed to make any of her own artistic decisions. She seemed a little sullen, and on a redhead I found this strangely disturbing. The two of them were in a tangle around the little Ape, so I slunk noiselessly into the main building.

Ducking my head into the chapel, I saw Rosa setting white votives into a wrought-iron devotional candlestand that they had brought back from their convent when they went back to change. The only thing missing was a coin box. Sofia was fussing with small crystal bowls holding green roses she couldn't quite trust to float. But the chapel dining room was exquisite, and the table settings caught the fading light, spreading the blues and reds and yellows of the stained glass. It was better than magic.

The common room doors stood open and inviting, and I marched into the center of the empty space in my kitten-heeled dress shoes, then I turned slowly. I would say that Cassina's of Florence outdid themselves, but I was new in Tuscany and didn't have a clue about Cassina's usual standards. The fire had burned down, but the embers still popped. If I stayed on past this evening, I would have to figure out a way to pay for these furnishings. I didn't think I could bear watching these chairs, sofas, desks, lamps, and rugs go out the door and get loaded back on a Cassina's truck. The rococo decorative screen had arrived in one piece and was angled in a way that hid the now moss-free wall.

Macy and I descended on the kitchen at the same time. Annamaria turned toward us. *"Dov'è?"* "Where is he?" She looked wonderful, like a disheveled, brilliant kitchen spirit. "I could use help." Little poofs of flour rose from her hands as she wrung them. She wore sleek black pants and a white blouse, with her thick salt-and-pepper hair making a nearly complete getaway from the knotted bandana at the nape of her neck,

Macy rubbed her hands together.

"Grazie," tossed off Annamaria as she pushed a green bib apron at Macy. "Wash your hands"—she glared at the farmer—"all the time. All the time"—she waved—"wash your hands."

A quick scan of the kitchen told me both ovens were working, all five spider burners on the Miele commercial stove were occupied, and the worktables were filled with baking sheets lined with parchment paper, with hardly an inch to spare. In the deep double sinks, mixing bowls were stacked high, and cooking utensils were scattered across the entire workspace. Clearly, not a night for beef stew.

"Presto" was about the closest I could get to Chef's ETA. While Macy peered into a pasta pot, I lifted one of the well-worn white aprons from a wall hook and eased the strap over Annamaria's head. *"Tutto bene,"* I assured her as I tied the apron and she crossed her hands on her chest in the pious way of the undertaker's handiwork. Then I gathered up her magical, wayward hair, twirled the ban-

dana into a twist, and retied it at the nape of her neck. She patted at it distractedly, then gave me a gruff *"Grazie."*

Since Annamaria was glancing at me, I troweled it on a bit, hugely sniffing at the room's aromas and uttering, *"Paradiso!"*

She produced dimples I had never seen and gave me the kind of playful swipe that back in New Jersey means "Go on widdya." Happily, at that moment in walked Chef, posing for a quick effect, one fist on his hip, a king regarding the court portrait artist. He turned once, showing off his dark gray pants and a signature Bugatchi shirt with the famous inked circles design. Black leather slip-ons. Nicely oiled skull. Fully toothed. Chef—I wrung my own hands in joy—was on his game. I was only hoping his game included the kitchen . . .

As he made his way to the breathless Annamaria, he tipped his head at me, blinding in the light from the pendant lamps. *"La Bella* Nella," he murmured. And again, this time to his far-mare, "Messy," who managed a tight smile. To Annamaria he held out his arms, and I thought I was about to witness a breakthrough in their relationship, after thirty-plus years. Instead, she produced a chartreuse double-breasted chef's coat she drew first over his one arm, then, scurrying around his back, over the other.

This ritual was followed by the kind of look that I'd expect to be followed by the unbuttoning of pants, but in the Orlandini kitchen it was followed by Chef slowly buttoning up his cloth-covered buttons. She patted his cheek. He swept a hand over hers. That appeared to be it. From over on the side counter where he had been reading the sports pages that morning he rummaged among the newsprint and pulled out a squashed black toque. This he hastily reshaped with his pasta-shaping fingers and set jauntily on his gleaming skull.

Peace fled as several things happened at once. Pete stepped inside the kitchen and caught my eye with a quick smile as he held the swinging door open for the human suction machine, Bu, alone, but with Ember's camera steadied on his shoulder. "Look natural, *tutti*," declared Bu, who pronounced it *toody*, and who had changed into pale pink drawstring pants and a black polo shirt. As he dropped into an inelegant crouch, I contemplated lending him the kitten heels. His direction to look natural was followed by a stream of other conflicting choices.

You're too good-looking for a dumb doorstop, Pierfranco or whatever your name is. Let's see some balls. Come on, come on, this is a kitchen, not a bus stop. You, you, lady with the crazy hair, grab a spoon, look like you just tasted something yummy and it's not in the pot, you capisce? This is television, televish, whatever you goombahs call it, if you don't mind my saying. Nell, Nell Valenti, insert hand, pull out rod already, I know you got it in you, and that's not the only thing. Macy, yo Macy, still gotta talk about your crop, farming's right on the cutting edge these days. Uncle Bu's here with his great big camera, so show some teeth, you stiffs. Tits would be better—not you, Chef, although you're plenty old. You're probably a D cup.

Gentle Reader, I kicked him in the pants.

Since I didn't want to leave anything in doubt, I hauled off and kicked him again, showing plenty of teeth. "*Capisce*, you jackass?" I yelled, enjoying myself more than I ever had with Bu, revving up for a bum bull's-eye with the kind of verve they like on television. As he started to sprawl, he fumbled the camera, fortunately in the direction of Pete, who dived for it and caught it before it hit the tiles. "Whoa!"

cried the trash-talking Bu. As Rosa and Sofia peeked anxiously into the kitchen, Macy got a jump on the rumor train to nowhere and shouldered them back out, all three of them disappearing. Bu Kaplan rolled over like a beached manatee and complained at me. "Trash talk is how I get my game face on." Disbelief suffused his doughy face. "You should know that."

I wasn't buying it. "How would I know that? Who the hell were you all those months at the Prajna Center?"

He looked furtive and held up pleading hands. "I was undercover," he spat between clenched teeth.

I realized I didn't care. While Chef and Annamaria stood paralyzed, I jerked my head toward the door. "Get out." I had a feeling I was overstepping, but I couldn't bear the thought that Chef and Annamaria understood any of that string of crap beyond maybe the words *Pierfranco* and *capisce*. Pete looked thoughtful. Then, as he handed Ember's camera back to the idiot on the tiles, he said, "We don't have to like this jackass, Nell, but we've got a contract with him." Bu's little eyes were squinting at Pete. "We'll give him tomorrow to finish his work here, and then he's out."

Bu started to bluster. "But I—"

Then Pete gave him a look I hoped never to see again, cold and menacing. He pointed at the prostrate Bu. "If you harass any of our dinner guests, any of our villa family, any of our neighbors, I will take care of you personally. Now, get moving. As you pointed out, this is not a bus stop." He tossed Bu's mangled glasses at him. *"Capisce?"*

6

The kitchen door opened a crack, and Rosa's face slid into view. "They're here," she announced solemnly, like the guests were a plague of locusts. But, on that score, she may have had insider information I was lacking. Then she disappeared.

Wordlessly, Chef and Annamaria turned to the stove, and Pete and I headed out to greet the dignitaries. The last I saw of Bu—at least for the next fifteen minutes—he was pulling himself upright, stroking his hands down the front of his shirt in the arch and pathetic dignity of some drunks. All he was missing was the alcohol.

He didn't meet my eye, but I sensed he was plotting to shoot me from every godforsaken angle he could muster—up my nose, down my shirt, next to the largest pores on my face he could find. Maybe the low-profile Ember would take over the camera again. Her I could trust.

In the dusky courtyard, empty now of delivery vans and pickup trucks and very nearly daylight, a bright blue Fiat Panda and a glossy taupe BMW were getting acquainted.

Stepping quickly behind Pete, I brushed off my battle-weary satin heels, then resumed my place. Out of the side of his mouth—while he smiled at a dark-haired woman alighting from the BMW—he said in a low voice, "You and Buford?"

A nondescript fellow looking a lot like a rumpled professor unfolded himself from the Panda. To them both, Pete called, *"Benvenuto alla Villa Orlandini, Ernesto e Contessa!"* His beautiful lips barely moving, he filled me in— Ernesto Treni, the food critic, and Contessa Aurora Ciano, the socialite.

I waved at the newcomers. *"Benvenuto alla Scuola di Cucina."*

He gave me the side-eye. "I repeat—Buford?"

I glared at him. "I don't want to talk about it," I hissed. "It was a lapse in judgment."

"Also, might I suggest"—he took a step toward the contessa—"taste."

I kept to his side, aiming for Ernesto. "It was a long, dark New England winter."

"And spring," he added, "apparently."

"Quit teasing me, okay?" I shot him an evil look. "Or I may have to dig into your past."

"Contessa! Sempre bella!" Smiling demurely at the cobblestones, she picked her way toward us. Under his breath, Pete said to me, "I'd better watch out for your pointy-toed shoes."

"Yes," I said primly, "yes, you'd better. These rosettes are glass, mister." What was happening? Was my idea of blood sport kicking Bu? I was spinning out of control. It had been a long day, and there is, after all, just so much you can expect from a navy blue sheath. If there was one thing I had learned in all those months at the Prajna Center, it was deep breathing. No time like the present to breathe deeply while somehow managing not to look like I was hyperventilating.

"*Signor Treni,*" I said, grabbing his outstretched paw and looking deep into his odd, golden eyes, one of which was shooting off in another direction altogether, "*parla inglese?*"

What was left of the fellow's hair was poised over his head, and his necktie was askew. He assured me he spoke excellent English. "In my field it is necessary."

He and the Roman socialite Contessa spent a few moments trying to nail down precisely which museum fundraising soirée they had last attended in common. In a cascade of laughter, she and I got tangled up in *signora* and *signorina* and finally made the kind of diplomatic decision that averts wars: I could call her Contessa, and she could call me Ornella. One of us came out ahead on that one.

Contessa was in her fifties, and her entire outfit was cashmere—even, I was pretty sure, her shoes, which would be useless in kitchen keister kicking. Someone in Rome worked hard on her artless locks, cut and styled in a retro Ava Gardner look, and if I were a betting woman I would say the rest of her face was tacked behind her ears. A combination of lip liner and Botox gave the contessa Ciano the kind of well-turned-out face that was expected in her social circle, I'd guess.

The contessa, who gazed dramatically at the sky and the grounds, trilled something along the lines of how positively *gioiosa* she would be to live in such a place as the villa— and then, in a clear cause-and-effect move, firmly linked her arm through Pete's. I decided her flirtation style needed some updating. Watching her put the moves on Pete was like standing by while somebody chose avocado shag carpeting.

The flirtation time warp was interrupted, though, when Rosa and Sofia appeared carrying solar patio lanterns, already shining brightly across the cobblestones as they strategically set them around the courtyard. Another set of headlights pulled into the short drive and came to a stop next to the Beemer and the Panda. These dinner guests were impressively tidy parkers.

Handing off the contessa to me, which caused her to pout, Pete said softly to me, "I'll meet you inside." Suddenly we were all awash in lights as Ember materialized with a light bar and Bu's voice seemed to emanate from behind the camera called the Red Weapon. "Ernesto Treni," cooed Bu, "is that you, Ernie? Always good to see you." With that, the bemused Ernesto slanted one hand over his eyes in an effort to identify the speaker. Bu, clearly recovered from my masterful shoe bashing, whooped: "And lookee here, it's Signora Ciano—hey, Signora, still calling yourself Contessa?"

Behind me, headlights were flicked off, and I heard Pete welcome the newcomer, Benedetto Ricci, director of Cortona's chamber of commerce. Ricci had the classic look of what Americans think is a middle-aged Italian male: a nimbus of thick white hair, heavy cheeks that make smiling a challenge, and hooded, dark eyes.

Next to me, though, the contessa's fingernails dug into my arm. "Who is that?" In the bright lighting, even her lip liner paled, and the Botox plumping lost some oomph.

"Who just arrived?"

"Not him—the clown."

"Buford Kaplan," I told her. "A filmmaker."

"Kah-plon?" breathed Ernesto.

"What is this person doing here?"

"He is filming the villa's new role as a *scuola di cucina.*

Just one segment in a Netflix documentary"—I suddenly felt tired and bored beyond belief—"about"—I curled one limp hand, trying to find the words—"oh, about Italy being the future of cooking. Or some such."

She stared at me, her reasonably new nostrils flaring. "The future of cooking?" You would think I had just declared myself her competition for the lovely Pierfranco. "Of course it's the future of cooking. It's the past and the present as well," she blustered. "What's so—"

"Ah," cackled Bu, who oozed over to us, camera rolling. "Contessa, always so diverting."

For want of anything better, I spoke the obvious. "Are you acquainted with our guests, Mr. Kaplan?"

"One or two," he replied coyly. Still invisible behind the camera and Ember's light bar, Bu went on, "By reputation," he said with the kind of equivocation that was dying to be called out. "While I was researching a film called *Italy Soddo Teeruh*."

"Soddo Teeruh?" I asked.

Ember put in, "He means *Sotto Terra*."

"Underground."

The contessa squeezed my arm. I turned, shocked by the alarm in her eyes. "I want to go inside now, Ornella, please."

Ernesto shrank, grabbing hold of the contessa's other arm, and in the kind of awkward huddle celebrities use when they try to avoid the paparazzi, we made our way past the cloister and into the villa. At the last minute, I turned back and spoke in the direction of the annoyance. "Remember, Mr. Kaplan," I said pleasantly, "Signor Orlandini said if everything isn't quite right, he'd take care of you personally." Anyone listening might think Pete was worried whether Mr. Kaplan had enough pillows.

But if poor Contessa and Ernesto thought ducking into

the villa was getting them out of range of the annoying Buford Kaplan, I wondered what they'd say when we all sat down to dinner.

*A*fterward, when I was questioned about the dinner, I described the first hour at what Chef Claudio Orlandini referred to as *a tavola*—at table—as the best. That night at the villa I saw fine dining as a superb achievement in the history of the species, bringing together as it did the human need for food, for shelter, for company . . . for beauty.

With a sweeping gesture from the threshold of the chapel, Chef called us all to table. Swanning in first on Pete's arm, the contessa smiled indulgently at everyone she passed. When she neared Chef, she lifted her hand, where diamonds sparkled, and Chef gallantly kissed it just beyond the pricey manicure.

I fell in, unobserved, behind Bu and Benedetto Ricci, who were whispering. "I'm telling you," Bu insisted, "I don't know who the hell you are."

"You are such a liar," sniffed the director of the chamber of commerce.

"Takes one to know one," retorted Bu, who was never very original in the heat of the moment.

"A restraining order? Such an insult."

"Take it up with Netflix legal, you pompous—"

"Would it have cost you so much, you pompous—"

Well, I thought, at least they had found common ground. At that moment, the two of them heard my stifled laugh, turned, shot me guilty looks, and hurried on ahead.

Whether the chapel lights grew dimmer or brighter, I couldn't say, as both the wine and Chef's charm seemed inexhaustible. When he raised his first glass with a *"Cin cin!"* and commanded all of our breathless attention, it felt to me like this villa, this splendid meal, this glorious company was all I ever wanted to know in my life. In soaring Italian I could only half understand, capturing ideas on the fly, Chef laid out his *disegno* for the evening's meal. A formal five-course Italian meal, one dish only at each step of the way, and each a signature dish of his own. In truth, he finished, a taste of things to come in the Scuola di Cucina at Villa Orlandini. Here he said something sweet, with a tip of his head, in my direction, and the others turned to check me out, mildly interested.

As Rosa and Sofia glided in with the antipasti—Chef's signature *crostini al drago*—so did the warm jazz riff of Sarah Vaughan's "Embraceable You." I smiled at Pete like I was twelve and free of my work life. There on my gold-rimmed plate was Chef's famous crostini with an incomparable rosette-shaped spread of red dragon fruit. First came a round of appreciative murmurs for the sheer beauty of the dish.

Benedetto Ricci beamed. "A good looker, eh?"

Even though Sofia blushed, it was clear to everyone else he was referring to his crostini.

Contessa lifted hers to her red lips, her tongue darting out for a taste. The rest of us waited. Through closed eyes, she lowered her voice. "Tell us, Chef," said the contessa, "once and for all—"

We were breathless.

"—at the heart of *crostini al drago*—" Here she opened her eyes wide at Chef. "Is it ricotta, or—"

In the candlelit hush, Ernesto Treni boomed, "—or mascarpone?"

Chef purred. "It is ricotta," and at the validated cries

from the others, he added wickedly, with an uplifted finger, "tonight."

Ah, that Chef, what a tease.

Half out of his seat, Ernesto pressed Chef on the subject of the drizzle. Again, a hush fell, but all of us held our crostini aloft, eyeballing the drizzle. Pushing out his lips, Chef asked Ernesto, "What do you think?" The words coiled around us.

Ernesto looked thunderous, weighing his culinary certitudes against the wiles of Chef Claudio Orlandini. Finally, he exploded, "Bay leaf infusion!"

At that, Contessa clicked her tongue. "Philistine," she twittered in Italian.

Chef lifted his shoulders like Atlas shifting a weight.

Even Ember weighed in. "This guy's a food critic?"

Bu drained his glass, licked his lips, and leaned toward her. "So he says," he drawled.

I sat quietly, savoring my *crostini al drago*. I knew the answer—because I had spent one winter Saturday in Gristmill Falls, Connecticut, sampling contenders for Chef's drizzle—but I didn't want to spoil the fun. But Chef caught my eye, and he grinned at me. He could tell. "Nella," he said, gesturing at me, "if you please."

I dabbed at my lips as all eyes turned in my direction. Pleased, Pete raised a glass at me. In English I divulged, "The famous drizzle on Chef's *crostini al drago* is"—I lifted what was left of mine—"an infusion—"

"Ha!" barked Benedetto.

"—of linden leaf and flower."

Hoots and claps went up, and in this excitement, candles flickered. Ernesto, looking surprisingly smug as though he had known it all along, jotted a quick note in his memo book. Suddenly, everyone *a tavola* seemed interesting to me, and I hadn't even finished my first glass of the Orvieto that Leo the vintner had delivered at the eleventh hour. I think at that moment I believed I had earned my place at Chef's table. Even before I arrived in Cortona. I had put the "pro" in produce. I was accepted. At that moment in time, everyone was getting along, wooed by the antipasto, and I could swear whatever secrets they held had to feel more gossamer than the rose mallow blossoms cupping the crostini. To me, they were all embraceable you. I gazed over at Bu, who glanced at his watch and pushed back from the table.

I just might stay. I twirled the stem of my wineglass and felt my smile spreading.

I just might.

When asked, many hours later, at what point did the evening change, I had to close my eyes to nail it down. It changed sometime during *primo*, I told them, the first course during the classic Italian meal. Chef's *primo* for the local dignitaries that evening was his signature *pappardelle di castagna con tartufo bianco*—white truffle shavings over wide, flat pappardelle pasta made from chestnut flour with a prosecco sauce harmonized with truffle oil. It is the dish that earned Chef the annual Golden Touch Award from *Le Mani*—The Hands—the premier Italian gourmet food and drink magazine. To perform the ritual shaving of the pricey white truffles and oversee the plating of the dish, Chef had slipped into the kitchen.

When Benedetto questioned the exact issue in which the Golden Touch Award was announced, Contessa remarked serenely, "It was the December issue," and she sat gazing off into the mental stores of irrelevant information.

Ernesto shook a pudgy finger. "No, no, never the December. It was the January issue." He reached for a roll. "The Golden Touch Award is always January."

"Never."

"Always the first of the new year."

"Always the last of the old year."

"Your memory fails you."

"Your memory plays tricks."

To settle what with enough Orvieto on board seemed like a fascinating dispute, I flowed out of the chapel to riffle through the magazines I had seen on the bookshelves in the common room, pausing in the dimly lit hall by the open door to breathe in the fresh night air. When I heard low voices just outside in the courtyard, I eased myself out of sight, my back against the wall.

"Back off, back off," said Bu.

"You've got a job to do," said Ember, who sounded angry.

"I'm doing it. Just because—"

"We're here for this dinner, not another one of your stupid, furtive little—"

"Oh, shove it, Ember."

"Where are you going?"

"I've got a meeting."

"You've got a job."

"This little start-up?" He gave a derisive laugh. "I'm sniffing around a bigger job."

"What do you mean?"

"I've stumbled onto something. Right here in this decrepit place."

Ember's voice got tense. "Are you edging me out?"

"Just laying some groundwork," he said soothingly.

"Like what?" She had her doubts, I could tell.

"All in good time," he actually told her. "It'll put me on

the freaking map, finally. It's that big," he hissed. "That big. And it's mine. Now go back inside"—his voice was moving off—"and finish your fungus like a good little girl. I'm working."

When I heard Ember swear, I could tell she was heading back inside, so I sprang double-time down the hall and scoured the bookshelves in the common room. No luck. The correct issue announcing the Golden Touch Award would remain a mystery, and one everybody would forget about by the time the cheese arrived. I returned to the dining room and took my seat just as Rosa and Sofia appeared with *primo*. They served it flawlessly. Then conversation dropped off as we consumed it reverently. Time passed. Sarah Vaughan did her hypnotic "Misty," Pete refilled glasses, and I lifted to my lips the last fleck of *tartufo* on the tip of my fork tine.

Chef hadn't returned.

Time passed. Time even dragged.

Guests leaned back in their chairs, fingers drummed, conversation popped along in little spurts. Any minute now someone would ask wonderingly, *"Dov'è Chef? Dov'è secondo?"*—the second course. I felt the beginnings of alarm, because if the delay got to the point that those questions were voiced, it was a fatal misstep in the progress of the evening. For an amateur, or even an untried professional, it might be generously overlooked. But for someone on the culinary world stage like Chef Claudio Orlandini, it would be unacceptable. It would be like glacial scene changes during *Hamlet* at the Old Vic.

Just then Rosa appeared at my elbow. I had to hand it to her; she managed a show smile. "Nella, *per favore*, Anna-maria see you inside now." I dabbed my lips, set down my napkin, and pushed back my chair. Standing, I realized Bu was nowhere to be seen. Nor for that matter, was the contessa. Had they disappeared while I was off thumbing through old issues of *Le Mani*? Across the table, Pete widened his eyes at me. We both knew he couldn't follow me, otherwise it would be a sure signal to the guests that something was amiss. I trooped out of the chapel behind Rosa, who squared her shoulders, and passed Ember, who was heading back into the dining room from the direction of the bathroom. My smile in passing felt a bit like a wince.

In the kitchen, Annamaria Bari, when she turned to us from the stove with a whisk in her trembling hand, was speechless. No English. No Italian. No sign language. We stared at each other. In a corner on a stool, Macy was dragging a chunk of ciabatta through a small dish of Pete's olive oil. "We will fail," Annamaria intoned with about as much emotion as the Oracle of Delphi.

"Where's Chef?"

She choked up. All she could manage was a shrug. Then she gnawed at the knuckles on the hand that held her whisk. "I don't know. I cannot leave to look. The *osso buco* is at the most—the most—"

"Delicate stage?" I put in.

She nodded vigorously.

The kitchen was chaotic. Newspapers were strewn, parchment paper had unrolled on the floor, a veal chop slipped off a platter and landed near Annamaria's feet. When she saw me staring at it, she emitted a high, keening sound that even Sarah Vaughan couldn't soothe. "No worries," I told the poor sous-chef, "nothing goes to waste." With a pair of tongs, I lifted the prodigal chop and set it back on the platter. I would give that one to Bu. I turned to Rosa, put my hand on her arm. "Please go get Pete." She fled. I grabbed a long, white bib apron hanging on a hook with others. "We'll help," I told her as I adjusted the straps and fastened the ties.

Annamaria flared at me. "How can Pierfranco help? Until Chef returns"—she let out a sob, then sniffed—"he is host." The king is dead; long live the king.

I stood my ground. "We need him. He will help." I held up my hands. "He will also host."

"But—"

"Annamaria." I took a deep breath. "Finish braising the veal chops, and let me think." No time to question her about Chef's movements. No time to question her about his mood. No time to get her to put a specific time to when she saw him last. "Macy." I looked at her, where she was washing her hands over the stainless steel double sink, and only took in that she had changed into different clothes for dinner, but still managed to look like she was just going out for pizza.

She stood up straight, ready for an assignment. "We'll put you on cheese and fruit, okay?" I said. A slow nod in reply. When I gave Annamaria the side-eye to see what she thought, she waggled her head a little equivocally, but then settled on a look that said surely the far-mare could put cheese and fruit on a plate, eh? How hard could it be?

Pete came into the kitchen, saw in a glance that Pop was absent, and exhaled mightily. Annamaria didn't even turn around, what with speed-braising a dozen veal chops. "Timing is all off," she said to the veal, to the utility table, to the overhead lighting. "Timing is all off." Macy lifted her eyebrows at him and dove into the Sub-Zero *frigorifero*. He leaned in to me as Sofia and Rosa slipped noiselessly into the kitchen with plates cleaned of the *primo*. "No sign of him?"

I pointed my chin toward Annamaria, who was sniffing

over the brazier, poking at the chops with her tongs. "She's on the edge," I mouthed at Pete. "Can we pull this off?"

He nodded tensely, walking quickly from counter to worktable, taking in the exact point in the meal preparation that Chef took a powder. He peeked under one of the four mini-muffin tins that had been overturned haphazardly. "So Pop's side dish for the *osso buco*—"

"*Sì, sì*," Annamaria said, her voice topping his, "*foccacine di polenta*." Then she added, in a flash more like her old self, "*Ovviamente*."

Pete explained, "Part of his signature *secondo con contorno*—second course with side dish. *Osso buco* with two different kinds of polenta mini-muffins. He hasn't made them in—six or seven years."

I stepped over to the stainless steel worktable. "Did he get cold feet?"

"I don't know, Nell. It was going so well." He scratched his forehead. "Can you make the *gremolata* for the veal?"

"The *gremolata*?" I looked around the chaotic kitchen in a panic. I hadn't made a *gremolata* since my junior year, when I had a bad experience with a food processor. "How could I possibly know what he had in mind?" *Gremolata* can have herbs, exotic greens, garlic, citrus, spice, horseradish, shallots, in almost any combination—

"Mix it up, anything you like. Just enough for garnish, that's all we need." Then, as he strode to the kitchen door: "I'm going back out to describe the plans for the cooking school."

I was aghast. "You don't even know what they are!"

He waved it off. "It will be fine. Half the guests must be out wandering the grounds, anyway."

"Along with Chef, apparently."

"The others have had three glasses of Orvieto. No one will remember what I say."

Suddenly, Pete grabbed the hand grater and shaved the remains of the truffle over the nicely rounded tops of a dozen polenta mini-muffins, slid doilies onto two serving trays, and divvied up the polenta between them. I was astonished at his speed. To Sofia he handed one with the instruction to circulate outside. "Wherever the guests are smoking. Try the courtyard. Lure them back inside. Tell them *secondo* is now appearing." To Rosa he handed the second tray, where he set a tiny pair of silver tongs. "Serve these to the guests still *a tavola*." Happy with a job to do, Annamaria's sisters disappeared, and Pete ran his hands over his face while I was dicing shallots and garlic for the *gremolata*.

At that moment I actually believed that improvising a *gremolata* to garnish the veal might send me over the edge that Annamaria had laid claim to—suddenly I felt I would be exposed as some kind of pathetic fraud, or craven imposter, or American goofball. Worst of all, anyone who thought so might very well be correct. I wore joke shoes and I couldn't keep track of my employer. Even my father the showman-shrink Dr. Val Valenti wouldn't want me in his business anymore. No empire for me. I would be penniless. I would be—

Pete made me jump when he left Annamaria's side, where he had been saucing up Chef's mystery signature sauce—it helped my mood a bit when I saw Pete squeeze miso—miso! *ovviamente!*—into the simmering prosecco. Suddenly he grabbed a handful of the strewn newspaper. This he held up high. "Annamaria—" he asked rather loudly, I feared, although he got her frazzled attention. In rapid Italian he asked her something along the lines of whether Pop had been reading the newspaper. She said something bland about scores. This morning. "No, no!" Pete was onto something, I could tell as I zested a couple of citrons. He was bothered by the scattering of the daily newspaper—not like his Pop at all.

With one hand, Pete Orlandini whisked the sauce that was smelling so wonderful it nearly swept disaster right out of my mind, and with the other hand, he fiercely scanned the first section of the newspaper, letting each page drop to the floor as he found nothing. I was taste testing the *gremolata* when Sofia rushed in, her platter empty. "Pierfranco," she breathed. The four of us—Macy, Annamaria, Pete, and I—stood very still. *"Per favore, Pierfranco—"*

"Che succede, Sofia?" What's the matter?

"The Ape is gone."

Gone? I believe three of us said, our faces looking as though the little can-do truck had tootled off the grounds on its own.

"What are you saying?"

Sofia spoke slowly, which made Pete chew his lower lip, then mimed passing her polenta mini-muffin platter—here she smiled at everyone's pleasure—when she, well, noticed. Because, here she banged the empty platter against the worktable for emphasis, the Ape is always parked right up against the dormitory.

"Was it stolen?" Macy asked quietly.

Slowly, Pete shook his head, trying to work it out. "He took it."

Every one of us was biting back the next question: *Where?*

With no answer, all I could do was chop cilantro and add a dash of cinnamon to three tablespoons of Pete's oil. This I then turned into the bowl with the diced shallots, garlic, and citron zest and tossed.

Rosa stuck her head into the kitchen, announced something about *tutti a tavola*, her little smile fading at the stricken scene before her. "Everyone is at table." Like a man confronting his fate with a deep inevitability, Pete found page one of the daily newspaper and glanced over it. In five seconds his eyes settled on one headline, and I saw him go pale.

"Di Bello," was all he said, chewing the syllables in the same voice that Holmes utters "Moriarty," as though it explains every wretched human act since the beginning of wretched human acts. Pete handed the page with a flourish to the woebegone Annamaria and turned back to the sauce. When she read the headline, she let out a wail, flinging herself at the *frigorifero*, where she stifled her sobs with her raised arm.

I grabbed the paper, my eyes drawn to the grainy photo of Dalia di Bello, the famous Italian movie goddess. "Has she died?" I asked no one in particular, taking my cue from the quantity of emotion in the room.

"Worse," said Pete, without looking at me. "She has sued for divorce from Rodolfo Impreza."

"Che donna terribile!" was barely audible from the muffled Annamaria, who turned her head just far enough to spit on the floor where just lately the prodigal veal chop had been. I'm pretty sure this act was followed by a time-honored robust *malocchio*, muttered into her sleeve. You don't have to understand Italian to know a fervent curse when you hear one, but you've really got to like a woman who gives it her all.

I bucked up. "So?" I ventured.

Pete swirled the saucepan and declared its contents finished. "Pop has run off to Rome." He shrugged, evoking a wail from Annamaria. "To plead his case," he added, as he began speed-plating the *osso buco*, reaching for a ladle for the sauce, "to the love of his life."

Somehow, we pulled off the remainder of the meal—almost. Macy, in a white apron, did a nice job with cheese and fruit, clearly earning herself a battle star from the doubting Annamaria. For his part, Pete turned on the charm and regaled the dinner guests with our plans for the *scuola di cucina*. Contessa offered her support and made it sound other than financial. Somewhere in the telling, Pete managed to slide in how hard at work Chef has been on his guests' behalf, and he sends his regrets at his fatigue. No one gave it a second thought. Chef Claudio Orlandini had almost literally knocked himself out! All for them!

Ernesto Treni, the food critic, seemed particularly gratified. That would be acknowledged in his review. Pete told amusing anecdotes about his years in the States. Ember told amusing anecdotes about working in Hollywood. The director told amusing anecdotes about his pedicurist, Alfonso. Guests flowed in and out at will—Macy offered a tour of the common room, the cloister, the nearest bathroom—although not until after poor Annamaria's beautiful plum and toasted almond galettes had been served. At the upraised sounds of their pleasure with her dessert, she stood just inside the kitchen door and lowered her head. It was her only triumph that evening. And even that—a galette she had fought with Chef to prepare—had been credited to him. But Annamaria knew the truth. So did the rest of us. And, for me at least, it had very little to do with pastry.

"Coffee and digestives in the common room?" Pete raised his voice as though he was asking around for a doubles partner for tennis. He eyed the intrepid Rosa and Sofia, who scampered toward the kitchen. I pushed back from the few flaky remains of my galette. With the high-spirited and inebriated guests sloping off to the common room behind Pete, I could safely return to the kitchen. I was feeling oddly peaceful at that point in the evening, maybe because it was nearly over, and the food had been superb, the guests breathless at the flavors and caring touches.

Annamaria, who, as far as I could tell, hadn't left her post the entire night, stood nibbling at a small hunk of cia-batta, staring at nothing, looking drained, the front page of the newspaper loose in her hand. Rosa and Sofia filled cof-fee carafes and set china cups and saucers on a tea cart that had miraculously appeared. It held two bottles of *grappa invecchiata*, a potent aged spirit distilled from the leftover skins and seeds of the Sangiovese grape. Out they went, young and tireless. Without a word, I started to rinse the plates and load the commercial dishwasher. When my hand slipped and plate scraped against plate, Annamaria did not flinch. Neither did I. She stood and stared, finally sinking onto a stool. I ran the faucet and tried humming "Embrace-able You" while I slid the rinsed dishes into place, but my voice seemed raspy.

About twenty minutes into the silence, all she said in a low voice was *"Grazie."*

All I said was *"Prego."* I still had questions. How was the goddess Dalia di Bello the love of Chef's life? What about Pete's mom? What about Annamaria? Would Chef abandon his guests on this occasion of his return to culi-nary celebrity? But any questions I had would have to wait for someone other than the sorrowful Annamaria to an-swer. In some ways, maybe the one real question was *Why does she stay?*

In the distance, I heard the muffled sounds of car engines and high, grateful voices taking their leave. Car doors slamming. Even, possibly, faint thunder. Before escaping out the back for some fresh air, I set down a plate of *primo* and *secondo* in front of Annamaria, who couldn't possibly have eaten, and slid a fork under her right hand, which rested inert and weathered on the worktable. Then I left quickly, not wanting to put her in a position of offering me yet another *grazie*. Too many thanks, too little to show for it. There was just so much pain I could witness.

Grabbing a solar lantern left inside the back door, I flicked it on and let myself out of the main building. The night sky was overcast, and an insistent little breeze struck up as I set out across the grass, holding my arms high overhead. I wanted to stretch, I wanted to breathe, I wanted to be alone. Swinging the lantern up, I got my bearings. To my left, up a small rise, the cloister, and past it, the courtyard. To my right, ah, to my right, the flagstone path to the broken fountain, and beyond that, the Abbess's room, and beyond that, Pete's cottage. I was learning my way. All I wanted was to fall into bed, depleted. Forgetting my bed was in the dormitory, I headed toward the flagstone path that circled the fountain that now, hundreds of years later, had no water and barely anything left of the marble Veronica.

As I neared the rubble, I swung the lantern toward something in shadow, sprawled on the stones. I pulled up short, recognizing the pink drawstring pants on the sizable Bu Kaplan. It struck me hard that I had lost track of him at some point during the meal. "Bu?" I called to him in the dark. How had he drunk that much that fast? Or had he started early? "Bu?" I said a little more urgently. "Come on, let's get you home." Say, to Albany. But for the night at hand, at least, Pete's cottage. When he didn't respond, I knew it was going to be tough going. I didn't want to have to call on Pete or Macy for help.

Holding the lantern high, I moved to the front of the fountain. In the bright light there in the rubble was Bu, his skull crushed and bloody.

7

I have an unspoken personal rule: Only one person gets to be hysterical at a time. In the matter of Bu Kaplan's murder, Ember turfed the hysteria right away—I never had a chance—so I became the handmaiden who brought her *grappa*. Followed by whatever else Pete dug out of the liquor cabinet. It was Pete and Macy who trotted down to the fountain to confirm my very strong suspicion, given the condition of his skull, that Bu Kaplan, late of Albany and my bed, was indeed dead. While Pete called the cops, Macy and I brought the news to Annamaria, who seemed to fault Bu for some affront to their hospitality at Villa Orlandini.

I sat next to the sobbing Ember on the chic leather love seat Cassina's had delivered just that morning. Somehow, Sarah Vaughan kept right on crooning, but when we hit the place in the loop where she eased into "Send in the Clowns," all I could picture was Bu in his pink pants, so I had Macy turn it off. "It isn't decent" was all Ember kept saying as I patted her hand. Finally she started alternating that with

"What kind of maniac—" A question she could never quite finish.

Rosa and Sofia had the misfortune of not having left for the convent at the same time the guests pulled out of the courtyard—before I had stumbled on Bu's body—so they were as stuck as the rest of us. At a loss, they straightened the screen and brushed nonexistent dust off the glass and mahogany coffee table. At length, they produced rosaries and sat silently fingering them in prayer. Macy hung out in the kitchen with Annamaria, whose anger at the bad taste of a murder on their grounds revived her.

It was Pete I studied.

He sat close to the fireplace, leaning forward, his clenched hands hanging between his legs. Whenever I caught his eye, some small part of his mouth managed a smile. I smiled back, but it took all I had. The *polizia municipale* arrived in the person of a helmeted blond on a motorcycle. Pete called her Serafina, and Serafina called him Pierfranco. She wore blue twill pants, a thick zip-up jacket, a white bandolier with a holstered gun, and no makeup. Her eyes swept the common room, then she nodded curtly to us and turned to Pete. *"Dov'è Claudio?"*

"On the way to Rome."

She outstared Pete, let it go for the moment. "The body," she said. "Show me."

Slowly, Pete nodded, started to stumble, then pulled himself together. With the cop at his heels, he walked toward the entrance to the villa as though he was carrying a great weight and it was clouding his thinking. The shorter way to poor Bu's body would have been through the kitchen and out the back. What was wrong with him?

Dov'è Claudio?

And suddenly I knew. All Pete had told the cop was that

his father was on his way to Rome. The question, then . . . and Pete got to it before any of the rest of us . . . was exactly when Chef had taken off. Was it before Bu Kaplan was beaten to death at the fountain? Or after? Was it possible that Chef's sudden flight had nothing at all to do with Dalia di Bello's divorce? Was it possible my employer, my culinary hero, had crushed the skull of my—in every sense of the term—late lover?

None of us got to bed before three a.m. Sometime after midnight, Annamaria put out apples, figs, and paper-thin slices of prosciutto slathered with mascarpone, rolled, and toothpicked. Rosa set out bottles of sparkling water, and Sofia made fresh coffee. Nothing helped. To the cop Serafina I reported how I found the body, with translation help from Pete. I spelled my name, told her I was employed at the villa to develop a cooking school—my head aching at the thought of the PR damper the murder would put on the start-up—and that I had recently ended a six-month casual relationship with the dead man. No, I had not expected to encounter Mr. Kaplan at the villa. The cop Serafina gave me long, appraising look. As to whether I knew anyone who would qualify as an enemy of Mr. Kaplan, I surprised myself by saying I didn't. Because I didn't. "Enemy" sounded like such a great and murderous monster.

True, Bu was annoying and insensitive, but that charitable view was based only on my own experience of the guy. Someone else at the Villa Orlandini that evening had a motive for murder. Bu Kaplan had fooled me for six months at the Prajna Center, where he had just seemed like a casual Buddhist hanger-on who was prowling around for sex or enlightenment, whichever came first, or at the same time—and at that point in my life, it seemed all right with me. Was he what he had hissed at me from the kitchen floor—"undercover"? In my heart I didn't believe him, and was cynical enough to think he was really just under the covers—mine.

Pete and Annamaria collaborated on a list of dinner guests for the police.

Ember provided them with the little she knew about the next of kin, a great-aunt in Albany and a cousin in Buffalo. It all seemed so pathetic somehow.

I watched, shivering, from a distance as a series of officials set up lights, took pictures, examined the body, bagged samples, including the apparent murder weapon, which was a rough and bloody red brick, and strung a red and white crime scene tape. My watch said it was 12:09 a.m. when a dark sedan pulled up and a tall, white-haired fellow with a long face like a death's-head unfolded himself from the car, stretched, adjusted his lapels, and admired *la luna*. It was a melancholy look he gave a wrapped hard candy he pulled from his pocket, unwrapping it as he headed our way on long, gangly legs that were peculiarly graceful. He popped the candy into his mouth and slipped the crumpled wrapper into his pocket.

"Ah," Serafina murmured to Pete, "it's the commissario, do you know him?" Pete shook his head. "Giovanni Battista Onetto, Joe Batta for short." As she stepped forward to meet him, her eyes glanced back quickly at us. "Count on a long night."

In the morning, I started my day with a shower in Annamaria's bathroom, where I stood under tepid water and clanging pipes. My brain was feeling to me like a heap of leftover pappardelle, with no relief from truffles, and I was drying off when it struck me I hadn't soaped up or shampooed. I kept right on drying, then laid an ear next to the door into Annamaria's room.

The creaks, I assumed, were coming from her footfalls as she paced. Had the woman even slept? Bu's murder and the disappearance of Chef overshadowed the triumph of the last evening. If I wanted to do some thinking about whether this news from Villa Orlandini was a dire game changer in terms of bringing American gastrotourists here to a cooking school, I would need at least one double espresso.

I cranked open the frosted window, and the steam met the morning air on its way out. My mind slipped back to the late night Serafina had promised. The commissario had a quiet, doleful manner that set me oddly at ease, although I didn't trust it. I answered his seemingly casual questions about how long I had been at the villa, how long I had known the deceased, how I felt about this former *innamorato* (here I felt Joe Batta was bringing a bit too much to my history with Bu), whether I could account for how the deceased and I happened to turn up here at the same time, whether I could account for all of my time this past evening, and whether I had even so much as a very little piece of chocolate I could kindly let him have.

After what felt like a never-ending night, I stayed right in the courtyard, just to be present when the gurney bearing the last of a body-bagged Bu Kaplan got wheeled up to the waiting mortuary van. It only seemed right. Bu never could have known he would die in Tuscany. Knowing the swaggering Bu, I was pretty sure he would have found it hard to believe he'd die anywhere at all. I felt lonesome on his behalf. As the van made its way back up the driveway, I lifted a hand. Ember had drifted off to the Abbess's room, and I headed to the dormitory on legs that felt wobbly—longing, oddly, for a cell occupied by a succession of nameless nuns hundreds of years ago. That night, at three a.m., if it had held only a mattress on the floor, and if all that mattress could offer was a clean coverlet, it would have been enough. Unlike Bu, all I needed was sleep and shelter.

In Annamaria's bathroom, the steam slipped out through the open window. I was grateful for the rain throughout the night, because it sharpened the smell of ripe grasses and the fullness of the fields. Not much different from yesterday, when I couldn't find the time in all the necessary mayhem to just stand—somewhere—with my eyes closed, taking in the light and warm Tuscan air. Today wasn't promising to be any better—in fact, maybe even a little bit worse, once the local media got a whiff of the crime.

Back in my temporary little cell—although suddenly I wondered just how long Ember would have to be on hand—I slipped on a lightweight jersey top and pants, pulled a brush through my hair, and grabbed a pad of paper. If I wanted to be useful, I could put my head to generating time-tables for the guests at dinner last night. Gaps and holes, I would turn to trusted others. Sinking onto the bed, I realized I had just posed for myself my very first problem. *Exactly who were my trusted others?*

Pete, Macy, Annamaria, Sofia, and Rosa?

Why should I assume I could trust any of them just because they were villa "family"?

Why should I assume I couldn't trust the director, the contessa, Ernesto, any of the other sisters, and even the truffle-hunting Vincenzo just because they weren't?

And what about Chef himself? Had he killed Bu and fled? Had he seen whoever killed Bu, and fled? Trust him or not, at that moment he was nowhere to be found—had a killer struck twice?—terrible thought—and I would have to look elsewhere for trust.

Just then, my best choice appeared to be Stella the dog.

With Pete, perhaps, a close second. Perhaps I could work the Pete line, not give too much of my suspicion away, and reassess his trustworthiness along the way. At 8:40 in the morning after the discovery of Bu Kaplan's body, and going on five hours' sleep, it was a plan. I grabbed my phone, my key, my sleeveless down vest, and my legal pad and stepped into the corridor of the dormitory. No sound from Pete's room. No sound from Annamaria's. Out I went into the fragrant Tuscan air, where not even violent death could interrupt the perfect beauty that had been around probably since the last glacier receded.

A lone in the sparkling kitchen, where there were no tell-tale signs of yesterday's culinary chaos, I found a small French press and made myself some strong coffee. Slicing a piece of leftover ciabatta, I headed into the common room to start working on a timetable of guests' movements the night before.

Macy stood on the threshold, her short, green-tipped hair wet from the shower. We nodded at each other, and she scrutinized the room. "Fire's out."

"No one was tending it."

"Other things to do."

"You could say."

"Want me to get it going again?"

I frowned. There was a slight chill in the room, but at least it felt dry, and I cranked open one of the casement windows. "No, we're good. Coffee's in the kitchen."

"Join you?"

"Please." At that, Macy, who was wearing a purple sleeveless jersey dress, disappeared. I sat down on the stylish love seat, swigged my coffee, and worked on the list, leaning over the blue marble coffee table. Racking my brain, I worked up a tentative timetable of others' movements based on my own observation.

"What have you got?" asked Macy, setting down a plate of chocolate biscotti and china cup of coffee. Dainty stuff for hands that had the signs of all-season work.

"Timetable for last night."

With great care, she dipped her biscotti. "Good place to start."

My smile felt thin. "Timetables," I asked, "or biscotti?"

Macy nibbled reflectively. "My great-aunt Etta used to say that it's a wise woman who keeps her truth under her baseball cap."

"She liked baseball?"

"She liked the Phillies." Macy sat back. "Also chickens."

"Kept a few, did she?" I realized I didn't know how to have a conversation about poultry.

"Farmed them." Then she added: "All by herself."

"She made a living?"

Macy narrowed her eyes. "I think that was one of those truths she kept under her baseball cap."

"Ah." I sipped my coffee and saw an opportunity. "Here's what I've got on you."

"Me?"

"Everyone's accountable, Macy." One minute more and I'd be full-out prissy. "No exemptions."

"Are you on the list?" she challenged, her eyebrows beetling up her forehead.

"Not yet," I admitted, but assuring her I would be, as I put it primly, "anon."

Macy raked at her wet hair. "Well, what have you got on me?"

I found her entry, fourth down. "Macy," I read aloud. "Helped R and S clear appetizer plates around eight fifteen, when Contessa chewed her out for removing plate from right instead of left."

She laughed, as they say, mirthlessly. "Good one, Nell! Please add that I flipped Contessa the bird."

"I hope she didn't see."

Macy crossed her tanned legs. "Oh, I made sure she did."

With a sigh, I added to the entry on Macy: *Appeared to flip Contessa the bird.* Then I read her the rest. "Helped R and S clear *primo* plates. Present for half of *secondo*, present for cheese and fruit."

"Correct." Then she sat up. "But the timing's off."

"Where?"

"Eight fifteen is way late, Nell. Rosa, Sofia, and I cleared the crostini plates more like seven forty-five. By eight fifteen, *primo* was half eaten." With a slow nod, I told Macy I would check the time with Rosa, just to be sure she was right, and then make the change. At that, she pushed herself off the couch, stacked her cup on her empty plate, and managed a smile. "Well, Nell," she said, widening her eyes at me, "it's been ghoulish." On her way out, she sidestepped Pete, who showed up with a coffee carafe—I really do admire useful men—and leftover galette from last night.

Wordlessly, he poured me a second cup, poured his first, and sliced the galette into quarters. "Two news bloggers turned up already this morning. Did you see them?"

"No." In my alarm, I paused with my coffee halfway to my lips.

"Plus," he went on, "a reporter from *Il Messaggero*. I handled them—told them the little I knew about Buford— and sent them on their way. I didn't want them stumbling over Annamaria. She's fragile right now."

I understood. "No details about the murder?"

"When they pushed, I told them to talk to Serafina or Joe Batta."

"Good."

Pete lowered his head. "It was all fine," he said sadly, "until they got to Pop. Where is he? Exactly what time was his flight from the villa? Did he kill the unfortunate American in a fit of passion? What was his motive? How would his arrest affect the plans for a cooking school?"

"What did you say?"

"About the cooking school?"

"Forget the cooking school. The other questions."

Pete sat back. "All I could say without losing my temper"— he chewed pensively for a moment—"was what I believe . . . that Chef left the villa on an unrelated matter." He widened his dark eyes at me. "What a fool," he muttered.

"Chef?" I said gently.

A short laugh. "Me."

"I don't think so," I told him with some spirit. "What you told the reporters gives them some new possibilities, Pete. Let's see what they turn up—"

His cup clattered to the table. "That's just it. I don't want them to turn up anything."

"About Dalia di Bello? They'll put that together soon enough. But maybe it'll buy us some time."

"To do what?"

I huffed. "To find the killer." Suddenly the room looked bright and white and strangely bare. I sounded ridiculous to myself.

"Nell," said Pete, leaning toward me. "What if it's Pop?" I pushed away the coffee—and my share of the plum and almond galette. "We have work to do." At that, I tapped my list. "Here's where we begin. Look it over, Pete." Grateful for something practical to do, he lifted the sheet and studied my timetable.

Bu: Last saw him toward the end of *primo*, just after 8:00, when he belched and pronounced the pappardelle with truffles "better than sex." Based on my experience, this was an understatement.

Chef: Last saw him halfway through *primo*, around 8 p.m. Assumed he was in kitchen, prepping *osso buco*. Ascertain with Annamaria exactly when in the kitchen he lost his mind.

Pete: Absent during appetizer. Present most of *primo*. Absent during *secondo*, say between 8:15 and 8:45. Present thereafter until guests left. Note: By then, Chef gone, Bu dead?

Macy: Helped R and S clear appetizer plates around 7:45, when Contessa chewed her out for removing plate from right instead of left. Appeared to flip Contessa the bird. Helped R and S clear *primo* plates. Present for *secondo*, present for cheese and fruit.

Contessa: See above. Present at original spot at table until halfway through *secondo*, when she switched places with Ember while Ember absent, thus enabling her to press boobs against Pete between 8:45 and *caffè*.

Ember: Hard to pin down, filmed till light gone, present on and off throughout all five courses.

Director: Present for appetizer, dropped *primo* when Ernesto caved under pressure to trade seats, demanded new *primo* from Sofia, who presented it muttering *"asino,"* and bent Bu's ear about his absent daughter Fabrizia's star quality, and would Signor Kaplan care to have a look at her portfolio? Absent from 8:15 to 8:45, claiming bladder. Absent again during cheese and fruit, claiming phone call.

Ernesto: See Director, above. Absent during appetizer, claiming phone call. Fumed during *primo*, during which time moved bottle of Orvieto next to himself and glared at Ember. Became aware of E's absence at some point during *secondo* when Director demanded to know where egghead went.

Rosa and Sofia: Not conjoined twins, Valenti, must not fall into trap. However, R & S moved to and from dining room throughout all courses like the Presto movement from Mozart Sonata in F. Could have beaned Bu between serving Contessa and Ernesto their *caffè*.

Annamaria: No appearance at table. As for movements in and out of kitchen, TBD.

Vincenzo: Not killer, no way. Owns nice dog and dead cow.

Here and there, Pete widened his eyes, or tilted his dark head. Finally, I asked, "What do you think?"

"I like the nice dog defense."

I nodded. "What else?"

He inhaled and exhaled as though he was majoring in yoga, and observed, "The entry on me is the most businesslike."

I said, "I'm not sure of your point."

"Are you protecting me?"

I felt taken aback, which is not a word I use frequently. "Why would I do that?"

He lifted a hand, then managed a small smile. "Because you think I did it."

As much as I felt like asking *Did you?*, I refrained, because there was a 50 percent chance I would vomit. "You don't need me to protect you, Pete," I said with admirable plainness. "Your entry is businesslike because"—come to think of it, why *was* it businesslike?—"your movements were clear to me, and . . . I see you as my colleague."

"Or maybe you just feel businesslike when it comes to me," said Pete.

The comment struck me as interesting in any number of ways. I found myself feeling as though I was standing barefoot at the end of a dock with my toes curled over the edge, staring into the water. Possibly a danger-free zone, but murky. The thing to do was to put on my shoes, turn right around, and come back another day. "What do you make of Ernesto?"

He scratched his chin. "You mean why was he glaring at Ember Weston?"

"That," I said, nodding, "and where in fact Ernesto Treni went."

Pete wiped his hands on a napkin, stood up, and walked to the fireplace, where he stood judging the ashes for a few seconds. "Another fire?"

I answered right away. "No, Pete," I said, "I want to get out. I want to fill in the holes on the list."

He turned toward me, suddenly sad again. "So do I."

I bit my lip. "When do you think he'll come home?"

"The question is . . ." he said as he cleared his cup and plate, "when will the cops bring him in?" And there it was, between us, more sinister than coffee and leftover galette. I had nothing to add. "About the list," he said with some spirit I was glad to see, "I do have one objection. And one correction."

"Oh."

"Yes."

"Go on." I readied my pen.

"I object to the statement that Contessa was 'pressing boobs' against me."

"Oh, please, Pete," I snorted. "I was there."

"What you saw was just a by-product of her hand on my thigh."

I think I blacked out. "With—with—*secondo* on the table?" I managed at last. She was feeling him up beneath a culinary treasure that properly belongs in the Uffizi if only it had a kitchen section? Had she no shame?

"I may have to take my pants to the tailor. See what he can do about the claw marks."

"Well, isn't she the sly one." When I'm truly shocked, I sound like a bad actress from a thirties movie, a bobbed blond flouncing through a noir script.

"Not really. But she's holed up at La Chiesina, south of town, so we have to question her."

"Together?"

"Oh, yes," he chuckled. "Or, if you prefer, you can go alone."

"No, no, we'll get farther with her if you're there, too."

"Good." He stared into his coffee cup ruminatively. Then: "I'm not ready to sacrifice myself in order to find Buford's killer."

"Unless it's Chef" was out of my mouth before I had a chance to censor it—so there we were, thanks to my drowsy censor, back to the central, painful question. Pete winced. We both sipped our way through the moment. "Truly, I wouldn't worry, Pete," I said urgently. "I can't imagine a motive."

"I can't either, Nell, but"—he gave me a raw look—"you see how he is." And he lifted a helpless hand. Then he muttered, "It all hinges on the medical examiner's report on Buford's time of death. That's everything." And he said again, "Everything."

Maybe not everything. But enough.

Aside from feeling jarred by his use of the name Buford, I understood Pete's point. Chef's disappearance—I could see how the media would spin it—"flight"—the night of the murder looked suspicious. If the ME's report put Bu's death after Chef's "flight," there was a good chance that would be all we needed to put him in the clear.

In the meantime, though, how much damage would already have been done to the cooking school start-up? And to the Orlandinis themselves? Suspicion makes for spicier headlines, and reputations don't always recover completely. Find the killer, yes, but a new priority felt urgent to me. "I think we need to find your father," I told Pete quietly. He nodded, and I changed the subject. "What's your correction?"

He lightly swirled the coffee. "It was Rosa, not Sofia, who called the director a jackass."

At the sudden peal of thunder, Pete cranked the window shut, and I hurried over to watch the unexpected storm sweep through the courtyard. "This won't last long," he told me.

I shoved my hands in my pockets. "Who should we tackle first?"

"The contessa. The police will have no luck with her, and she'll leave for Rome at the very first opportunity, which," he said, locking the window, "is why we need to hurry. And then we'll find Ernesto. Unless the cops tell him otherwise, he could be harder to track down, what with making the rounds of restaurants."

"Then the director?"

"Right. He's not going anywhere."

Together we watched Annamaria make her way awkwardly along the cloister, her shoulders bent against a chill that probably had only a little bit to do with the rain. Her arms were tucked under the transparent folds of a thin, hooded plastic poncho. To me, following her as she headed stiffly along the passage, she could have been one of the nuns from the villa's early days in the fifteen hundreds, where the disappointed, seduced, abandoned, pregnant, and imprisoned women found shelter here among the vocational women. Which of these was Annamaria Bari?

"Tell me about Dalia di Bello," I said quietly, as Annamaria disappeared into the kitchen. Out of one storm. Into another.

8

D alia di Bello.

Pete went on pretty efficiently to describe the great Italian beauty, the Oscar winner, multiply married goddess with Olympian charm and talent, now in her late sixties with, as she confides to tabloids, "no regrets," leaving in her irrepressible wake—and with seeming unawareness—capsized men, homes, hearts, yachts. Over forty years ago she and Claudio Orlandini had what any reasonable person would call a fling, and she sallied off to Hollywood, where she married her first director, and young Chef mourned her loss forever.

Pete's mother was a rebound move. She was his pastry chef, and willing to get married, have a baby, make pastries, and somewhere find enough oxygen to breathe in all the rooms haunted by the departed Dalia, who was soon on her second husband. As for Annamaria Bari, she preceded them both, a child who fell in love with a dashing neighborhood chef earlier than girls should fall in love at all. She is always present, and always invisible. She is considered minutely, and overlooked utterly. She endures, she waits, and not for a moment does she ever believe the future will not be hers.

We agreed to meet down at the barn, where Macy bunked. "You can get the key from her."

"Key?"

"To the garage." He loped off to check in with Annamaria and tell her our plans.

With my luck, we would wind up in a second Ape. Or a motorcycle.

What Pete called the barn was a wood and stone structure that couldn't have been more than a hundred years old. A newer addition to the villa, flung up close to the beginning of the drive turning off from the main road into town. A necessity, I guess, in a motorized age. It was actually two attached buildings, both with the kind of plank double doors that take some tugging to swing open. The set of doors on the left was padlocked, but the set on the right stood open.

I peeked inside, peering into the light, warm shadows to see a kind of quick renovation of animal stalls into a living space for humans. A concrete floor had been poured. Track lights had been installed. One corner was a tack room—bridles and saddles were draped over sturdy posts jutting from the rough walls—left pretty much intact from the old days, except for the toilet, sink, and stall shower that had been added. Sash windows were screened and shuttered, now open wide to the fragrant morning air.

No Macy. But I scanned a neatly made up single bed covered by a colorful woven quilt, the tired lounge chair that—just two days ago—used to take up space in what was still a moss room, and a very basic kitchen, what with an apartment-sized *frigorifero*, a basin for washing up the dishes, and a counter that was big enough to hold a knife block and a two-burner hot plate. Her few clothes were split between an open shelf and wall pegs. No TV, no sofa for entertaining, no poker table, pool table, strewn books, or photo albums.

On the floor beside the single bed was a huge, framed Gregory backpack, the kind that strapping wilderness geeks use, where, if you saw it from behind, you'd swear the wearer was transporting a small hiker. Stepping around a cultivator, I glanced quickly at the small stall just inside the open barn door, where a long row of farm tools stood ready for use—a shovel, spade, fork, hoe, and a couple of rakes, plus, on narrow shelves, hand tools.

In the open doorway, I called, "Macy?"

Through the pine boarding of the old walls, I heard her faintly. "Back here!"

I circled the building and found Macy up to her ankles in tilled soil. She was wearing worn jeans, a tie-dyed T-shirt a boomer somewhere must have donated to a Goodwill store, and muck boots. I eyed this part of the Orlandinis' property that I hadn't seen. Here it leveled out and was being cultivated over time. Toward the back of what looked to me like a quarter acre were a couple of fruit trees that had seen better days—or, at least, better care. Still a few fruit hanging, but not plentiful. "Lemon tree?" I smiled at her.

She pushed her gloved fingers through her short hair, then frowned as she looked toward the trees. "The one on the left," she said. "The other's"—here she squinted—"a pear."

I nodded. "So what are you planting?"

With a firm thrust into the Tuscan soil, she gave the

pitchfork a little turn, then raised it. From a small burlap bag slung over her shoulder she pulled a bulb. "Garlic," she declared, held it up for a speedy inspection, then pushed it into the hole and swept dirt over it. "Tomorrow it's asparagus. Annamaria's been hankering for a crop. She's got something in mind about a new bruschetta she wants to try that uses asparagus puree."

I thought about it. "If she keeps the San Marzano tomato, basil, and oil, it sounds pretty good."

Macy raised a hand. "Don't know," she went on. "All I know is I want to surprise her with a spring crop of the stuff." With that, she poked the pitchfork back into the soil, breaking up some clods.

In the distance I caught sight of Pete heading our way, so I got down to business and explained to Macy that I needed the garage key. Pete and I were off to see the contessa. Wordlessly, she pulled a key off the carabiner hooked on a belt loop on her jeans. I could swear in that moment Macy was remembering the body in the rubble of the fountain. We looked at each other with pursed lips, sad and speechless.

For just that moment she and I could push back the memory of that sight, but as I turned away, we both knew the trouble was just beginning. She pulled out another garlic bulb. "This is easy," she said softly. Then: "Good luck with the contessa." She gave a small laugh and dropped the garlic into the new hole. "You can be Pete's wingman on that one." As I smiled, Macy smoothed the dirt carefully over the bulb, more carefully than before. "Hey, Pete," she said as he reached us. "Today's the day I've got to burn all that brush."

"Not too wet?"

"Nah, I got it covered with a tarp."

"What's the forecast?"

"Wind, lots of it, and they'll put the fire ban on again."

"Then go ahead."

She nodded, turning back to her burlap bag.

The gem in the padlocked garage turned out to be a 1955 Ford Thunderbird in a green the shade of the ocean off Key West. The eggcrate grille and eyebrows over the headlights gave the car a slightly manic expression, which may explain why she required a certain amount of sweet talk. The Bird had wide white radials and wire wheels, and the door on the passenger's side was wired shut. For the first few minutes we drove through Cortona and downhill toward the Airbnb the contessa had rented, bumping along companionably in the T-Bird.

To its credit, it was clean and interesting, sporting a vague scent of tuberose. While I balanced my legal pad with the timetable of everybody's whereabouts last evening, I felt distracted, wondering whether I had ever ridden in a vintage T-Bird and why the Orlandini family didn't own a single normal vehicle. Their wheels were the misfits of the automotive world, like a DeLorean. But why the lovestruck Chef didn't take the T-Bird on his swoonfest to Rome instead of the little Ape that chugged along at 40 miles per hour, I had no idea. Pete offered an explanation.

"The Ape was closer."

"By thirty feet," I pointed out.

"In his extremity," Pete tried it another way, "the closer car meant all of one minute more with di Bello." It seemed like an adolescent stunt to me, and although I said nothing,

Pete caught the sour look I felt on my face. "One minute more to hold her in his arms." When my flat expression didn't change, he gave up good-naturedly. "I know it doesn't make sense. To get it," he added, "you'd have to be in love." He spoke it in the way my optometrist let me know I could certainly choose the less expensive prescription sunglasses. But my heart beat a little quicker.

"It's a stereotype, you know, Pete." I can never resist soggy ground.

"What do you mean?"

I rolled my hand in a dismissing way. "These grand gestures Italians make." I watched the countryside, glistening in the leftovers of the rain, slip by. "It's all for show." Am I really so cynical? Blinking a few times, I managed to glance over at him. It wasn't irritation; it was something else. My breath caught in my throat. Pete Orlandini was sorry for me—and kind enough to say nothing.

I said nothing, too, and watched the clouds thin out over the faded green hillsides as we splashed along through navigable puddles in the T-Bird. Then, when two cows lumbered across the road, heading south, we felt merry. Not even fifteen minutes later, three goats crossed the road, heading north, which made us merry all over again. Maybe we were both looking for reasons to laugh. And to put our minds to things other than Chef's lifelong passion . . . or my lack of one.

Suddenly I had a sobering thought. "Tell me they won't end up in the olive grove."

"They won't. I hired a couple of locals to put up chicken wire fencing." When an Italian version of a truck stop wasn't turning up, I expressed a need for a pit stop. At least I didn't call it "the facilities" to Pete's face. If he'd been traveling with my mother, she'd call it "the little girls' room." She has

a prissy streak someone once must have told her was ador-
able. Probably my father. Pete pulled over to the side of the
road, where we idled. Gesturing toward the kind of high
grass you see in remote areas of Laos, he said, "You'll be
fine," with the breezy confidence of someone who wasn't
getting out of the damn car. The man waited patiently for
me with his head averted while I bemoaned the lack of roadside facilities to myself and plunged into the knee-high
grass. My eyes swooped around truculently, thinking woe
betide any asp that ventured into my zone just then.

When I finally sprang back into the car on the driver's
side and slid across to my seat, I was blitheringly happy to
report that the high grass was—when all was said and
done—just high grass. He gave me a tight smile that held
no scintilla of mockery, and I decided that my ally in solv-
ing Bu's murder was a fine, truth-telling kind of guy.

It was then, as Pete tried to get us off the wild grassy
shoulder of the roadway and back into paved splendor, that
the wheels spun in a slick of mud and slid sideways. In a
flash we went off the road and partway into a ditch, where
the Bird listed at a sickening angle. *Hey, hey, hey,* Pete was
barking, and *Whoa, whoa, whoa,* I was yelling, and when
the noise stopped all I could hear was the front right tire
spinning in helpless protest high off the ground. The door
next to me gaped open just enough to show me what more
it could do if the wire that held it shut were to fall off. In my
mind, we were teetering.

Swearing, Pete sprang out of the car and threw his jacket
onto the seat, where it landed alongside a thermos. Then he
grabbed for my arms, which presented a problem, since I
was clutching my legal pad to my chest. "It's not so bad," he
told me, and as I scooted uphill across the seat, he tugged
me the rest of the way. "My briefcase!" I cried as I landed

both feet on the running board and jumped to the ground. The car was listing less now that we were out of it, and Pete swung my briefcase out of the space behind the seat and set it on a square of dry ground. Together we trotted toward the front of the T-Bird to have a look at what Pete was calling "our little problem."

Hitting a slick of mud, my feet went right out from under me. As Pete made futile grabs for me, I hit the ground flat out on my back, and he went tumbling past me, hollering. Overhead, squawking birds rose out of the trees. As I tried to stand, I swiped my face with muddy hands and flipped over, this time flat out on my stomach. Finally, I managed at least to sit up, gasping, my legs flopped straight out in front of me, and I looked around.

Crawling toward me on his belly, covered in mud and with a determined look on his face, was Pete. "Well," he said through gritted teeth, "this sets us back." I nodded, squinting past him. Would we miss catching the contessa? Next to me, the Bird's airborne wheel finally stopped spinning.

While Pete caught his breath, I stared into a roadside forest. "What's in the thermos?"

He swiped mud from his face. After a moment, he replied, "Scotch." Then he gave me the side-eye. "But it's been there awhile." Was this a test?

I forgot everything I had ever learned about beggars and choosers. "Single malt?"

Pete gave me a wounded look. *"Certo."*

I brushed with no luck at my jacket, which would probably never come clean. "That would be lovely, thank you."

It gave us an achievable goal. With a full-on smile at me, he jerked his head toward the road, and the two of us crawled to a patch of dry earth where we could get a foothold. Standing up felt original. Pete set about pulling down on the driver's side of the Bird, directing me with his chin to reach for the thermos. At that moment, a bright red Jeep pulled alongside us and idled. "Pierfranco," called the driver, leaning toward the two of us, offering a tow. The shadowy face grinned. "You and your Elvis car!" he brayed. Then a breathy smoker's laugh ended in a string of *hee-hee*s. "Need a tow?"

Pete turned to me. "Second shift foreman at the marble quarry." He was about to turn back, but then added quietly: "An idiot from my school days. Besides," he said with a sigh, "everyone knows Elvis drove Cadillacs." Then he called back to our rescuer. *"Mille grazie, Lorenzo."* The quarry man pulled ahead of us just far enough for the two of them to go to work with a rope while I stood around brushing mud from my legal pad—notes, still legible—and consoling myself that my lovely Coach briefcase was getting a mud mask.

After much negotiating about how and where to tie the ends of the rope, the men were ready to go, and the burly Lorenzo climbed back into his Jeep. "Stand back, Nell," called Pete, slipping behind his steering wheel, and I hot-footed it well away from the vehicles as engines strained and wheels strove mightily to get some traction. Finally, the ocean green T-Bird lurched and followed the Jeep back onto the pavement.

While the men, laughing, shook hands, and relived every little detail of the rescue, I shoved my briefcase behind the seat, rewired the passenger's door shut, and climbed into the T-Bird on the driver's side. The quarry man hurled the rope into his Jeep through its rear cargo door, tossed me a breezy salute, and roared off down the road.

The mud we were wearing had started to dry.

Pete poured a generous helping of Scotch—which turned out to be a peaty little Oban—into the cup of the thermos and offered it to me. I sipped, approved, and smacked my lips. From where I sat drying off thousands of miles from my Weehawken studio apartment, both the mud and the Scotch smelled earthy. A moment later I remembered with a pang that I had let the apartment go in order to do the work at the Prajna Center, where I got room and board—nice perks for a nearly thirty-year-old trying to build a career away from her pushy pop. I was, I realized as I savored the Scotch, really rather homeless. An interesting thought. Pete sipped long and hard and let out a sigh of pleasure, and we both sat back. Then he recapped the thermos, which he handed to me, and let in the clutch, shifting.

In less than two minutes we were pulling up at La Chiesina, the little church-turned-into-guesthouse the contessa had booked. As we stepped out of the Bird, I took in the square, converted chapel built out of stone and mortar a shade of red bleached nearly pink over centuries of sun. The roof was cedar shake, and black lacquered shutters framed the natural finish of the front door. There were two steps up to a flagstone patio, where a grape arbor shaded a table and two chairs.

The grapes were dark and heavy and plentiful. Surrounding the wide gravel driveway were lavender bushes, their high, thick stalks bent from the slight breeze that was helping to spread the scent. There was the kind of sleepy peace to the place that lavender always seems to provide, and I was standing on tiptoe to pluck a couple of particularly plump grapes when suddenly the front door was flung open.

Out stepped the contessa in a leopard-print coat and a state of perturbation. Her hands were shaking as she struggled to button up—Pete blocked her way, murmuring in that conciliatory tone made famous on-screen by Dr. Val Valenti—but her voice was shrill and indignant. I couldn't follow all the Italian outrage, but I popped the plump grapes into my mouth and approached the poor woman.

She was missing a shoe, her wet hair was slicked back, and I was pretty sure the leopard-print coat was the only thing she was wearing. Stumbling, she whirled and limped back inside La Chiesina, hurling Italian left and right, *poi* this and *anche* that. It all sounded so very cynical and ambivalent that I think it had something to do with men. But there's a possibility Dr. Val would say I was projecting.

Pete and I followed the contessa into the rental she couldn't abandon fast enough. Still raging, she attempted to close her overstuffed Louis Vuitton suitcase by slamming the halves together like she was a cymbalist who had failed anger management. While Pete soothed her in just about every way except any that included removing her coat, I hunted for the missing shoe, finally finding it up in the choir loft that had been turned into a bedroom.

I eyed the scene below, where the contessa deflated into a colorful chair, and Pete crouched in front of her. All the game she'd had last night hadn't returned with a night's sleep—or with anything else of interest up in the choir loft—and she looked scared. But she started to listen to Pete, even though she punctuated his points with whimpers.

I joined him in a crouch, where I slipped the shiny black patent stiletto onto the contessa's foot, which led to a kind of keening from behind her pursed lips. Pete gave me a quick update. "The police have been here."

"I guessed."

"She didn't like their attitude."

"So it seems." I gave her a smile. She brightened. She tucked a stray wave behind my ear and—burbling at me in Italian—gave me a patronizing once-over with the kind of baffled hand gesture that seemed to wonder, *Why would you look like—like—this when you could look like me?* I muttered to Pete, "Did she just say she wanted to do a makeover?"

We kept smiling. "Pretty much."

I chuckled. "What were her exact words?"

He chuckled, too. "She offered to take you on as a style pupil—"

"It sounded longer than that."

"—and that with her help you might—no guarantees—attract a man who drives a bus."

I smiled broadly at the contessa, who chirped. After a moment, I said, "I'm liking her for the murder."

He patted my arm, which made the contessa suck in her breath. "I think we can move on."

I sprang over to where I had dropped my poor briefcase with its dried mud shell, then pulled up a chair in front of the contessa. Over the next few minutes, with translation help from Pete, we nailed down the contessa's movements during the dinner last evening. There was an unexplained (I thought, despite moving on) murderous gap in her alibi.

Although I had her down for pressing her boobs against Pete from eight forty-five through the final *caffè*, she admitted to returning to her car to look for her phone sometime between nine and, oh, half past. Her wide-eyed innocence was unconvincing. "Half an hour to look for your phone in your car?" I asked in my best prosecutorial voice.

She seemed to be enjoying herself, and her expression went feline. "It's a very small phone." When I asked if any-

body could corroborate her tale, she said offhandedly that
perhaps the director could. Then she stroked her highly
waxed right eyebrow. I persisted scornfully, "You mean to
tell me it takes two people half an hour to look for a phone?"
By then, Pete was elbowing me. She purred that no, it required only thirty seconds to "find" the phone. And then I
got it. She flashed me a woman-to-woman look.

Sucking in my breath, I took a different tack. "Prior to
last evening," I began, nodding at Pete to translate, "were
you acquainted with the murdered man?" At my own
words, I felt a sudden pang, my mind crowded with the image of poor bashed Bu. The contessa got impatient, ruffling
her hair with both hands and spitting out a few fragments
of Italian.

I eyed Pete, who nodded at her and said, "She has already told the policemen she never met him before last
night." Now she yawned—stylishly—and dismissed poor
dead Bu with the kind of imprecision that suggests paralyz-
ing boredom. "Keppler, Korman, *come se dice* . . ."

We took turns staring at each other, yielding nothing. As
I was just settling on becoming annoying for the sweet sake
of annoyance, Pete weighed in. "I believe her," he said,
which pretty much put to an end that avenue of questioning.
I felt stymied, but I wasn't about to show it, not to my style
coach. I made a note to check her alibi with the director,
and I racked my brain to think of a new direction for my
questioning, but as it stood, if she said she only met Bu last
evening, where could I go?

And then I had it. Straightening my spine, I turned easily to my colleague. "Ask her if she knows where Dalia di
Bello lives." For a second, Pete was about to ask what possible relevance di Bello's address could have, but then he
caught on. Among last evening's dinner guests, it was the

contessa who was most likely to have information that could lead us straight to Chef.

Pete laid a sacrificial hand on her knee. "Contessa," he crooned, having her full attention, "*conosci* Dalia di Bello?"

I could tell the contessa was so encouraged by the placement of his hand that she would claim to be the movie star's BFF if she thought she could get away with it. Both women were Romans, both ran in expensive social circles, and both were close to the same age. But could the contessa add anything else? With Pete's prodding, which led her to scrutinize me like she was trying to figure out how to get rid of me, she apparently knew di Bello a little bit, just by chance, showing up at the same occasional party or opera gala. As to where di Bello was living, she scoffed something to the effect that absolutely everyone knows she's still in the Piazza di Spagna, third floor of the corner building overlooking the ugly boat sculpture by the Baroque artist Bernini.

"Dalia," ventured the contessa, working hard to contain her glee, "has been there almost as long as the Bernini boat"—and at her catty implication about the movie goddess's age, the contessa simpered.

"Enough?" Pete asked me.

It was enough to go on, if Chef didn't turn up instantly. I nodded.

Pete gave Contessa's knee an affectionate, brief squeeze and let go.

Having satisfied herself that she was witty and well connected, the contessa rose regally, brushing Pete and Nell cooties from her fine fake leopard skin, and sidestepped us. This time, her Louis Vuitton suitcase closed with no drama whatsoever, and she gestured—princess to peons—toward the door.

"*Scusi,*" she nearly sang in a triumphant aria, going on

to explain her imminent departure, something about a pressing engagement *a Roma*. We watched the contessa check the pearliness of her capped teeth in a gold compact and then apply a scarlet red lipstick in sleek, practiced strokes.

We had been dismissed.

9

After a couple of calls to mutual acquaintances who might possibly know the whereabouts of international food critic Ernesto Treni, Pete hit pay dirt with a local reporter. We bypassed Cortona and steamed up the A1, shooting for a place called La Chiocciola, between Siena and Arezzo. To me, the T-Bird was beginning to show some disinclination for long road trips. To Pete, the Bird was out of alignment, due to the cliff-hanging mudfest. While we rode in silence, I looked over my timetable notes, hoping to get a good sense of where the interesting gaps in Ernesto's movements were.

As Pete turned off the highway, we passed a boxy beige Fiat pulled over onto the shoulder and a young guy wearing sunglasses changing a flat. I began to Google Ernesto Treni, just to see where his most recent food and restaurant reviews had been published. We turned down a two-lane paved country road, then entered what looked like a campground. Pete and I exchanged looks, and I could swear the T-Bird growled when we pulled into the grounds of Camping La Chiocciola. We drove slowly, swerving around children, Frisbees, and other cars, none so fine as the '55 ocean green T-Bird. There were pitched tents, mobile homes, and trailers that looked about as old as the Bernini ugly boat sculpture in Rome.

I ventured, "This can't be right, Pete."

"Snob." He slowed alongside a woman wearing a broad-brimmed sun hat and a muumuu. Her hair was thin from a lifetime of dye jobs, but her smile was friendly. In Italian, Pete asked her where we could find Signor Treni's . . . house.

She laughed gaily and made a series of gestures that suggested the signor had a big head and screwy eyes, followed by a flat hand accompanied by a sound effect of *splat*. By this I took her to be referring either to a terrible fall or a sexual encounter. She pointed to a beige and white mobile home situated at a bend in the drive through the colony.

We pulled up in front of the home, and Pete turned off the engine and got out of the car. For a long minute, the two of us sat and stared at the metal steps on wheels that led up to the plain white front door. The house was raised up on cinder blocks, and a satellite dish topped the old shingled roof as though it was a gaudy bow on a little girl's head. Pete hopped gamely up the steps and rapped at the door.

A group of three wild-haired children gathered by the single canvas deck chair on what back home we would have called the lawn. Two of their T-shirts proclaimed LEGAL-IZE MARINARA, and one, on the youngest—a wiry girl with hair pointing off in all directions—had a drawing of a winged and fiddling red goblin. *"Cerchi lo scrittore?"* asked the oldest—"Looking for the writer?"—who crossed his arms and looked as authoritative as only a ten-year-old can.

I answered yes, we were, and the little gang gave us a practiced once-over—they slowed when they scrutinized me because I was carrying a smart leather briefcase. Or possibly because I was covered in mud. My eyes narrowed at them. I was betting they were figuring the odds of making off with the smart leather briefcase. I held my ground, staring down goblin girl, who seemed the fiercest. At that moment, the front door to the mobile home was wrenched open, and there—looking like we had interrupted a hard day at the Barcalounger—was a very different Ernesto Treni from the one at the dinner last night.

He seemed strangely happy to see us, remembered my name, and swept us inside the mobile home. During a flurry of Italian, which Pete translated for me as delight in his new digs, so much more affordable and quite decent, really, Treni dragged two folding chairs to the center of the room. He patted each, inviting us to sit.

The living room was painted almost as beige as the exterior, and green low-nap wall-to-wall carpeting seemed chosen to match the shade of the Tuscan landscape. But the notable thing about the food critic's home was that it served as a kind of command center. There was an economy to the setup that appealed. Cookbooks, textbooks, Zagat's guides, maps, framed photos of restaurants across the Continent, food industry publications, and a twenty-seven-inch iMac desktop computer. Presiding over the happy, organized disarray was a large blue cat, sitting motionless, its yellow eyes deceptively narrow.

His cheerful expectancy—*"Che magnifica sorpresa!"*— "What a wonderful surprise!"—suddenly struck me with misgiving. Treni sprang up, full of self-recriminations about his flawed hospitality, and attacked a stash of Montepulciano and wineglasses.

While he unearthed a brass tray under a bunch of back issues of *La Cena*, I whispered to Pete, "If he isn't the killer, I'm thinking Ernesto hasn't heard about the murder yet."

Pete let out a low whistle. The cat stiffened.

Ernesto, wearing a polo shirt and loose jeans, pulled his shoulders back and lowered the tray to where we could choose glasses. "A Montepulciano," he explained, and then added, "stronger than usual." Pete and I lifted our glasses. All three of us sipped, and Ernesto Treni settled back into high-speed Italian.

Pete turned to me. "This grape was—as he puts it—found near an Etruscan necropolis he enjoys visiting."

I smiled appreciatively. Ernesto puffed up. Always the mood killer, I leaned toward Pete. "Tell him about the murder." And he did. Our host spilled his wine, invoked God several times, and actually wrung his hands. Something flickered across his face, for only a moment, and I wondered if Ernesto Treni was musing about something that had been left out on the kitchen counter. The cat, on the other hand, stretched from stem to stern, jumped off the table, and ambled toward the litter box. Scratching ensued.

Ernesto was filled with basic questions. First, was it the food? We assured him that no, it was not the food, and we jollied him into a pact never to voice that question again outside these four prefab walls. Second, could the dead man have fallen and hit his head? We assured him no, several times. Then Ernesto Treni made a fist and glowered at what might have been a clutch of red-winged goblins. He informed us in a low voice that somebody will pay.

Figuring that was as good a time as any to fill in the Ernesto Treni gaps on the timetable, I motioned to Pete to begin. Right away, he jabbered at the food critic in Italian, asking for what sounded to me like an opinion on the *dolci* course. Treni's reply seemed genuine enough, considering

I was hoping he'd pretend to have actually been at the table when it was served. But he seemed a bit shy to admit that when he saw it was Chef's signature galette—he is terribly allergic to plums—he took that time to return to his automobile and call in for work messages.

And *secondo*? Pete persisted pleasantly. Did Signor Treni enjoy Chef's pork *osso buco*? I was about to correct Pete when I tumbled onto his strategy and instead sat waiting to see how it played out. It is an insider tidbit comparable to knowing, say, Jason Momoa's swim fin size, that Chef Orlandini never makes *osso buco* with pork—asserting in high-handed Italian, *You can, but why would you?* But Ernesto Treni might not know that, and if he wasn't present for *secondo*, he would fall into the trap.

Treni was confused. Pork? It was veal. Trap averted.

I corrected my mistake in the timetable: Ernesto Treni was present throughout *secondo*. But I hoped to trip him up on the subject of Ember. On my behalf, Pete asked the food critic whether he knew Ember Weston before last evening, to which our host said no, only he always had a hard time concealing his contempt for (in other words, unwilling attraction to) Out There women like that. With a long, cooling swig of wine, Ernesto surveyed the framed photos of himself wearing a beret and standing with out-thrust chest at the site of a Milanese bistro that had closed after his scathing review.

"And so," I asked slowly, totally leading the witness, "you enjoyed Chef's dinner last evening?"

Pete translated quickly.

"Ah, sì," waxed Ernesto. *"Che magnifica sorpresa,"* he said for the second time in fifteen minutes. With delight, he pushed his hands at us and said something coy in Italian, which Pete told me was "wait until you lovely people read my review."

I clamped a hand on my chest. "We are honored, Signor Treni."

He beamed.

It was then, in this moment of good fellowship, that I asked him whether he had recognized Signor Kaplan.

Paling, he demurred.

I persisted. "He called you 'Ernie.'"

"Did he?" was all Ernesto Treni could get out.

We were all of us—except the presiding blue cat—still smiling. Ernesto Treni seemed to sense something more was required. What followed was a burble of Italian. I turned to Pete, who explained that Treni said perhaps their paths crossed sometime in the past—after all, both are artists.

I tried a different tack. "Have you lived here long in La Chiocciola?" I put to him.

Absentmindedly scratching his cat's fine head, Treni replied, "Galileo here and I grew tired of big flat in Siena. We move out here to our summer home just for change." He went on to describe how he happily takes rich Americans on Treni Tours of great restaurants in northern Italy. Studying his cat Galileo balefully, he went on, "The Americans, all they want to know about is food."

As we said our goodbyes, we slipped in casual comments about the likely imminent arrival of Commissario Joe Batta, leaving poor Treni looking bemused. Off we went, none the wiser, but there was something going on. Something despite Ernesto's sidestepping denials. Treni Tours? Why would a respected international food critic be busking around the country with tourists on buses? Were restaurant review outlets dropping off? If so, why?

While we bounced back along the A1 in the Orlandinis' 1955 T-Bird, which now desperately needed wheel alignment, Pete called Benedetto Ricci at work. *Yes? Yes? Fifteen minutes? That will be fine.*

Had Ernesto Treni just put one over on Pete and me?

If so, he had been coached by his familiar, the blue and slow-blinking Galileo.

I sighed. Bu Kaplan had been a careless man. A rough-shod man. A trash-talking shooter of film who grooved on quantity over truth and diligence. No wonder he had ended up dead. I only wished it had been back at the Prajna Center where some yogi could have led all the rest of us through a guided meditation, urging us to stuff our thoughts into a car and watch it ease on out of sight.

Pete parked the car on a short, winding side street three blocks from the Piazza della Repubblica, and we walked to the center of town. When his phone rang, we slowed down as he answered it. "The vet," he mouthed at me. As he listened, he paced, uttered a few *capisco*s and *grazie*s, and ended the call. There was nothing in the way of a smile when he stood in front of me. I watched him. Finally, he said, "Vincenzo's cow?"

"Yes?" Already I was wondering if I'd need an alibi for the attack on the bovine.

"It was aldicarb poisoning."

"What's that?"

I heard him sigh. "A very toxic weed killer," he said. "It's been banned for twenty years."

"'Banned' doesn't mean unobtainable."

"You're right." He took a deep breath.

"So what are we looking at here, Pete? A terrible mistake?" It was the easy answer, but in my experience the easy answer was rarely the true one. "Is there some leftover— what is it?—"

"Aldicarb."

"—stored somewhere at the villa?"

"To my knowledge, we've never had any of the stuff." He explained, "We've never grown vegetables."

"Not even tomatoes?" What self-respecting Italian doesn't—

"All right, tomatoes, herbs, just enough for ourselves. No large-scale needs to address pests."

I went on slowly, "So . . . someone brought in the pesticide."

"That's how it looks."

"The trees, the murder—these two things have got to be connected, although I don't know how yet, but—" I clutched at my hair, feeling thickheaded. "Let's figure it out. How could Bu's work intersect with yours?"

A beat. "It can't," he said plainly. "It doesn't."

"But—"

"They're two different crimes, Nell."

We started walking, and I found myself wondering where else could there be a stockpile of the banned weed killer. And . . . who had access to it? I slid a look at Pete, who had so much on his plate, so much at stake, what with the murder at the villa. If the killer was close to home, how would the Orlandinis survive it? I decided to do some discreet poking around about the poisoned trees. But I couldn't get away from the fact that the culprit had to be somebody with easy, regular access to the grounds at Villa Orlandini. Someone whose presence might not even be noted.

It was a sickening thought.

So it was a relief to arrive at the heart of Cortona. There's nowhere better to understand the age of a place than the center of town, and if I looked past the colorful plexiglass awnings over the *tabacchi* and florist shops, Cortona's expansive piazza, with its broad, rustic pavers, soaring archways, and stony, inscrutable facades, flung me back several hundreds of years. I found that point of intersection between invincible and holy. Square, fortified, open for market day business, open for everyday, strolling humans, enjoying what the Italians call *passeggiata*.

Director Benedetto Ricci's office in the *camera di commercio* was on the street level of the piazza, a storefront next to a brightly lit pottery shop, where everything round or flat was glazed in many colors. If I had been wondering the day I arrived about stray dogs in Cortona, I found them. They were all scoping out goodies in the hands of the director at the chamber of commerce. Thirty-two sets of toenails tapped excitedly on the varnished wood floor of the one-room office. Brown, white, black canines with spots and streaks, with bull's-eyes and mittens and an unintelligible scrum of yaps like late night at a popular bar, chomped sausage cubes flung from the director's own meaty mitts.

When he noticed us, he herded them to the door—*"a domani!"*—and they squeezed and bounded through to the piazza, vocalizing their delight. A four-legged flash mob. I am such an unyielding sleuth, I allowed myself a full minute before eliminating this great humanitarian from the list of suspects on the assumption that no one who feeds homeless dogs can commit a murder. Theft of sausage, yes, possibly. Kidnapping of dog warden, yes, possibly. Murder? No chance.

But I needed to appear stern and as full of possibility as the director's pockets.

Pete appeared to be softening him up with some dog jokes. Although—maybe it was the wine I had on board—Benedetto Ricci was seeming pretty soft already. Lovely man. A prince who takes on the contessa in the back seat of a car, a charming homage to any decade you can name from the time of the Model T. Yet one more Italian with an adolescent's devotion to the sweatier celebrations of life.

I was feeling plenty serene when the director proclaimed, "I didn't do it!" The man who just five minutes ago was single-handedly crooning to a dog pack was now confronting us like a pugilist. At that moment I wondered whether the Cortona chamber of commerce came equipped with a pistol or two. He went on: "I do not know what you are talking about, and besides I have an iron-clothed alibi." Which, he added, he mentioned to the *carabinieri* fellows who had come by earlier.

But the exact time of his automotive interlude with the contessa still needed to be proved. Warming up to the inquisition, I cracked my knuckles and sang out, "Are you saying—"

Pete closed his eyes.

Over the threshold clambered two white-blond tourists in knee socks and matching white shirts. *"Guten Tag,"* the one with bigger, whiter, straighter teeth greeted us. Then the two of them looked around with their noses high, as though that's where they expected to see the Valkyries arrive. "Haf you a mep—"

The director sprang into manic action, swiping maps and tourist trifolds from various metal racks, yelling, "If you think I—I—I—had anything to do with the murder, then you have gnocchi for brains, you two." Shoving the tourist information at the cowering white-blondies, Benedetto went on, "I do not kill people with rocks." His tone implied that other methods were perfectly acceptable, but rocks? No. He drew the line. The hapless tourists shook their heads ever so slightly. The director whirled, storming toward the counter by the back wall.

"We—we—" the bigger, paler tourist stammered.

My nightmare was rendered in real time when the director produced a pistol the size of a hanging sausage at the local butcher's and brandished it. "This," he declared, "this is a man's weapon, not a silly rock, let me tell you, and my papa, God rest his crazy-ass soul, put the end to many a gutless enemy during the big war with this baby." He came around the counter with surprising speed and made it over to the cowering tourists in three bounds. One brochure he tapped with the barrel of the gun. "Fill out the online survey about the *camera di commercio* to be eligible for a gift card—"

They babbled.

"You hear me?" he hollered.

"Ja, ja, danke, danke—"

He waved his pistol. "Your opinion matters to us."

"Ja, ja—"

The director wrenched open the door to the office. "Now get the hell out of here," he snarled. Their knee socks were just a blur. "And have a nice day." Slamming the door, he stomped back to the counter, stashed the pistol, and pulled out a white box. As sweet as Annamaria's plum galette, Benedetto smiled. *"Pizzelle?"*

10

We decided to leave the T-Bird where it was—an easy choice since I didn't know where it was in this medieval maze of a walled town anyway—while we took stock of where the investigation stood. In other circumstances, I would have called it a date. I was coming to the conclusion that all of the serpentine streets in Cortona ran in two directions only: uphill and downhill. From a fruit stall, Pete bought a mango, then he produced a pocketknife and did a quick peel. He silently offered me a slice, and I took it with a smile. Together we chewed placidly as we dodged idling tourists and sidewalk café tables. Coming toward us was a young couple wearing Ray-Bans on a red and silver Vespa, purring around an old woman wisely wearing hiking boots, squeezing out the tune "Santa Lucia" on her accordion.

We passed nannies grabbing hooting children out of rain puddles while shopkeepers smoked inscrutably in their open doorways. Another day in the life of Cortona, a place that predates even the Etruscans.

"He admitted pleading with Buford to give Fabrizia a part," noted Pete, slicing another hunk of mango and passing it to me, balanced on the blade.

Savoring the slice, I half closed my eyes. "But did you notice he made it sound as though his whole interaction with Buford occurred at the table?"

"So?"

"I followed them inside when Benedetto arrived, Pete. It sounded to me like the director had already been making a nuisance of himself."

"How? Why?"

I hesitated. "Something was off in his account, but I don't know what. Either's he's got a motive he wants to hide, or"—I held up my hands—"or he's downplaying the interactions with Bu because he knows it looks like a motive whether he had one or not."

Pete pointed toward a lovely stone building with a flat facade festooned with a great, white hanging banner. "This is not a man who kills with rocks," he said sagely. "And here's another odd thing about Benedetto Ricci—"

"Besides the pistol waving?"

Pete shrugged. "This is Italy."

"Then what?"

"This little Netflix gig, filming a few European start-ups in agritourism—" With that, he stood still, turning slowly to me. "Exactly where's the part for his daughter?" It was a good point, and I felt irked I hadn't thought of it myself. "Right," I said. "Maybe the edited footage on the Villa Orlandini Cooking School gets down to, what, fifteen minutes?"

"If that."

"A quote from me, a quote from you, and from Chef—"

"Establishing shots of the buildings, the grounds—"

"Some good shots of the dinner—the lighting was beautiful—"

We looked hard at each other. After a moment, Pete made the conclusion. "Why plead?" he said softly.

I took a shot. "Maybe he doesn't know what a promotional video is."

Pete shook his head. "Ricci's the director of the chamber of commerce. He's seen plenty of promotional videos." That did seem likely.

I had an idea. "Why don't you talk to Fabrizia? Maybe she can give us some insight into Benedetto's state of mind."

After a couple of quick calls, Pete got Fabrizia's number. What followed was a conversation in cheerful Italian. Finally, with many *grazie*s back and forth, he clicked off. Then he turned to me, giving me a waterfall of English, he was so excited. Apparently, Fabrizia was thrilled not to get a part in the American's little promo flick. She wanted to be an architect. But for now her papa could enjoy his California dreamin' for his only child a little while longer. She had thought she was off the hook, that it was a nonissue with Signor Kaplan, until last evening when her papa and the American filmmaker turned up at the same dinner party, small world. And—from what Pete told her—it sounded like Papa had taken up the cause all over again. Pete looked at me meaningfully.

I heard it. "'Again'?"

"For almost a year now," he explained, "the director has been pestering the filmmaker Buford Kaplan to cast his beautiful daughter, Fabrizia, in an upcoming feature film."

"Not just the segment on the Orlandini Cooking School?"

"No." Pete finished, "Tough letters exchanged hands. Through Netflix, Kaplan threatened her persistent papa with a restraining order; Papa threatened to make public his terrible treatment at the hands of the ugly American."

I nodded, agreeing at least with the *ugly American* description. The director believed the Kaplan fellow was far too brittle for a man in such a tough business—he should be able to take well in stride the repeated blandishments from someone with a talented and beautiful daughter, but no. Kaplan was immovable.

I cast my mind back to last evening. Had Bu and Benedetto found themselves by the fountain in the dark, starry night, both men driven past the bounds of accepted social behavior? When the director told us—and the hapless tourists in optimistic knee socks—he did not kill men with rocks, did he mean . . . not unless he had no other weapon at hand? Was I making too great a leap of faith in the case of a man with an office full of a pack of feckless pups? Was I blinded by sausage treats? It would not be the first time.

B ack at the villa as fast as the wounded T-Bird could manage, Pete dropped me off in the courtyard, heading to neighboring Arezzo, where he had some errands. No one was in sight, and the Ape was still gone. What is there about silence and solitude that always gives me a sense of impending doom? It was the sort of question Dr. Val always liked to tackle on the air in the TV studio, if the audience had nothing more confessional to offer up.

The smell of a bonfire came from somewhere down past the dormitory—Macy, I was guessing. But hardly doom. As I headed toward the cloister, thinking I might find Ember Weston holed up in my room, a door slammed, and I turned. Annamaria hurried to catch up with me, with Rosa on her heels. The impending doom had arrived.

Without Pete, I didn't know how far the conversation would get.

Today my bathroom colleague was wearing a blue floral wraparound dress and an unbuttoned navy cardigan, minus the apron, minus the flour. There was even an asymmetrical prettiness to her salt-and-pepper hair, pulled back on only one side with a comb. As the two of them pulled up beside me, Annamaria started to wring her wiry hands, and I noticed her professional manicure. When her hands weren't wrist deep in dough, the blue-violet fingernails could really shine. *"L'hai trovato?"* she said breathlessly. When I took a second too long to figure out what she was asking, she added, "Chef?"

All I could do was wince and shake my head. "No Chef."

She deflated almost imperceptibly, and I could tell the woman who singlehandedly kept the villa together was grappling with something. Either the futility of her love for this man, or whether she should set one less plate for dinner. Without any answers or volume two of *Italian for Idiots*, I couldn't help. But I remembered the sound of her fretful pacing in her room this morning.

For all I knew, Annamaria Bari could have come to the end of her frayed rope and was now debating whether this was indeed a good time to decamp from life and from her work at the Villa Orlandini. After all these years, what hope did she have? Always present and always invisible, as Pete described her, she was up against the spectacle of a long-loved man who runs out on a dinner that holds the key to his future professional life—for a woman who must loom like a specter for Annamaria herself. Dalia di Bello.

Off he went in a joke car with no other information or preparations, sticking the rest of them with an event that— when it came right down to it—meant nothing to him. It struck me that Annamaria's competition wasn't Dalia di Bello. It was the idea of Dalia di Bello. And that made it worse. Was that what brought on the pacing? Did she finally see it—see her life—for what it was? Yet another question for Dr. Val Valenti.

When I asked about Ember Weston, Annamaria gave me a look like I had *panna cotta* for brains. And not even very good *panna cotta*. She made an airy gesture with her hand that didn't narrow down the possibilities as to where on the fifty-acre property I could find Bu's assistant. Rosa, then, clearly feeling bad about her sister's difficulty, launched into charades. As Annamaria turned and headed back to her kitchen domain, straight-backed like a mythic figure, Rosa tried to communicate something that included rubbing her hands together, scribbling in the air, and pinching her nostrils together against a terrible smell. "The moss room, Rosa?"

"Em-bear, *sì*." With that, she winked at me—now, who was around to translate that?—and bounded off after her sister. Narrowing my eyes at them, I reminded myself that although I could pretty much account for Rosa and Sofia's movements last evening, my entry on Annamaria was still TBD. I'd have to catch her alone.

Still clutching my briefcase, still sporting my muddy clothes that had dried to dust, I found Ember Weston right where winking Rosa had told me. But when I realized her back was to me, and that she was on her cell phone, distracted, I hung out in the doorway, easing the door shut behind me. From her tone, I could tell it was a business call, which made complete sense to me—with Buford Kaplan murdered, what was the fate of the Netflix documentary on new start-ups in European agritourism? How far had poor dead Bu gotten in the filming before last night, when rock and career had come crashing down on him?

"So you saw it online?" She lifted her head, listening. How close to Bu's fate was Ember's own? I wondered just how employable she'd be without Bu there to keep her in a paycheck. Could she always count on the filmmaker Bu Kaplan, or—I studied the back of her dyed red asymmetrical hair, her stark white neck, her soft and collarless black leather jacket—was she the prop, the talent, the better half of the moviemaking duo? "The *carabinieri* are . . . investigating," she said into the phone, and I found myself betting the Netflix exec on the other end was not someone she knew well. Ember was speaking carefully. No matter what Bu's assistant felt about his death—possibly, let's face it, even less than I did—this was a stumbling block the size of a boulder.

"Not much here yet," she said, answering what had to be a question about how much film they had shot. "We just arrived. I'll send you what we've got, if you'd like." Then she added with some spirit: "Pretty great stuff, you can take it from me." I slid sideways just enough to catch Ember widen her eyes at her own starch. As long as she still had a connection and an audience, she said with some spirit, "Kaplan and I had mapped out the rest of the segments. I can certainly finish it up without him," she said, then threw in an obligatory "—if you'd like, and I can handle the final segment in Albarracín alone."

She bit her lip, trying to keep from squealing at the picture she was painting. "Or," she ended on a casual note, "you can send me an assistant." For all her bravado, I could tell she was anxious about suggesting herself for the top spot—and it seemed like a new idea, maybe not one she had killed to get. "All right," she said, keeping her voice neutral, "all right, I'll do that." Then she took a chance: "Let me know what you think—although I think you'll be pleased. As for carrying through on the rest of the project—" She was holding the exec's feet to the fire.

But whatever the exec was outlining on the other end, Ember was looking like a taxidermist had gotten to her. "Albarracín day after tomorrow? I don't see how—" How it can happen? Neither did I. She listened. "Of course I'm a team player, H.L. But last night the other half of my team got himself killed. Now I'm the team. The cheapest way forward for you is to pay me what you were paying Kaplan, and I'll finish things up. But until the *carabinieri* make an arrest—or settle on someone they like for Kaplan's murder—I can't leave."

While Ember waited out the exec's final word on the matter, she bit her nails, her restless eyes flitting around the common room of the Villa Orlandini Cooking School. "Okay," she said finally, not entirely pleased. "I'll see what I can do. Bye."

At that instant, I pulled the door shut so hard it sounded like the end of time. Ember whirled where she sat. "Oh, hello," I said, deciding between exactly which fake I was going for: surprise at finding her there, or pleasure at finding her there. From Ember's expression it didn't seem like she was buying either one. "Ember, can I ask you some questions, if you've got a few minutes?"

As I sat down next to her on the love seat and pulled my notes from the briefcase, out of the corner of my eye I noticed she oozed away from me by about three inches. Interesting in a woman who has a tattoo of Minnie Mouse decked out in a bustier on her biceps and gauges in her elongated earlobes. How had I missed those before?

"What the hell happened to you?" she said aggressively. I forgot I hadn't changed clothes.

"Ah," I said, pretending to root around in my case for something—anything at all—that was proving exceedingly difficult to find in an otherwise empty bag, "it was a whole mud thing." I had meant to set her at ease, or suggest Nell Valenti was capable of some pretty unexpected behavior in deep dirt, but instead she was just scowling at me. Which was when I realized I could see the time on the mantel clock through her gauged earlobe. I patted my hair in a finishing-the-toilette kind of way. "So"—I looked back at Bu's assistant with my eyebrows raised—"a few questions?"

"Someone make you a deputy?" If she had been swirling coffee in her mouth, it would have sputtered all over both of us, she was so amused at herself.

I countered, "Someone make you a suspect?"

A beat. Then: "No more than you." She slung me another wily look and bounced another two inches away.

"I can account for my time last night," I said, adding weight to every other word. "What about you?"

"As I told the commissario, I was out getting shots." She made a face at the ceiling. "Until the light failed." I think she was trying to dazzle me with her filmmaking lingo. "And then I had food."

Pen poised, I barked, "Tell me what you were served." I couldn't picture her *a tavola* at all last evening. "Appetizer?"

"Glop on toast?"

I felt stunned. The woman was sitting in Chef Claudio Orlandini's very own moss room calling his signature *crostini al drago* "glop on toast." Far be it from me to concede the point. In that second I had her pegged as a Philistine. But was she also a killer? "And *primo*?" I felt relentless.

Ember spread her hands. "Macaroni?" I believe my heart stopped. "Big whoop."

"Can you be more specific?" I choked, trying to get the pen to write the word *macaroni* on my list.

She scratched Minnie's red-inked bustier, trying to recall. "Red sauce. Some kind of white shavings on top—I thought maybe it was seaweed. Had that kind of OMG-I-just-swallowed-some-swamp-water taste."

So much for *tartufi* that cost a hundred bucks an ounce. "And *secondo*?" I asked, steeling myself for what I was sure would be her pithy critique of the number one *osso buco* on the planet.

"Well, it was totally dark out by then, so I had nothing else to do but sit there picking at the veal." Grudgingly, I had to give her points for recognizing the meat. "But Chef's showing his age if he thinks it's cool to support factory farming." She shook her head at a dying generation clinging to their old ways. "Nobody, but nobody"—suddenly we were girls gossiping in the locker room—"is making baby cow anymore. It's so yesterday. Actually," she corrected herself, "it's so the day before yesterday. Really."

"What should he use instead of baby cow?" I had to know.

She sniffed out a small laugh, surprised I had to ask. "Lentils." Warming to her subject, she added, "You'd be surprised what they can do with lentils these days."

"Yes," I said slowly, "I would be."

"Very underrated legume."

"Its day will come."

"Totes." She added as an afterthought: "After it got too dark to shoot, I asked one of the servers to bring me what I had missed, just all at once, no worries. I ate right here." She patted the Cassina sofa. "They fixed me a plate. I was fine."

No wonder I couldn't place Bu's assistant at the dining table. At this point, I think I was slipping into a fugue state, and my voice sounded very far away while I tried to wrap it up with Ember. "The cheese, the tart, the *caffè*?"

She temporized, "Pretty good. Listen, I won't dwell on any of the rest of the meal in this segment. No worries. Go right ahead and make your little cooking school," she actually said in a munificent sort of way. "I'll make it look good."

At that, I blew. "You don't even know if you've got a job—"

"You listened."

"—so don't tell me you'll keep our little secret. There's no little secret. Not about Chef, and not about his cuisine."

"Then where'd he run off to so he could hand us over to the B Team?"

"He had an urgent call away. Not that it's any of your business."

"It's my business that you had a thing for Buford."

I stood up, furious. "How did you—" It's difficult to tower over a woman with tattoos and gauged earlobes. She was impervious to threats. "I didn't have a thing for Buford. I had a thing *with* Buford. There's a difference." Nell Valenti, ever the wordsmith.

"Not the way he told it."

"Before you brained him!" Where did that come from? Oh, Nell, tut, tut.

She stood. "Why would I brain him? He was my"—here she made a gurgling sound—"meal ticket."

Suddenly I felt sorry for her. Was that an awful truth—that the dead man was her meal ticket—for a woman like Ember, a talented assistant just waiting to step out from behind her boss's big frame and reputation? Had she pleaded with Bu to give her more artistic freedom? Did she finally just break out of frustration? Something Bu had said in the courtyard the day they had arrived, and he had stretched and swaggered, came back to me. "Tell me about *Sotto Terra*, Ember," I invited her, forgiving her instantly for her dull taste buds. "The Italian high society exposé."

All the spunk squeaked out of her. A cold breeze wafted through her earlobes. She drew a useless little cardigan over her shoulders, and I watched Minnie disappear. *"Sotto Terra,"* said Ember quietly, fondly, as though dimly remembering a dead lover. "By all rights it was mine," she said, and her smile couldn't even crease her face. "I did the shoots, I wrote the script, I did the final edits, I drove the car, I damn near made the coffee and peanut butter sandwiches." Oh, she went on wearily, it was Buford's "vision," all right, this exposé of Italian high society, and Buford talked to the brass, and he did a director's cut that was hardly different from her final edits, and Buford—she lifted her chin, which was the first time I noticed a small tattooed fist on it that looked like it was landing a KO—got the money and took the credit. Ember gave me the side-eye. "We had words."

"I can imagine." For a moment we just looked at each other.

"And then the Emmy noms came out," she said with some final reserve of energy. "And it included *Sotto Terra*."

"And you had more words."

"By then, it was too late, of course." During that time, Bu Kaplan reminded his assistant that he had done all the research on *Sotto Terra*, lest she forget. He had gotten all the verifiable dirt on the subjects of the exposé. It was his best argument, back in the day, for her continued silence.

Chalk it up, he told her. Lesson learned, he told her. Make no mistake, he told her. The jackass was actually giving her advice about why she shouldn't trust a jackass like him—but, since she had, to what he called her "monumental disadvantage"—chalk it up, lesson learned, make no mistake. Slowly, Ember Weston looked at me. "And I won't. Not ever again." With that, Ember buttoned up the cardigan that could have been her granny's.

11

Did you kill him?" This time it was better framed than
when I had yelled at her about braining Bu, and I honestly didn't know what I'd say or do if she told me she had.
But for some reason—maybe I was as gullible as Ember
had been with the dear departed—I felt Ember Weston and
Nell Valenti were founding members of the Wish I Had
Killed Buford Kaplan club.

"No," she said musically, drawing out one of those long
notes of self-awareness, "I didn't have the stuffing for it."

"The cops might think you did."

She widened her eyes at me. "The cops might think
you did."

"Why? Because I had a thing with Bu?"

"Bu?"

"Buford."

"Did you hate him?"

I had to think about it. Then I answered, "I disdained him."

She snorted. "Try telling the Italian cops that difference." She topped herself: "In Italian."

"I will not underestimate them. These are subtle people." I pictured gangly old Joe Batta, sucking on a hard candy he'd had to be reminded to unwrap.

"Who want to make an arrest."

"A just arrest."

"Are you sure there is such a thing?" It was a warning look she gave me then. "Chalk it up, lesson learned, make no mistake."

"Well"—I lifted my hands in a way that meant nothing whatsoever—"there you are."

Then she declared, "I'm forty-two, Nell."

"You don't look it." She shot me a look. "I mean it. I took you for ten years younger."

She tossed her phone up, caught it, slipped it into a pants pocket. "I've got holes in my ears and cartoons on my skin, and I wonder why nobody at Netflix takes me seriously."

"You don't know that."

She gave me a flat look. "You heard the call."

"It doesn't mean they won't let you finish up the project, just the way you want."

"Not if I can't be fancy-free in Albarracín in three days, they won't. If I can't get out of here, they'll shelve the whole thing." I didn't want to keep flinging around easy answers, so I said nothing. "I need a smoke," she declared. "In fact, I need several smokes. Then"—she sucked in a big breath—"I think I'll check out of your room, nice as it is, and into the inn in town, and I'll let my hair grow in gray. How's that for starters?"

"Let's have a drink later."

"Sure." She stuck out a hand, and we shook. "We've got some time to pass."

"Well—"

"All right, all right. You've got your list of suspects.

Very healthy approach, I must say. Me, on the other hand . . ." Together we headed for the door to the courtyard. "I've got some time to pass. And maybe a career to pass. Sometimes," said Ember, "I think I only try so hard because I think that's what I'm supposed to do."

As she shouldered the door open for the two of us, Ember Weston worked a mangled pack of Marlboros out of her pants pocket. She squinted in the bright sunlight. "Only I'm so old now and I've been doing it so long that I honestly couldn't tell you whether—really deep down—I even care."

I watched as she buttoned up the rest of her cardigan. "It's just . . . what you know."

"Right."

"Worth something?"

She lit up. "Maybe."

"Ember," I said suddenly, "what was Bu doing at the Prajna Center for six months? Do you know?" Clearly she had been working with Bu before that time, so maybe they had kept in touch, even though they weren't working together while he was there, "undercover."

"Oh, that?" She took the kind of deep drag I hardly ever saw anymore and headed toward the cloister walk. "He had a nervous breakdown. Or whatever the hell they call it these days. I thought you knew."

"No."

"Six months at a meditation center. Nice gig."

"He tell you that?" I jerked my head in the vague direction of the villa. "To the rest of us he let on he was doing some undercover work."

"Nope. He broke down. I made some calls when I couldn't find him. Never let on I knew about the breakdown, though." She turned suddenly and walked backward. "Poor Bu." Moved, she ran a knobby fist over her nose.

Something occurred to me. "Tell me," I said, my words coming slowly, "how did this gig at the Villa Orlandini come about?" It suddenly struck me as a potentially interesting piece of information, and I wondered if I was the only one on the property who didn't know the answer.

The answer might very well be a clue to the motive for murder. And we thought the only ones who had been invited to the villa had been last night's dinner guests, the local "dignitaries" who could spread the good word about the new cooking school. Maybe—maybe the dinner was just a blind for a more sinister reason.

Was Bu set up?

The thought made me sick.

Ember seemed perplexed. "You mean how did we get the job?"

"Yes."

"Nell," she said, spreading her hands, "this project got the green light a couple of years ago. It didn't just happen."

"Who suggested it?"

Her eyes narrowed. "You mean did Netflix approach Buford, or did Buford approach Netflix?"

"Yes. Which was it?"

"I can't be sure. He did the first segment all on his own. A start-up cooking school in Alsace-Lorraine. I think he thought he could do the whole project that way, without bringing me in, but he couldn't. So when he brought me in and up to speed, he told me he used the Alsace segment as part of his pitch to Netflix."

"And it flew."

"Big-time. Wingspan of a condor sort of thing."

"So it sounds like Bu approached them."

"Not necessarily."

She was right, but I really wanted to nail it down. "Then what?"

"We worked our way through the start-ups that had made the list approved by the producers at Netflix, and"—she pulled out another misshapen Marlboro—"and we had nearly made it through when Buford broke down and checked himself into the Prajna Center for half a year."

I felt so close to the choice bits, and it wouldn't be glop on toast. "What were the approved sites, Ember?"

She rattled them off. "Bruges, Salzburg, Dubrovnik, Bath, Bern, Albarracín, and Colmar—the site in Alsace—seven start-ups over a two-part miniseries. That was the concept."

My skin tingled. "Cortona's not on the list," I pointed out.

A beat. "No, it wasn't." She looked interested.

"When did it get added?"

"Sometime during Buford's time out, I guess. After he left that meditation center, he mentioned they'd added Cortona, Italy, to the project. Cooking school start-up at Chef Claudio Orlandini's villa in Tuscany."

"How did he seem about it?"

"Fine." So, for Bu, no obvious red flags. Then: "And by me, great. More work."

"Did he tell you how Cortona got added?"

"Nope. I just assumed it was the producers. It would have to be."

I said softly, "Would it?" What if Bu had made the Villa Orlandini cooking school start-up an unofficial stop, a chance to scope out something else, meet somebody, take care of something altogether else under the cover of the current project for Netflix? Could it work? Wouldn't Ember Weston and the Netflix execs wonder at the Cortona latecomer?

Or down the road—with his real, covert reason for show-ing up in Tuscany behind him—could Bu just edit out the entire Cortona segment, casually claiming it didn't work, wasn't up to the others. Who would question it? Was Bu that devious? I could certainly picture him thinking he was that devious, and then failing spectacularly at it somehow—the murder, finally, being the strongest evidence that he wasn't as clever as he thought.

"I suppose," said Ember reluctantly, "but"—she clapped a hand on my shoulder—"Nell, I just don't see it."

She was so sure of herself I felt my chin sink to my chest. "Did he mention any names?" I was sounding plain-tive. All right, desperate. "Anyone you met at dinner last night? Anyone else he hoped to see while in Cortona? Any-one who may have had something to do with the addition of Cortona to the Netflix series?"

"Top of my head? No." She turned, heading toward the cloister. "But I'll give it a think while I pack my crap. You could check Bu's files. After he broke down, he got so paranoid about getting scooped on his projects in develop-ment that he made hard copies of his research notes and carried them around in that briefcase he never let out of his sight."

"Oh!" Pulling herself up short, Ember looked over her leather-clad shoulder at me. "Did I mention," she called, "the commissario is coming at four o'clock? He called ear-lier and asked if I could make myself available." With a quick laugh, she added, "At his age, I figure he means for questioning." I was beginning to doubt whether Ember Weston would make it out of Cortona in time to keep her Netflix job. And I discovered it mattered to me. "And he wants me to turn over Signor Kaplan's suitcase, briefcase,

equipment—all of it." Ember gave me a wan look. "All of
Bu's effects are now the property of the police."

"Ember," I said softly, "I think I need those files."

I wanted to give Ember assurances that I would eventually
turn the files over to the cops, but she made a face,
turned the three folders over to me, and re-fastened the
briefcase. Then she wrinkled her nose. "Still plenty of crap
in here for the cops to paw through." Next to her she had set
Bu's suitcase and whatever filmmaking equipment did not
include her precious Red Weapon. As I tucked the files into
a tote bag, I saw Joe Batta's official car turn into the villa
driveway. We actually winked at each other as she turned
brightly to the approaching car, getting on with her day like
any other day.

I slunk off to hide the spoils in the Abbess's room, where
I could do my own pawing through them in my own good
time. But then I couldn't resist. *Just a quick once-over,* I
told myself. Overview. Lay of the land. That sort of thing.
And then I just about fell all over them. Bu's files were
surprisingly well organized: manila folders with color-
coded tabs, arranged according to whether the film project
was current, future, or past. In the Past Projects folder, I
came across *Sotto Terra*, no surprise, and set it aside for
quick review.

In the Current folder was his paperwork for the cooking
school start-ups. A page of scrawled possible titles—*On the
Boil, To the Bite, Whisked Up*—all crossed out. Hasty
notes from phone conversations with the heads of the start-
ups. Signed waivers. Signed releases. Signed contracts.
Hard copies of narration for each segment, written by Bu

himself. Anything pertaining to the Orlandini start-up seemed unremarkable, although a couple of Post-it notes included a lot of punctuation. *Arrive afternoon of pre-launch dinner party?? Get guest list ahead of time??? List of villa employees, residents, yada yada?? Put EW on dirt detail! More ahead of time, better innuendo—school de-signer is Nell Valenti?! WTF!!* Clipped to one page was a photo of the Villa Orlandini, across which Bu had scrawled in a Sharpie, *Holy cow! Lucky me! Glad I agreed to add it.*

Someone had indeed emailed Bu the guest list for the dinner party. There they all were: Contessa Aurora Ciano, food critic Ernesto Treni, and Director Benedetto Ricci. The table also included Pete, Macy, Ember, Bu himself, and me, but the only names on the list that had been sent to Bu ahead of time were the "dignitaries"—the well-positioned Italians who could spread the word about the superb food at the Villa Orlandini Cooking School. Aside from the names, there was nothing added by Ember or Bu in the way of any dirt that might be interesting either to allude to in the narra-tion or for him simply to have in his back pocket.

Had Ember dug but uncovered nothing? I couldn't believe it. Not in any way. The dinner party itself was so last-minute there wouldn't have been any time to dig—besides, I couldn't imagine Ember having much taste for that sort of thing. Pure background on a subject, yes. Dirty little secrets laid bare, not so much. Bu and Ember were shooting a docu-mentary on European cooking school start-ups—so different from *Sotto Terra*, an exposé from the very start.

But how did a Netflix film crew get invited in the first place?

I decided to assume that Bu himself had added the Tuscany segment because someone—some mysterious someone—had sold him on it. What is it about human nature that lets us refuse to entertain the obvious? When I was talking with Ember, was I making everything too complicated? I wasn't ready yet to ask myself that key question about Bu's murder—namely, who benefits?—but I could start small and ask myself who benefited from bringing the Netflix filmmakers to the Villa Orlandini.

Now the obvious was surrounding me like Girl Scouts during cookie season. Who stood to gain from the exposure? Who needed to jump-start his world-class bocce-derailed culinary career? Who disappeared the night of the murder? It was a good thing I was planning on quitting that impossible job, because there was a very good chance the one thing the Villa Orlandini Cooking School would be missing was Chef.

The sooner I got to the bottom of Bu's death, the sooner I could get back to my metro New York haunts and browse the listings on the Good Food Jobs website and let my parents know about half a year later that I was back in town and still not coming to work for the empire. No more time for the overview. The quick review. The lay of the land. Stroking the three folders Ember had slipped me, I pushed aside my mattress, huffing and puffing, and stuck them there.

Then I pulled out one file willy-nilly—couldn't quit cold turkey—and stuffed it in my tote bag, just to see me through any slow moments in either tracking down a cold-blooded killer or savoring a double-shot espresso—and this I would keep with me nonstop until the killer was found, the way my mother does with her pink silk tote from Fiji—it's her version of eco-consciousness when she falls prey to a madcap shopping spree. With boundless satisfaction I pulled the mattress back in place, wondering if I might be missing a thrilling career in the CIA.

In the meantime, I stalked straight to the source of insider information on Chef. I pushed open the door to the kitchen sanctuary, where I found Annamaria and Rosa sitting across from each other, silently sharing wedges of ciabatta and cubes of fontina. The back door was held open with the knife block, and the afternoon sun hadn't quite made it to the windows. Silence and shadow—those two went together very well.

At first, I tried to get across the question of how the Netflix filmmakers got invited to the villa by doing the classic charades mime for movie: one hand open vertically, the other twirling alongside, like a projector. This move I sketched several times in midair with my hands. I got nowhere. In response, Annamaria drizzled some lovely green-tinged olive oil into a saucer and dragged her ciabatta in a lazy line through the goodness.

Finally, I tried English. "Who invited the—how best to put it?—dead movie guy? *Capisce?*" Annamaria simply stared at the slow, slow drips of Pete's small-batch olive oil as though they held the secret either of human existence—or of Chef's whereabouts.

It was Rosa, always willing to please, who nailed it. "Movie guy!" I nodded enthusiastically. *"Sì, sì, capisco tutto, cara* Nella.*"* For Rosa, this was effusive, and I suspected her beloved sister's ponderous silence was getting to her. She acted out someone prowling around with a camera, lifting high, swinging low, and although it resembled someone acting out a Babar book, I was feeling optimistic. But when she got a sour look on her face and pounded at her earlobes with her fingers rounded around huge holes, I knew she had got it wrong.

"No, no, not the woman—"

Rosa gave me a quizzical look.

"Il uomo," I corrected her.

"Ah, il uomo," she said, but had nothing to add.

I half turned to Annamaria, who met my eyes. "Annamaria," I started and pretty quickly came right up against the limits of my *Italian for Idiots* book. *"Chi ha invitato"*—just making it up here—*"il uomo morto alla villa ieri?"* "Who invited the dead guy to the villa?" or words to that effect.

This graceless Italian was met with a faintly put-out air from Annamaria, who was looking at me as though I had asked her what exactly was pasta. Lingering somewhere inside that look, though, was something else: fear. I had to do it. Rosa, who took suddenly to shredding her lips with her teeth, saw it coming. "Annamaria," I said more sharply, "Chef." Her shoulders stiffened. I cobbled together my question in a new way. *"Ha Chef invitato il uomo mortissimo"*— very dead guy—"to the villa?"

She shrieked, and I jumped back by a foot. Rosa's nails were clawing the air beseechingly. *"Ah, per favore, no, no, no, no, no—"*

Annamaria stood so quickly, so tragically, that for a second I was pleased to see some life in her. *"Vattene da qui!"* She literally showed me the door. Her hands went *shoo-shoo*, which helped downgrade the awfulness of the moment, but she was angry. And I still didn't get my answer. Not directly. Without another word, I let myself out of the dim, sad kitchen.

I made a quick mental list of where the others on the property were, as far as I knew, at that moment. Ember, my room, checking out and going gray. Annamaria and Rosa, moping in the kitchen over cheese. Macy, burning brush somewhere in the vicinity of the barn. Pete, in Arezzo, on errands. I couldn't account for Sofia, but a cart with a laundry bag just inside the archway to the dormitory gave me a pretty good idea where she was out of sight—and busy.

Leaning against the arch, I called Pete, hoping Chef had given his son the key to the dead bolt for his room. Had it been my father, Dr. Val Valenti would have given keys to his lawyer, his financial advisor, his executive producer, his personal assistant, his banker, his bodyguard, my mother, and (I'm pretty sure) me—all with a showy interest in matters of trust in interpersonal relationships. Not, however, Chef. My heart sank when Pete told me his dematerialized dad had not shared that important object with his son. But then he went on to explain that Chef had called the dead bolt a *grande abominio*—great abomination—and had refused to use it.

My father could take a lesson in trust from Claudio Orlandini, although Dr. Val would publicly call that kind of behavior, with his camera-ready rueful smile, "dangerous disingenuousness," sending his studio audience off to furtively look up the word "dis," "dis," "dis something" on their phones.

On the upside, Chef's dangerous disingenuousness meant his door was unlocked—and his apartment open to all sorts of malefactors. I'd start with me. From my pocket I pulled out the pair of ultrathin disposable vinyl gloves I had taken from an unused box in the kitchen. These I worked over my fingers now.

Thrown out of Annamaria's kitchen, I was feeling like the day was one characterized by slipping—slipping out of the kitchen, slipping on the accoutrement of crime scene techs, slipping into the dormitory . . . here I went, proposing to prowl around my culinary hero's rooms, looking for something. A clue. Better yet, several. Given Annamaria's recent behavior, she was as good as telling me there was a connection between Chef and the *mortissimo* Buford. If she wouldn't provide it, I'd find it for myself.

Only, as I approached the great abomination of a dead bolt in the recently painted glossy black door, I could tell said door was ajar. Not standing open, not in the slightest, but not fully closed. It had been opened—at that moment, I was experiencing a rare moment of thinking Dr. Val Valenti had a certain amount of prescience—and then pushed shut just enough to look undisturbed from a distance. Well, I was closing the distance, and moving as stealthily as I could, considering my knees were knocking together. Ever so quietly I breathed the door open and slid noiselessly inside. *In your face,* I thought, lording it over the *mortissimo* Bu, then suddenly recalling his recent lack of face altogether and cursing myself for my bad choice of gloats. Still, who was the clever one?

At the sound of a dresser drawer being pushed shut, I slunk toward the squeak, not for an instant anxious about what—or who—I would find, me in my crime scene hand wear. I stood in the doorway to what had to be Chef's bedroom and did a fast impression of Annamaria standing on the moral high ground. (The threshold was roughly an inch higher than the floor.) "Sofia!" I said indignantly.

She whirled.

I stood even taller. In her left hand were a few small whatnots she had scooped up from Chef's underwear drawer. This piece of detection I based on the fact that it was the top, narrow drawer, the traditional domain of unmentionables, and that her right hand held a magenta spandex negligible garment I astutely figured to be underwear. Coupled with the underwear was a passport. This was puzzling. Had the missing Chef called Sofia and asked her to send him these . . . essentials?

"Che pensi?" I improvised grandly. It was the closest I could get to that timeworn expression of wronged adults everywhere: *What were you thinking?*

Patting the spandex back into the drawer, Sofia sputtered something by way of feeble explanation.

Waving away the unintelligible Italian, I felt emboldened by the sneak thief. *"Che Chef ritorna questo minuto?"* This was meant to convey, "What if Chef returns this very minute?" As soon as I put the idea out there in the air between us, I realized it implicated me, too, but I think she was still undone by my sudden appearance.

Puzzled, she waved the passport around, stammered something more at me, and then wept.

"Tell me," I said imperiously.

"No passport no go," she explained miserably.

After staring at each other for a full minute, I thought I understood. Chef hadn't taken his passport. Chef wasn't eloping with Dalia di Bello. Or . . . perhaps Sofia had a little thievery in mind. If she snatched and hid Chef's passport, he couldn't take off to parts unknown with di Bello. Either way, I held out my hand, and with great reluctance the resourceful Sofia turned it over to me. For all of three seconds, I took in the poor Sister's ungloved hands. Amateur. I shook my head. I happened to notice the bed was half made, the old sheets lying on the carpet, the new sheets half arranged on the mattress. I preferred to think that Sofia had settled on bed-making as a subterfuge. But right then I had the upper (gloved) hand. Ripping a page from Annamaria's playbook, I declared, *"Vattene da qui!"* In a word, "Begone!"

And as she deflated her way over to the floor sheets and swept them up into her quaking arms, I added something questionable along the lines of *"Cha, cha, cha."* I pointed like one of those very stern gods at what Sofia still held. At that, she shook out her clenched hands, and everything scattered on the floor. I rubbed my forehead.

So hard to find good help.

She was gone.

As I set Chef's passport back inside his drawer, I was left to ponder whether it might be a wise precaution to close the door all the way, in case the banished Sofia returned with reinforcements—only one, the tragic Annamaria, would be all that was required to set me off at a run. I shut Chef's door, then glanced around in a stymied way. Big shot, Nell, big shot. Now what? The first course of action seemed to be to see what Sofia had scooped up as booty and to replace it. Them. Those. First, the underwear I had to believe would look infinitely better on someone Pete's age.

I'm happy to report I was able to move swiftly past that image, which, had I not been detecting, deserved a whole lot more time than I was giving it. I dropped the item back into the top, narrow drawer, noting similar items in other colors. Chef definitely had some youthful tastes. This was one of those things you find out about a parent that forever rearranges the lobes of your brain. Bad enough if it's a parent, but a culinary hero? For a brief moment I wondered if I would ever be able to watch Chef deglaze a pan in the same way again.

Since I had forgotten to bring my notebook, I took out my phone and took a picture of the scattered items. A dried-up boutonnière. A foil packet I thought was the Italian equivalent of a Handi Wipe but, when I felt it carefully, realized was a condom. A foil packet I thought was a chocolate and, when I felt it carefully, realized was a Handi

Wipe. A wedding ring. A couple of black-and-white photos: curled edges, nobody I recognized. And one photo I did recognize—practically anyone in the whole wide world would recognize that great beauty, Dalia di Bello, every perfect feature caught in a moment of fun, shared with a young and strong Claudio Orlandini, their arms around each other. In their eyes and smiles, not a hint of anything less than the sheer joy of being together. Someone— Chef?—had laminated the photo, preserved it in a kind of plastic amber.

And yet these two had gone on to marry other people.

Dalia first.

As I set them all back inside the drawer, I saw other objects Sofia hadn't chosen. A few euros, an English phrase book, a pocket datebook from 2016, a blue index card with a series of numbers that looked like phone numbers—some with international prefixes—an unopened pack of Gauloises cigarettes, two matchbooks from restaurants in Rome, and a digital pen thermometer. The thermometer was, naturally, the only object that made complete sense to me. I felt a wave of nostalgia for a metal stick whose sole purpose was to tell you whether your turkey was done. After the events of the past couple of days, I longed to run everything in my life on the thermometer principle: done, not done. Forget the pine barrens of the in-betweens.

We Jersey girls are absolutists, and as I stared into Chef's top drawer of private crap, I discovered how deep my Jersey point of view went. Either Secaucus was a pig farm, or it wasn't. Either you evacuate the beach during the hurricane, or you don't. Either the Boss is the greatest pop star ever to come out of the Garden State, or he isn't. Either Chef Claudio Orlandini and Buford Kaplan had some point

of intersection that led to murder and disappearance, or
they didn't.

I found myself picturing the moment I surprised Sofia
pawing through Chef's stuff. She had started to remake
Chef's bed, but all of a sudden, midsheeting, she had turned
instead to ransacking the top drawer. Was it just a spur-of-
the-moment bright idea? If so, what was so bright about it?
This I pondered while I completed the making up of the
bed, smoothing out the creases.

The stuff she'd had in her hands—the foil packets, wedding ring, photos, undies, and boutonnière—wouldn't give
any of us a clue about whether Chef and Bu knew each
other from the Great Before, or where we could lay our
mitts on Chef and Dalia di Bello. I reconsidered Sofia's
handful. It was seeming less like she had picked out these
items to stash in her pockets and present to Annamaria than
she had simply been sifting through all of the drawer's contents. Trying to see up close the possibilities in each of the
items.

So what were those possibilities?

I studied the things.

Finally, from Chef's closet I pulled a spare toque, which
I used as a carryall. I kept all of the photos—maybe Pete
could identify the background of the one with Chef and di
Bello—and I kept anything with a number on it, with the
exception of the digital thermometer. In the short run, I had
to set aside my own weary absolutism—turkey done or not
done—nothing a good night's sleep wouldn't help—in favor of gray indistinctness.

Maybe Chef and Bu had met in passing and might not
necessarily recognize each other. Maybe Chef had lost
weight; maybe Bu had lost hair. Maybe they had only ever

spoken over the phone. Maybe Chef had contacted Bu on a whim about filming the dinner party and Bu had run with it—which might account for why Ember thought the idea had come from Bu himself. It was Bu who had pitched it, she had recollected.

But something had to account for the fact that Cortona was an add-on. I'd have to fine-tooth-comb those file folders as soon as I could, hoping something would jump out at me.

Who had suggested adding Cortona? Just Bu himself? Or someone else?

A killer? A killer who had used a gig at the villa as a lure? But why? Why lure Bu Kaplan to the villa—wouldn't it be too close to home? Wouldn't suspicion fall on the denizens of Villa Orlandini? Could those official suspicions be exactly what the killer counted on? A side benefit to the murder itself—kill Kaplan and ruin the good name of the Orlandini clan. Which, in turn, would pull the plug on the cooking school. Who could hate all those people quite that much? A rival?

One by one, I remembered the dinner guests: Ernesto Treni, the food critic; Contessa Aurora Ciano, the Roman socialite; the director of the Cortona chamber of commerce; Ember, the filmmaker's assistant; Pete, the olive-growing son; and me. Not to mention the other key villa people, like Annamaria and her sisters. And not to mention Macy Garner, the farmhand placed with the Orlandinis through the efforts of Global Farm Friends. On the periphery was the neighboring truffle-hunting Vincenzo. And, finally, the tradespeople who had been the worker bees that day—could one of them have seen Bu and felt a murderous resurgence of hatred for reasons that had nothing to do with Chef and the cooking school?

I found a rubber band and tightened it around the opening of the toque.

I was at a loss. Rather half-heartedly I kept opening other drawers and cabinets in Chef's apartment. All I accomplished was to still feel at a loss and now slimy to boot. Maybe over a glass of Montepulciano, back in the Abbess's room, I could spread out Chef's lists of numbers—even the datebook from 2016 had the phone numbers of some appointments—but at that particular moment there was just no getting around the fact that Chef Claudio Orlandini—by virtue of the bad timing of his disappearance—was looking like a prime suspect. The rest of his rooms were a shrine either to bocce triumphs or to Dalia di Bello.

In a troubling flash, I suddenly saw Chef's one spot so tender that he might bring a rock down again and again on someone's head: It could only be di Bello. If Buford Kaplan had filmed anything mocking about Chef's bocce team, Chef could swallow it in pieces, over time. And the Orlandini Cooking School? I couldn't picture my hiring as much of anything beyond a buoyant whim, fueled by wine and bonhomie. If Bu had filmed something unflattering along those lines, I actually had a hard time picturing the sweat-flinging, toothless Chef giving much of a damn.

His kitchen felt to me like something slipping from his capable hands for complicated reasons that had nothing to do with the done or not-done of a digital thermometer: He was past it, and he was watching his world-class career whistle off over a horizon in the fading light. It seemed very possible that Chef's kitchen was sliding unstopped into history—all that excellence locked up with tenderly guarded recipes in his recipe vault. Chef might mourn Pete's mom the pastry chef, and maybe competitive bocce had pulled him into an utterly different world at a vulnerable time.

But as I turned slowly in his living room, taking in walls covered in framed magazine covers and newspaper front pages and team photos—and movie stills from the great di Bello's glamorous career—I knew it was only Dalia di Bello and a malicious slam on her reputation that could drive him to murder.

Had Bu gone too far?

12

Did *Sotto Terra* include Dalia? Had Bu as good as taken a knife to the love of Claudio Orlandini's life? The exposé had come out in 2018. Two whole years for Chef to work up some homicidal pique. Was it possible? Could he have turned down his anger to a comfortable simmer, only to find an irresistible opportunity for revenge—some kind of cockeyed chivalrous slaying to avenge the lady love's honor?—did people still do that?—did Italians still do that?—had they ever? The other possibility was that Chef hadn't seen *Sotto Terra* in its first run and had only just caught it recently. Less simmer that way, more first-run rage.

Only, in my short personal acquaintance with him, Chef seemed to be a pretty happy sort of guy. Bocce wins, bocce losses, bocce team postmortems at local pubs, the career CPR of a cooking school at the villa, arguments with souschef Annamaria over the relative virtues of fig and plum. His life—despite the absence of Dalia—seemed complete. Exhibit A: pairs of colorful spandex briefs. I took those as a symbol of hope.

*   *   *

*A*s I left the dormitory with my suitcase repacked, I
caught sight of smoke from the bonfire rising over the
barn roof. Macy must be keeping an eye on it. But then I
saw Ember slipping into the passenger's seat of the T-Bird,
with Macy at the wheel. "I'll call you," Bu's assistant yelled
at me with a grin and a fluttery wave. "The cop's meeting
me at the inn in Cortona. Wish me luck." I flung her a salute
and realized I didn't know how to say good luck in Italian,
French, or Spanish, for that matter.

"Macy!" I called.

"Yep?"

"Bonfire okay to leave?" I was amazed at how relaxed I
sounded.

"Sure," she hollered. "Rosa's babysitting it."

"Ah."

"Back soon," she said. With that, she gunned it, and they
sped off down the short drive.

Cupping my hands around my mouth, I yelled "Good
luck!" to Ember. Once they were out of sight, I hotfooted it
around the side of the barn. Macy might trust Rosa to baby-
sit the bonfire, but I didn't trust anybody. In a flat, wide
open section of the villa property, far from any overhanging tree branches, I spied Rosa sitting with outstretched
legs on a log set close to the bonfire.

As I drew up alongside her, I saw her grooving to the
music flowing through a set of earbuds. Her fingers were
easing a nicely browned marshmallow off the end of a long
stick. The fire had burned down, but the ashes still smol-
dered, trails of smoke blown skyward. Little flames
erupted, and the unmistakable smell of "campfire" encir-
cled us.

"Ah!" said Rosa, noticing me as she chewed. Happily, she grabbed another long stick, speared a marshmallow, and presented it to me.

For the next ten minutes we said nothing, instead just enjoying the gooey sugar load that had nothing to do with fine dining. And maybe the sugar sharpened my brain, because I suddenly saw an opportunity, if I could make her understand me. "Rosa," I said with as wide-open an expression as I could muster, what with licking goo off the corners of my mouth, "I want to make a little garden. Garden," I repeated, louder, doing the charades for digging and planting.

"Ah, sì?" So far, so good.

"Do we have weed killer?" When she gave me a puzzled look, like burned marshmallow was gluing her lips together, I tried Italian for "bad grass." *"Erba* bad. Bad *erba."* If Rosa was the tree poisoner, this line of questioning was a nonstarter, but I took a shot.

Rosa gave me a stifled look, a pensive look, then a look of utter disinterest. "No, no, no," she rumbled at me, and then she seemed to perk up, and as she trilled something at great length, like minor royalty explaining why yard work is so utterly beneath them, I had a flash. Rosa Bari hated gardening. And, if I understood her correctly, so did Sofia, and, come to mention it, Lisa, Laura, and Annamaria.

Someone was missing in the litany of garden-hating Bari sisters.

At that, Rosa raised both her hands and lowered her head. Giada was a different matter, she said reverently. Then she went on to mime the sheer floral abundance of their sister Giada's activities at the convent. Sunflowers, roses, verbena, violets. Rosa wound down finally, suggesting I should ask Giada about bad grass killer—here she popped the offending weeds with a pretend pistol—since she's the only one who uses the shed and has *la chiave*. I took it the word meant "key," although her actions seemed to suggest inflicting a nasty death with a switchblade.

I kept my face neutral. "*Grazie*, Rosa."

Humming with my new information, I skirted the edges of the dying fire, browning my marshmallow, poking at the ashes whenever I saw something glittering in this spot where the Orlandini family had burned brush for many years. A couple of coins too hot to rescue, a can with its identifying paper all burned off, a metal buckle, a pair of mangled eyeglasses, a small fork that could have been a child's. Once upon a time, Pierfranco's? How do little household objects end up in the bonfires that get rid of yard work prunings?

With thanks to Rosa, who was watching the remains of the burning brush, I licked burnt sugar off my fingers and headed back to the Abbess's room, where I was pleased to find the Victrola and the birdcage in their proper places, if not the piano. Ember had left the place undisturbed—bed neatly made, only one bath towel damp. No smell of cigarettes, no coffee rings on the nightstand, all good. As I pushed open the window, I realized I could glimpse the broken fountain where Bu had met his end and the red and white candy cane–striped *Polizia Zona* tape. For now, the white-coated techs were as gone as Sofia's laundry cart.

From this distance, the fountain looked rather small and mild, as though the most important thing to have happened there was someone's stumble or pee. I could see the top of marble Veronica's head, quick to offer her veil, guarding the spot with her brawny arms and determined eyes. Had the killer stood on the lip of the stone basin to kill Bu—or was he tall enough not even to have to leave the ground to bring down the rock with enough force? It seemed like an interesting question, one that could narrow the field of suspects.

On the table by the window, I opened the chef's toque I had used as an evidence bag and set out the items I had taken from Chef's rooms: the datebook from 2016, the list of combinations, the list of phone numbers, the photos.

After I booted up my Mac, it didn't take long to find *Sotto Terra* on IMDb. It was a start. I clicked on **See full cast & crew** and scrolled down the page. Buford Kaplan and Ember Weston were listed as directors and as writers. There was a lengthy list of executive producers, coproducers, archival producers, consulting producers, and just plain producers. If they were Netflix people, they might have some overlap with Bu and Ember's new project about the cooking school start-ups. The "cast" consisted of whistleblowers, journalists, and subjects of the exposé, who appeared in on-screen interviews. Fast-forwarding through the movie, I saw there was archival footage of sleazy ancestors, bewildered descendants, and dazzling villas, yachts, and balls. But nowhere could I find the names of Dalia di Bello or Claudio Orlandini.

Was I smart enough to know a dead end when I walked into one?

If Dalia wasn't Chef's motive for murder, then what or who was?

What other possible connection between Chef and Bu could there be? Something altogether aside from filmmaking? Something personal? I cast my mind back to the moment last night in the courtyard when Bu and Ember had driven up and we all turned out to welcome them. Had anything passed between Chef and Bu that indicated an acquaintance? Hard to say. But it did strike me that if Bu had any advance warning of bad blood, he wouldn't have shown up. Would he?

Bu had a reptilian sense for other people's tender defenses and exposed jugulars—but I didn't think he had much in the way of radar about his own. Could he have excited homicidal rage in someone and not even known it? Just how many hooks over the course of his life and career had he slipped himself off of? Was he egotistical enough to think he was blameless when it came to pretty much everything? That he could destroy lives and careers and not assume any personal responsibility for it?

With a chill, I told myself that yes, he could.

Maybe the camera gave him too much of a false sense of insulation, a digital eye on others' secrets and failings and little crimes, as though there could never be any blowback. For Bu, anything hidden was fair game. He'd dig it out like Stella the dog uncovered *tartufi*. I didn't sense, standing there in the courtyard, that Bu had set Chef up somehow—that Bu had taken the job to expose and ridicule Chef. But what accounted for the sudden addition of the Cortona segment in the new Netflix project?

I'd spend a while longer online, then it would be back to the mattress. I'd dig out the files I'd stashed and see what they yielded. This time I'd go more carefully through the names of Bu's other producers, because if they liked his work, one of them might have been likely to see an opportunity to put Bu on the scene at Villa Orlandini. Who was that absent puppet master? Last night I had been so mindful of the known guests, those food-loving dignitaries invited for their promotional powers, that I found myself wondering whether if it had been possible for an unknown to get onto the grounds, unremarked, unobserved, and kill Bu. If so, it was a damn near perfect crime, hidden behind the chaos of sisters and tradespeople and vans and villa residents all pushed to their breaking points, the murder itself hidden behind Veronica's marble veil.

That person, like Chef himself, had disappeared.

So much depended on timing. When had he bolted out of his kitchen? And when exactly will the *medico legale* determine the time of Bu's death? On my legal pad of alibis, which were beginning to look more and more like hieroglyphics, I made a note to ask Pete, Annamaria, the sisters, and Macy whether they had seen anyone they didn't recognize on the grounds. Even during daylight, there were plenty of places to hole up, lie in wait. In the meantime, I could concentrate on Treni as a suspect. I was scrolling through Bu's other film credits—still scouring the information for any clue of a Chef connection, Dalia or otherwise—when the knock came at the door. It was Pete, dressed in jeans and a faded gray long-sleeved T-shirt, back from errands in town. I nodded him inside.

He strode past me and dropped into the easy chair.

I sucked in a breath. "Pete," I said sadly, "I think there's got to be a connection between Chef and Bu Kaplan. I just haven't found it yet . . ."

"Dalia di Bello?"

"That's been my line, but nothing so far."

He sprang up and started pacing. "His disappearance looks bad."

"And once the time of death comes back—"

"Maybe even worse."

"Right." I motioned him over to the table, where I handed him the photos. "Recognize any of these people?"

"Pop and Dalia a hundred years ago. The others—" His voice slowed. "Maybe the one in the uniform is my grandfather; he was a member of *la Resistenza*"—a quick look up—"the Resistance, along with his brother, probably the one on the left. Both killed after the Armistice. Pop doesn't remember his father." I said nothing. "As for the other photo . . ." He turned it over, checking the back. No handwritten identification. "More of the same?" Then: "Where did you get these?"

I smiled and tried to toss it off lightly. "Chef's underwear drawer." When he gave me a long look, I explained, "The door was unlocked, Sofia was there first, and it had to be done."

"Sofia!" He looked bewildered. Mud and bewilderment—it had been quite a day for Pierfranco. He murmured, "If Sofia was in Pop's room, it has to have something to do with Annamaria."

"It does. She wants to hide his passport so he can't take off."

"Thereby helping Annamaria."

"Depending on how you look at it."

"So true."

"Otherwise, there are these." I held up the two cards with the lists of numbers. "Any ideas?"

"Well," he said, stretching his back, "what do you say we make a few calls?"

"Maybe one is Dalia di Bello."

"And maybe Pop's there." He neatened up the little pile of photos.

Time to spring the new information about Giada. "And it's been a busy day for the Baris altogether."

He came to a sleek stop in his pile neatening. "What do you mean?"

I went on to describe my marshmallow roast with Rosa.

"Giada!" His shoulders drooped in disbelief.

I ticked off the facts. "She has easy access, she's the only one who uses the garden shed at the convent, and she's the keeper of the key."

He was nodding slowly. "But we don't know why."

"First," I pointed out, "we have to determine whether her shed's got some aldicarb. And if it does—" I left it unfinished.

Pete sucked in a deep breath. "I'll get to it, Nell. Until then—"

"We'll keep an eye on her."

For a minute, we were silent; then the mood changed. "I came over to ask if you want to join me for dinner." He seemed to want to elaborate, so all I did was lift my eyebrows at him encouragingly. "The cottage. I'll cook. A bottle of the Montepulciano, a nice chicken scarpariello." He seemed a little unsure of me, so he was describing the menu, like it was just the food that would get me to have dinner with him. It was sweet.

"Any drama?"

A tip of his fine head. This could be a deal breaker. "No drama."

"I'll come anyway."

He laughed. "Good. Let's go."

"Right now?"

"The cannellini beans are already pureed—"

"For . . . ?"

"A new bruschetta I'm trying."

He handed back the booty from Chef's underwear drawer, and I slipped the thin stack into my pocket. When I saw the dried mud, I said, "Give me fifteen minutes. I'd like to clean up." Pete bounded toward the door, calling some high-speed Italian back at me as though he was so pleased to try his new bruschetta on me that he'd plumb forgot I had no idea what he was saying. Out he went, striding toward the cottage, and I closed the door quietly. Then I tore around the room in a sudden, wretched sweat over what I should wear to this dinner.

I decided to go for what I call a "studied casual" look—my light gray Banana Republic ankle pants topped with—what? Satin button-down blouse tries too hard, because it needs to. Anything with ruffles would look too much like the contessa and put Pete right off his bruschetta. Cami plus cardi, hello I'm available, not to mention out of style. Bell sleeves, okay for Popeye. And then I spied my pink V-neck sweater, and, like the first time I entered the meditation room at Prajna Center, I knew it was right. I fondled it by way of imparting high hopes. Maybe I'd get to sauté the chicken . . .

A speed shower, speed shampoo, and manic dabs of blush and swipes of lipstick later, I squared my pink shoulders, grabbed my phone and legal pad, and went out of the room. Bringing a list to a potentially romantic dinner for two is like bringing a kid brother with you on a date. A mood killer, if that's what you're looking for, or something to attend to if you've misjudged the mood in the first place. You can't buy a better defense system.

I felt very nearly happy in that moment. In the distance, I saw Macy cutting across the field in light overalls, and the breeze was blowing the scent of fresh-cut grass, which smells the same, I was betting, the world over. It's how the color green smells. For just the rest of that day, I wanted green to push off the sight of Bu, bloody and still, from my mind. Even big things and big people, like Bu, can crumple.

I slowed as I approached Pete's place, suddenly knowing how determined I was to solve this murder—not even for Bu's sake, or to clear the Orlandinis, or to save the cooking school that was hardly a page of notes at this point. But I had some dawning sense of how murder leaves something broken behind, long after the body has been removed and the suspicions dispelled. I might not have been planning to stay at the villa—when was I going to tell them?—but I liked this crazy place enough to keep them from breaking beyond repair after the murder was solved, if I could.

Pete appeared in the doorway, sleeves pushed up to his elbows, a glass of red wine in each hand. With a swift look, he took me in. "Fashionista," he chided.

I took my glass. "Olive grower."

He smiled at me, and it seemed like a new smile, one I hadn't seen before, a different smile. Then he noticed the legal pad, tucked under my pink-sweatered arm. "Oh, good," he said ambiguously, "you brought your list."

With that, I saw for the first time that the legal pad defense system was more far-reaching than I had appreciated. Perversely, I found myself wishing I had left it back in my room, and now I flung it haphazardly onto a chair. Pete was smiling serenely, and we silently toasted—what, exactly?— more things than we had a right to expect from a single clink. Chef's safety came to mind. Chef's success with Dalia di Bello. Chef's innocence in the matter of Bu's death. Chef's ability to prove that innocence. "Have a look around, Nell, while I finish up the bruschetta."

The cottage was nearly three hundred years old, and in terms of villa buildings, it was the newcomer. I loved it all at once, and completely. It was a perfect wood and stone hobbit hole. A place apart from olive groves and uncertain futures and murder. The whitewashed stone walls, the broad, natural wood rafters, the wide plank flooring that had to be original. A tough old straw basket filled with a few trim logs and kindling. The deep-set windows, the fireplace with a low rocker set in front of it. A thin Persian rug in faded reds and blues gave the cottage an exotic touch. Pendant lights of different lengths were hung from the joists spanning the ceiling.

Next to a small guest room, an open doorway with a rustic natural wood frame led to Pete's bedroom. Hooks held some clothes, and one wall of handmade shelves held books, a library through the ages, with old leather bindings and bold paper bindings, cookbooks—including *The Compleat Housewife* and *The Art of Cookery Made Plain and Easy*, two of the very first cookbooks ever published— histories, maps, novels. Pete's bed had a comforter hastily pulled up, and a trunk alongside that served as a nightstand. A rustic armoire stood open, and on the floor next to it, a basket for his laundry. A small addition with a sloping roofline held a toilet, basin, and stall shower.

I met him in the kitchen—a beautiful state-of-the-art concept built along the back stone wall—and set down my wine. "*The Compleat Housewife*?" I teased. A Bose sound system was shelved over the quartz counter, along with a line of cascading herbs in pots. Pete tapped a remote, and Miles Davis's *Kind of Blue* slunk into the room, carrying all its story and allure right along with it.

"My ex-wife's." This was news. I grabbed a knife, and together we chopped red onions. "I got the cookbooks, she got everything else." At that, Pete pinched a couple of sprigs from the pot of fresh thyme and handed them to me. "Just a teaspoonful." I nodded, set about the thyme, and waited. As he pinched some parsley for himself, he went on, "If she had wanted the cookbooks I would have thrown them in as well." He pushed the chopped parsley into a little pile with the side of his hand. At the first smell of toasted Italian bread, he grabbed a dish towel, pulled the sheet from the oven, and leaned closer to me. "We were

young and stupid," he explained. "Of course," he added
with a laugh, "that was all we had in common."

I nodded. "Ever see her?"

"Haven't seen her," he said oratorically, giving me a thin
package of prosciutto—"a few slices to set on the toast"—
and I set to work, as he picked up the story, "haven't seen
her, haven't wondered about her, just someone else left behind in the mists of my Cornell days, along with Bread
Club and *Crème de Cornell*."

"Bread Club?"

He laid a hand across his chest and said solemnly, "I was
president."

"Very impressive."

"Being young and stupid didn't affect my dough."

"Ah," I whispered, "so lucky."

"Then there was a coup." He sniffed in mock indignation. "Led by those who favored using rapid-rise yeast."

I was laughing so hard I could hardly get out the words.
"What happened?"

"I was sent into exile." He patted his hair. "Otherwise
known as graduation." Then: "It wasn't until much later
that I discovered wine and olives. Less young"—he raised
his glass—"less stupid." Then his eyes crinkled. "Pop was
so pleased." I watched him assemble the bruschetta, which
he plated and swept gently under my nose. Oil, vinegar, red
onion, cannellini beans, and, best of all, fresh thyme and
parsley—each with its own blended scents and flavors. I
was suddenly ravenous. As we settled into the single other
modern note in Pete's cottage, the sofa—in saddle-brown
leather with clean lines—I found myself thinking again of
Chef.

I took a napkin, a slice of bruschetta, and a big bite.
Heaven, I often think, lies in beautiful food. "Delicious," I

murmured. For a few minutes, the two of us munched in contented silence.

"What about you, Nell? Any ghosts of grooms past?"

Maybe it was the final spray of setting sun angling through the front windows. Maybe it was the red onion. Or the freshly showered scent of the man next to me. I came to a stop against a moment of real honesty. "You would think." I nearly glanced at him. "But no." I dabbed at my lips, more to stall, which he could probably tell. Then: "Considering I'm still young and stupid."

Pete sat back and scrutinized me. "Don't judge yourself by Bu."

We both laughed a little, but kind of feebly. Struck, I think, by how awful the situation was outside these walls. "You know," I tried, because I felt I had to, "it doesn't look good for Chef."

"I know." Still, Pete looked at me.

"Although I can't find a motive."

"Neither can I."

I set my wine down on the very old overturned crates that had been stained black and served as a coffee table and pulled the little stack of photos and numbers out of my pocket. "Maybe there isn't one," I said, feeling suddenly cheerful.

He got into the spirit. "Want to make some calls?"

"And if we find him, Pete—" I sighed. "What do we do?"

"What do you mean?"

I gave him a steady look. "Do we give the cops the number?"

Once we had agreed we'd have to totally play it all by ear—which we both knew was just kicking the question down the road—we divided the list into four calls apiece and found a couple of pens for notes, and I tore a sheet from my legal pad and handed it to Pete. To take the chill off of the early evening, Pete set a match to a small fire and then quickly sautéed and lemon-glazed the boneless chicken thighs for the scarpariello.

The mysterious list yielded mostly nothing—a chiropractor in Arezzo, a couple of bocce pals in Bologna, the convent where Rosa and Sofia and all the others lived, the Florence law offices of the improbably named Baldi, Berti and Betti, a couple of restaurants in Milan, and two women in Rome—one sounded young and shrill, *No, no idea where Claudio is, not at the villa?*—and the other, breathless and throaty, hung up on us.

This last, I felt sure, was Dalia di Bello. Wasn't that the Voice that had made celluloid men swoon in her series of Hollywood movies set in ancient Pompeii? Or had I simply heard what I wanted to hear? The hang-up did not bode well, unless it wasn't Dalia di Bello, just some acquaintance who didn't want to be bothered. But if it was di Bello, would she have hung up on us if Chef was with her, next to her, finger to his lips, signaling to her not to give him away? And why on earth would he do that . . . unless he was in fact running from the police?

Later, while Charlie Parker's sax kept us company from the Bose, we savored the chicken and tossed green salad dressed with lemon and Pete's olive oil, comparing notes from the day's interviews. Something about the contessa was troubling me, but I couldn't nail it down, and Pete wondered whether the director was downplaying the ugliness of his argument with Bu Kaplan. We cleaned up in silence, turning on a table lamp, the only other source of light besides the dying fire. Finally, we gave up the evening with soft laughs.

"I'll walk you home," said Pete, setting aside the dish

towel. The space felt full of everything unseen and unspoken and imperfectly understood, and we both knew it didn't all have to do with questions surrounding the murder. For that evening, it was fine. In the silence as we stepped out into the night, I told myself it's always good to see that partial things aren't necessarily imperfect things.

I felt brimful of more than wine and Moraiolo olive oil from the Silver Wind grove, a taste that found its way into everything else—the bruschetta, the chicken scarpariello, the dressing. Like Pete. I slid him a look as we reached the door to the Abbess's room. Like Pete, the taste finding its way into everything. I unlocked my door.

Then, in a sudden move that seemed a little awkward, I stepped in, slipped my arm over his shoulder, and set my cheek against his. *Stay, don't rush off, Nell, just let it be a moment, skin to skin.* His cheek pressed against mine in a way that felt more expressive than almost anything else I could name. All I said was, "I don't want to be young and stupid," and I couldn't even say what I meant by it.

We inched apart, and he took my hand and squeezed. "You're not," he said, believing it more than I did. *"Buona notte,"* he said softly, and as he turned away, he added, "I hope you don't leave, Nell. I know you want to." His shoulders hunched against the night breeze. "See you tomorrow." I watched Pete become shadow, just black moving night air, in the overcast night sky, no starlight, no moon to draw outlines into something human. A man can seem so insubstantial. Finally he disappeared, whether before he got inside the cottage or not, I couldn't say. The shadow flattened out, past indistinct now, and I was watching nothing at all. As I turned to step inside the Abbess's room, I heard a sound coming from the direction of the cloister. The rasp of footsteps on the walk, then a different sound—a sob.

It would have been so easy just to duck inside my room, close the windows against the distress out there in the night, shove my tired head under the pillow. But I couldn't do it. None of the sensible cautions running through my mind got any traction—to be honest, the one that went *There's a killer out there* at least slowed my steps—but I pressed on the flashlight on my phone and made my way up the path to the cloister. A slumped figure was hunched against one of the colonnades, and I didn't want to shine the light directly, so I swept it nearby. "Rosa?" I said into the dark. "*È* Nella."

When the sob turned into a moan and the figure huddled into something smaller, tighter, I stepped into the cloister. Shining my light on the figure's feet, I knew right away it wasn't Rosa, who wears sensible runners. "Annamaria?" Why was I so surprised? This proud, brilliant, unlucky-in-love woman had the most to lose, the most to mourn, the least to cling to—and all I, the bumbling American, had managed to do was expose her here. By now she had slumped all the way down and sat hugging her knees while she wept.

Cheering her up seemed like a classic American approach to any misery, so I didn't—one American who invaded the villa had gotten himself murdered, and now here I was, the other one (I could fairly picture her spitting the words out), exposing her, cheering her up. What a collective nuisance we transatlantic folks were. How had poor Annamaria ever agreed to turning Chef's villa into a cooking school for American foodies? That, I thought, nodding slightly, must be love.

I settled myself next to her, and we sat in chilly, companionable silence—Annamaria hugging her knees in a tight little ball like a potato bug, and me just staring out into the darkness. Had she been on her way from the kitchen to the dormitory, and just succumbed to whatever grief over Chef she had been holding off until that very moment? I had just decided to try slipping an arm around her shaking shoulders, friendly, not maudlin, when she suddenly scrabbled at my sleeve.

Wretched, she ran her forearm over her head and under her nose, then clutched my arm again. "Nella," said Annamaria hoarsely. It seemed she was working herself up to something, so I waited. "Nella?" Her voice rose as though she wondered where I had gone. I hadn't moved.

"*Sì?*"

Finally, she intoned, *"I saw him."*

13

I didn't know what she meant, but it made my skin crawl. Encouraged by my silence, she bunched up my pink sleeve. Then she said it again, this time as if someone's hands were around her neck, squeezing. "I saw him. *L'ho visto!*" She punctuated this accusation by circling her hands around her eyes, the way the fourth-grade boys had done when I had shown up at school for the first time wearing glasses. *"Capisce?"* she whispered, then sobbed. Annamaria was certainly keeping up her end of the terrifying conversation. In this miserable twosome, I was the slacker. Undaunted, she wiggled two fingers fiercely at her own eyes. By then I took it to mean that she had seen something.

"What?" I tried. And "Who?"

With that, she bit her lip, averted her gaze, pulled me close, pushed me away. "Chef!" came out at last. This was followed by blubbering.

"Chef?" I said encouragingly. "You saw"—now it was my turn to twiddle my two fingers at my own eyes—"Chef?"

That seemed like rather good news, considering he'd been missing for twenty-four hours.

She flared, calling me *idiota*, comparing me, I believe, to Giada. *"Ieri sera!"* Two hands majestically moved what appeared to be invisible piles of dirt from right in front of us to somewhere behind us. *"Ieri sera!"*

I saw all. "Yesterday." Now it was my turn to grab her sleeve. "Yesterday evening. *Dove?*" We turned to face each other, and Annamaria launched into a rapid description in Italian of what she had witnessed. I tried very hard to keep up, nodding, translating one word out of twelve. Chef, Kahplon, fountain. Apparently after Chef ran from the kitchen during *primo*, Annamaria followed him out, wondering what was wrong. Where was he? Where had he gone? There was *osso buco* to plate! She peered around the courtyard—here she made sweeping gestures back and forth in front of where we sat—no Chef. Then she started toward the back of the property, and she saw him, finally.

But it was odd and strange and a little bit awful, the look of Chef as he stood there like a very old man. She kept to the wall of the main building and made her way closer. Closer still. When she came near enough to get a better look, she had no voice. There he was, staggering, his chest heaving, his arms useless, without a sound, looming like a monster over a heap. After a moment, he stumbled backward—how odd, always so good on his feet, like at bocce—and then he fled. Soon she heard the Ape start up.

She fell silent.

Had Chef witnessed the murder?

Had he committed the murder?

Or had he just happened upon the corpse?

Or . . . had Bu still been alive, and Chef left him to die?

I felt strangely collected. *"Andiamo*, Annamaria," I said.

"Time to sleep." It was all I could think of in the night air. She had just explained her moody behavior of the last day—what I had mistaken for grief at Chef's taking off for Rome to win Dalia di Bello once and for all. Maybe that still explained his flight, but of all people it had been Annamaria, who loved him best, who had seen him, who could place him at the crime scene at the key time. Now more than ever, the *medico legale*'s report on time of death was critical.

In the meantime—and I was so very grateful for a meantime—I walked Annamaria over to her room in the dormitory. Her hair had found its way out of its pins and clips, and her handsome head was bowed. Sniffling all the way into her room, she stood like a lost kid in an unfamiliar place. I pulled down the bedcovers and nodded her into lying down. She turned on her side away from me. "*A domani*, Annamaria," I managed with a reassuring little lilt.

I didn't know any Italian lullabies. I smoothed her hair, slipped off her shoes, covered her up, and felt sad to think she would probably hate me in the morning, when it came right down to it. Because it's human nature to resent whoever's around when our defenses are down. And there would be nothing I could do. I slipped out, closing her door without making a sound, and made my way slowly toward the Abbess's room—now with a feeling of dread.

When I couldn't fall asleep after two hours of valiant attempts at mind-emptying, I quit, punched my pillows into some cooperation, and gazed at my legal pad. I rearranged a few items, crossed out a couple of others, and came up with some observations. I would call them "concerns," but even that word didn't come close to what I was feeling—"objects of dread/terror" was spot-on, but already I couldn't sleep, and I didn't want to wind myself up with more anxiety. So at the top of the list I penned: *Observations*.

- Why has nobody mentioned to the commissario that I kicked Bu Kaplan flat out onto the kitchen floor just hours before his murder? Could they possibly want the cooking school so badly that they're protecting me??
- Why did Bu's breakdown occur after *Sotto Terra* came out? Any connection? He lost half a year's work.
- The contessa. There's something.

I had no answers, but I booted up my Mac long enough to run through my Junk Mail, where I scan and trash daily. From CBDGummyBears, promising Five EZ Tips. From KetoFuel, promising Five EZ Tips. Sometimes I believe it's all we ever want—Five EZ Tips—just five, just easy—about things that matter, like love and life and keeping boneless skinless chicken breasts moist while baking. With my last bit of energy, I closed my laptop, switched off the lamp, and floated off, light and free. I didn't wake up until morning.

*E*arly the next day, I had a shock that actually jolted me. In a spurt of self-care, I decided to take a walk somewhere, possibly down into town, just as the sun was rising, but I didn't get very far. I was pumping my arms, trying to get some oxygen to my sleepy brain, when I crossed the cloister and hit the courtyard.

There, in its usual spot against the dormitory, was the Ape.

Instinctively, I sprang backward.

I could only assume that Chef had returned. But I didn't know what to make of the stealthy, middle-of-the-night appearance. A quick look around showed that the only life in the courtyard was a finch trying out its early morning song with Five EZ Tips. I saw no one. Approaching the Ape quietly, I peered inside. No Chef, but two other interesting discoveries. An empty large-size cup, with the Golden Arches of McDonald's, tipped sideways next to a half-crumpled take-out bag with wrappers visible. This discovery alone made me feel about as mentally rearranged as I had when I stood looking at Bu at the foot of the broken fountain and tried to make sense of what I was seeing.

And that—no denying it—was murder.

But this. This was Chef Claudio Orlandini tooling down the highway shoving a bacon double cheeseburger in his piehole. It felt like murder of a different sort. Goodbye to image. Goodbye to hero. Goodbye. The second discovery was the chef jacket I hadn't seen since the night of the ill-fated dinner party—well, ill-fated for Bu, although everyone else appeared to have a good time—the night of Chef's disappearance. There it was, cast off in a heap on the tiny floor of the little Ape.

For some reason that might have something to do with good sense, I didn't want to touch anything, inside or out, until the commissario's team had a chance to go over it. Who knew where Chef had been, or what he had done? But the sudden reappearance of the Ape put me right off my power walk. Wake Pete? Wake Annamaria? Make some coffee? I scratched my head. The third option won, but first

I'd scope out the dormitory. After all, I couldn't be sure the Ape had been returned by Chef himself.

I slipped into the dormitory and passed silently by Annamaria's door. No sound. Absent, or asleep? With a tiny tug at the door handle, I knew it was locked. So I let myself into the bathroom we had shared and tiptoed over to the door that led into her room. At least she wasn't in there pacing. The door handle gave under my touch, and I eased the door open just enough to peek inside her room. I could swear she hadn't moved the entire night: still dressed, still turned away from me, poor thing. Was that natural?

And in that single second I felt clammy.

Was she breathing? Had the killer struck twice?

If so, it wouldn't look great for me to discover a second victim in less than forty-eight hours. Nell Valenti, one-woman crime spree. Still. Was this moment the source of dread I had been feeling the night before? I squinted toward the bed, willing something obvious to strike me that wouldn't actually strike me, and then I remembered what someone at the Prajna Center had scribbled on a white-board: *Run toward what scares you.*

As Buddhist teachings went, this one didn't get much traction with me, it seemed so entirely counterintuitive, and I frankly had to question what little value anyone could gain from following it. At the time, I had concluded it was meant for entertainment—even monks get the blues, right? Still, I couldn't turn my back on Annamaria, so I moved closer to her bed. Nothing moved. On the upside, though, I saw no blood. I gazed at her intently, exquisitely ready to snap up any sign of life.

It came.

She let out one long, sonorous snore.

With that, I turned hastily and slipped out of her room,

back through the shared bathroom and into the corridor. At Chef's door, nothing helped. The door was shut up tight. Nothing was thumbtacked to his freshly painted door. No confession to the murder of Buford Kaplan. No apology for his impulsive departure. No disclosure of how things had gone with Dalia di Bello. No thanks for the team effort for the dinner party. No bocce scores. I left, dissatisfied. If there was any banging on the door to be done, I'd leave that to Pete.

Off to make that coffee. Then, call Ember to make a plan to meet. I figured her for my best source on the run-up to Bu's breakdown. And with any luck at all, maybe sometime today we'd get word back from the *medico legale* about the time of death. Chef might be holed up in his apartment, with or without the goddess di Bello, and I could ask him outright what he had discovered standing over Bu that night by the fountain, but the only proof would lie in the time of death. As I was heading toward the Ape for one more look inside, in case I had missed something, I found myself remembering the fateful evening two nights ago.

The mountain of work that had miraculously been accomplished that day by way of prep. The moments we stood out here in the villa's courtyard, car after car pulling in. The orderly parking. The elegant dress. The niceties exchanged as we all stood out in the fading sunlight of the courtyard. Bu and Ember. Treni—rumpled and nearsighted—and the contessa. Eyes for Pete, a custom of some long standing, I could tell right away. I couldn't fault her taste. Or even her persistence. Her grace, her fashion sense, her self-assurance, her title.

There seemed something especially wonderful about Italian aristocracy. All the same tastes as the commoners, only with more dough to put into them. Generations of good breeding as familiar as Stella finding prime truffle spots. All the indisputable self-assurance that comes from knowing the names of your ancestors hundreds of years back—and the kind of charm that even lets you laugh it all off. *What's a title, dear one?* It's all so easy when you have that kind of history and connections and familiarities. It's all just *la dolce vita*, only, for the aristocracy, it's just a little more *dolce*. Nothing opens doors or the best bottles of wine quite like a title.

And then the scene from that evening shimmered before me, as the contessa tried to get past Bu and scurry inside. I remember how jovial he'd seemed, his hands on his hips, watching her go. I heard it then. I heard him say, *Still calling yourself Contessa?* It had seemed playful, but so much was happening at once that I may not have caught an undertone. If the contessa was divorced, or widowed, wouldn't she get to keep the title? Wouldn't she still get to use it out in society—wouldn't they let her continue to be the contessa out of some kind of respect? As though some things endure, and matter, even when marriages fall apart. What could Bu have meant? What did he know?

The kitchen was cool and dim, and I was alone. Measuring out some beautiful, dark grounds into the French press I had used yesterday, I added boiling water and set my phone timer for a hefty seven minutes.

I heated water, scooped grounds into the French press, and stood waiting. So all I could conclude was that coffee was not an area of particular Orlandini interest or expertise. With the advent of the cooking school, this could change. Measuring out six cups of near-boiling water, I poured it into the French press, then set the stopwatch on my phone for four minutes. In the meantime, I dug around in a basket of baked goods.

Pete arrived, his hair uncombed, tucking a well-worn faded teal shirt into his pants. "You saw the Ape?"

"Good morning." I poured us both a cup. "I did." I set a plate with flaky, ricotta-filled *sfogliatelle* and flaky, Bavarian crème–filled "lobster tails" on the stainless steel worktable. Pete perched on a stool across from me and stared moodily at breakfast. I went on, "Did you knock at Chef's door?"

"Should I?" His fingers tapped restlessly. "The way I figure it, Nell, he might as well get all the sleep he can, because"—he sucked in a deep breath—"once Joe Batta gets wind of Pop's return, not much bocce is going to get played." He had a point, especially as I recalled the confessional nighttime scene with Annamaria. Picking apart a *sfogliatella* seemed to revive him, and Pete suddenly looked around. I knew what was coming. "Where's Annamaria?"

Usually I prefer to address bad news with generous helpings of chocolate brandy hazelnut torte paired with a couple of shots of Dr. Val's fifty-year-old Glenfiddich Scotch whiskey. (This was the fare the evening I told the parents I would not be joining the empire. The first time. Also the second.) But today it was just seven a.m., and too early for whiskey, if not for chocolate. "She's asleep, Pete. She's a mess."

"A mess?" His cup came to a stop in midair. I filled him in on my time with Annamaria after Pete had said good night and gone back to his cottage. The look on his wonderful face kept shifting with each blow. Her pursuit of Chef after he lurched out the back door during *primo*, her stealth when she saw him standing agitated in front of the fountain, her discovery of the dead Bu, her shock at Chef's running off, her despair, her despair. Pete sat quietly for a couple of minutes, then looked up at me. "Of all people," he remarked. "Annamaria. No one loves him more—"

"What about you?"

Pete shook his head tightly. "Not even me. Believe me, no one loves him more. And she's the one who can place him at the crime scene."

A wider net. What we needed was a wider net. And I remembered what had just occurred to me about the contessa. "Pete, what can you tell me about the contessa?"

Macy darted in, dressed in her lightweight overalls, rumpled Pete's hair, and grabbed a lobster tail pastry. "Rumor has it Alfonsi's got ants, Pete."

Pete slid her a skeptical look. "No ant would dare."

"Alfonsi?" I put in.

"Olive grower close to Arezzo," said Pete.

"Still," Macy countered, adding a second lobster tail to her score, "I'm checking out our trees."

She had started to bound back out of the kitchen when he called after her, "If you find any—"

With a mouth full of flaky pastry and Bavarian cream, Macy mumbled, "Check with you first." She saluted breezily and disappeared.

"Contessa," I prompted. "How long have you known her?"

"She's"—he spread his hands, trying to explain—"a famous Roman socialite. I've known her name for as long as I've known my own, probably. The Conte and Contessa Pamphili—"

"Pamphili?"

"Her married name." He went on, "The conte and contessa were high society for—well, decades. They represented something that still had value, for a lot of Italians, but to tell you the truth, not the glamour of someone like Dalia di Bello. For the young, that Hollywood glamour became a new kind of aristocracy."

I felt thoughtful. Maybe that's what Bu had meant, recognizing the contessa, a very public person, drawing her unwilling attention to the "plight" of the nobility—lack of relevance. *Still calling yourself Contessa?* He might just as well have added, *Nobody cares.* In a world of Facebook and Instagram and Twitter, where we manufacture multiple identities and the truth is nothing else but slippery, the titled nobility seem like a quaint throwback to a simpler time, and a simpler understanding of the way the world works.

If it ever had. *Still calling yourself Contessa?* Maybe someone like the contessa was patiently waiting it out, still drawing on her name, her title, her role as a tastemaker. How long would all her influence last? How long could she weather this phase of passing irrelevance? How far would she go to cling to the top of her very own little mountain?

"What else?" I pressed him. "What about her husband?"

Pete sat back. "Aldo. I never met him. He was considerably older than the contessa, and he died maybe fifteen years ago."

"Any kids?"

"No. Not him, not her, not them."

"So she's a widow."

He nodded slowly. "There was something, though, I don't know exactly what. I never did. It was a scandal, a rumor. Something. And"—he shot me a look—"before you ask, it had nothing to do with me. I've always kept my distance."

"Could Bu have gotten his hands on it?" I wondered.

"Maybe. I just don't know." Then Pete added, "It was old. Old stuff. Nothing recent."

I was intrigued. "How would I find out about it?"

Pete was about to make a suggestion when Chef appeared. He stood just far enough over the threshold that the kitchen door swung into place without bumping him in the butt. For a few moments, the three of us froze, wide-eyed. For a man who had loomed like a monster over the battered

Bu, sped to Rome to declare his love, and consumed a bacon double cheeseburger on the way home, Chef Claudio Orlandini looked surprisingly good. But not happy. Not, actually, much of anything.

"Pop," said Pete, by way of breaking the ice.

The older man couldn't meet his eyes. Or mine. I watched him take in enough of me to remember who I was, which flattened his expression in a way that spoke, *You still here?* Chef wasn't wearing kitchen attire, and he wasn't dressed for bocce. To me, he looked altogether like someone else, straightening his shoulders in a colorless polo shirt and pants that might work for a truffle hunt. On his feet were slip-on shoes that had seen better days.

Without looking directly at his son, Chef addressed the leg of the worktable. "Pierfranco." In my direction he added a mumbled name that could have been Nell or Gemma or Giulia. Silently, I grabbed a clean mug from the cupboard, poured coffee—grateful for the sound and the smell in that dead zone—and held it out to him. His lips moved in the shape of *"Grazie."*

Pete and I watched him breathe. I can't speak for Pete, but for my part, I was concluding that Chef had left his personality back in Rome. Along with Dalia, was my guess. "Sit down, Pop," said Pete, pulling out a stool. Chef shuffled to the seat and then seemed a bit undone by how to manage setting down the mug and inching the stool closer to the table. We waited. He figured it out. One hand was flopped in his lap, the other clamped around the handle of the mug, which bore the colors of the Italian flag and the words IF YOU LIKE MY MEATBALLS WAIT TILL YOU TRY MY SAUSAGE.

Pete caught my eye. "An American fan," he explained.

"Ah."

"Came in the mail."

"Ah."

Turning to Chef, Pete laid a hand over his shoulders. "What happened, Pop?"

Chef shuddered, squeezing his eyes shut. In English he said, "I am so ashamed." In the two and a half hours' drive between Rome and Cortona, he seemed to have settled into a full-body guilt that had ossified. Not the kind of workable guilt someone can jolly you out of, signaled by shy laughs and a confidential air. *I feel so guilty,* wink, wink. *Waiter!* Without a glance into the basket, Chef reached for a *sfogliatella*. "Fresh?" he asked solemnly.

"Fresh enough," said Pete. "So?"

"I am ashamed."

"We understand that, Pop."

Since I was getting the idea that this shame could cover anything from running out of a dinner party to murdering a guest, I pushed for clarity. "Tell us more," I urged him, the way I had heard Dr. Val ask some sap from the studio audience, his beefy hands clasped prayerfully. But Chef said nothing at all, which was certainly different from the studio audience saps, as he sat peeling off gossamer-thin layers of pastry as though freeing a self-adhesive postage stamp from its sheet. I sensed something more was needed. "Annamaria saw you bending over the dead guy." Too much? Pete shifted on his stool.

Chef looked up in alarm. Several things were spoken at once. "Annamaria?"

"The dead guy."

"Saw me?"

"Why did you do it?" I bleated at him.

"Bending? What is this bending?"

"Pop, no one is saying—"

"—kill him?" I wanted to be clear.

"Nell, please—"

"Annamaria?" Chef seemed bemused.

"Pete, really—"

Chef heaved mightily at us. "I am so ashamed."

"Are you saying—"

"Head like a crushed *pomodoro*."

"Are you saying—"

"Kah-plon *morto*."

On this score, Chef seemed forthcoming. The violent death of Kah-plon was not the source of his shame. I cracked my knuckles. "So you say," I said with a slow tip of my own head, not crushed like a tomato. I added tritely, "Time will tell." Pete rolled his eyes. Chef set a layer of *sfogliatella* on his tongue like a communion wafer.

At that particular moment, Annamaria herself walked into the kitchen with her head high. She took in the presence of Chef, who made a begging gesture toward her. Love? Understanding? A fresher *sfogliatella*? Better coffee?

From where I sat, I saw tears spring to her eyes—relief, I thought. He had returned in one piece, still had a heartbeat. She said nothing. Instead, she sniffed and wrenched open the Sub-Zero fridge. The cold air that rushed out seemed like a punctuation mark to her attitude. The woman stared motionlessly into the fridge. Everyone waited. I expected her to ask—while she scanned the shelves looking for who knows what—whether Dalia di Bello had welcomed him into her bed, or whether he had clobbered the American filmmaker, which was certainly how it appeared.

When she spoke, it wasn't a question at all. In her Hanging Judge voice, Annamaria noted, *"Sei scappato mentre il secondo."* It was the tone of voice that had sent suspected witches to the gallows. It sounded to me as though in her eyes his great sin was leaving at the critical point in the meal.

With his head bowed, Chef flogged his chest with his fist. *"Ho peccato,"* he agreed. "I have sinned." And for good measure, because she hadn't heard it yet, he added, "I am so ashamed." It sounded sincere, if a little shopworn by now.

Annamaria drew out a carton of eggs and a small bowl of chopped onions and tomatoes. "We managed."

He sensed a thawing. "I knew you would."

He had misjudged.

She whirled on him. "You—you—you knew nothing."

14

🌿

What followed was a barrage of Italian invective, an aria of anger and hurt, a presto movement of pain and accusation. One of her hands slicing like a sharp knife edge at her other, she oratorically told a tale of years of—many things, all lousy, no denying. I wondered if he could be court-martialed for dereliction of *osso buco*. Chef sat and took it. He had no choice. He had sinned mightily. He had let down his side. Had he been wearing epaulets, she would have ripped them off.

Rosa and Sofia slunk in, landing quick little kisses on his face before emptying the dishwasher. Apparently wound down, Annamaria turned majestically to her All-Clad frying pan, where Sofia had drizzled Pete's olive oil, and sautéed the onions and tomatoes in an act of violence. None of us looked at each other, but as the delicious smell rose from the pan, Annamaria's hand spread it toward us. If I read the gesture correctly, she had forgiven.

Rosa handed her the bowl of whisked eggs. A nurse handing a surgeon a scalpel. At exactly the right moment, Annamaria poured the eggs into the pan, sprinkling diced fresh basil like a benediction, and humming the crescendo of "Nessun Dorma." She interrupted herself just long enough to give Sofia a direction that had something to do with slicing ciabatta. Then she fretted about a missing apron—aprons do not grow on trees, she informed us—and ricotta left out of the *frigorifero*. "Do you want to kill us all?" she asked no one in particular.

When Sofia shot us a quick little sourpuss face, Chef pointed a piece of pastry at her. *"Ascolta tua sorella."* He was telling her to listen to her sister. The world had been set back on its axis, and Annamaria preened. Sofia started slicing happily.

Pete winked at me.

I blushed. It's a terrible trait, and my tell.

He grinned and looked away.

In the kitchen of the Villa Orlandini, something even better than peace flavored with onions and tomatoes flourished. In a flash, napkins, utensils, butter, and hot sauce appeared, the six of us clustering around the worktable as plates filled with second breakfast slid in front of us. When the conversation turned to what was now being called Chef's recent trip to Rome, I watched Annamaria communicate something to Pete with her eyes. For her part, she buttered her toast inscrutably as Pete asked Chef, "Pop, did you see Dalia di Bello?"

Chef glanced at Pete. *"Sì, sì."* Then he asked me to pass the plate with extra basil.

Pete swirled the remains of his coffee. "How is she?" At that, I knew I was dealing with a secondary roads kind of guy, someone who sends his GPS into rerouting fits.

Now Chef motioned for the hot sauce. *"Sta bene,"* he

replied with a noncommittal shrug. The health of Dalia di Bello had been covered.

It was Rosa who exploded, a study in conflicting desires. She dropped her toast. *"Lei vivrà qui?"* On the one hand, she seemed excited by the prospect of a star on the premises. But a quick side-eye to Annamaria prompted her to add, *"Quella strega!"* That witch! And then Sofia took it up a notch. *"La sposerai?"* Are you getting married? Collective breath was held while we all watched Chef drag a crust through the hot sauce on his plate as if he were raking sand in a Zen garden.

Encouraged by his equanimity, Sofia bumbled on in Italian along the lines of *Will she get the villa when you die, will she bring her boy toys with her, will she give the orders now, will we have to obey the witch?* Poor gabbling Sofia was half off her stool. Pete patted her back to a sit, and the rest of us—including Chef and Annamaria—looked dazed.

This was a Vesuvius moment, I could tell, but I didn't know where to look.

Finally, Chef turned red, and his chest, inside his colorless shirt, swelled. "No!" he shouted, more at the world than the rest of us, I thought. Beyond that, the man didn't have much to say. Dalia di Bello is reconciling with her husband, that was one piece of news. And then Chef's face went dark as he muttered that this beloved goddess actually asked Claudio the Faithful to drive her back!

"Dov'è?" I believe we all asked at once.

To the palazzo of Rodolfo Impreza, her husband.

We all sat back, digesting this dreadful, comical news. I could hardly believe it.

He spat in English, since it seemed to make a point. "I give a—lift!—to the husband's arms!" And still he did not call her *quella strega*. What followed then was a chorus of varying opinions that pretty much covered calling her a witch and him a sap, a fool, a good friend, a knight, a clown. Everything was in Italian, except "sap," which was my contribution to the name-calling.

In a dark mood, Chef raised his hands. There was more. "On the way to palazzo, she point to drive-thru. 'Mickey D, Mickey D,' say di Bello." So he, he, world-famous Chef Claudio Orlandini, finds himself ordering a bacon double cheeseburger and a McFlurry. Driving, ordering, paying, delivering.

"No wonder you're ashamed," I whispered. Rosa nudged me, Annamaria nudged Pete, Sofia pushed at Chef. To lighten the unsettled mood, which had been so joyful just minutes ago, when the only flaw seemed to be that the eggs were a little dry, I brought up what had been on my mind, keeping my tone light and casual. Pete assisted with Italian. "Do you remember how we were all right here"—I gestured around the kitchen, patting the air into place—"Macy, too, all of us right here just two days ago—"

Chef grunted. "Before McFlurry."

"Yes, yes, before that. You remember?" Bored nods won the day. "Do you remember when I gave Mr. Kaplan a swift kick in the pants and then, well, told him off?" Pete's translation included some foot action and finger wagging, which led to some gentle chuckles. "Well, what I'm wondering"—here I dropped and slurred my voice—"considering what happened to Mr. Kaplan . . ." I glanced around at the silence, where crusts and coffee cups were stalled in midair. "I'm wondering why none of you has mentioned that incident to the *carabinieri*." Trying to look as innocent as possible, I widened my eyes and opened my hands.

Sofia asked, "You mean rat you out?"

Rat you out? This I took to mean there was a sense that I had gone and done it, after feeling oddly unsatisfied by the kicking and tongue-lashing, that I had killed Mr. Kahplon later that night. If they had told me they had forgotten, or that they weren't sure what to do, or they were worried about the cooking school—whatever, I could have heard it and tumbled it around my mind until it was all buffed and polished. But as I studied their faces—with the exception of Pete's—I saw something deep and furtive at work there, something on which they all agreed. There would be no straight answer for me.

They thought I did it.

And they were protecting me.

I didn't know whether to be touched . . . or horrified.

Figuring she was my best source on Bu's breakdown, I made a plan to meet Ember Weston at the Hotel Italia on Via Ghibellina in Cortona, where she invited me to join her for what would turn out to be my third breakfast of the day. On his way to water the olive trees with Macy, Pete suggested I take the Ape, but I didn't want to add parking to my first solo experience with the little farm truck, so I said I'd walk.

The hotel was right off the Piazza della Repubblica, where Pete and I had collared the director yesterday. I knew my way. The weather was fair. I needed the air. Chef and the others had wandered off to various tasks—one of which was reconnecting with a bocce team. In short, nobody needed me. In fact, after I got nowhere in the kitchen with my question about my kicking Mr. Kaplan flat and telling him off, I would say they were avoiding me. Paranoia has a way of sharpening the senses. And if there's one thing growing up in New Jersey teaches you, it's that a little paranoia is never amiss.

Even Pete seemed thoughtful, scrutinizing Chef, Annamaria, Rosa, Macy, Sofia, trying to figure out what lurked behind their weird united front. At least, if I guessed right, he was content to let them suddenly remember what pulled them together—it got them all past the high-handed drama of Chef's return. "So that's that for Dalia di Bello?" asked Rosa in her blunt way. All heads turned to Chef. After all, how much humiliation could one Chef take?

For him, though, he apparently had a capacity for humiliation the size of the Mariana Trench. *"Per adesso,"* he said with some recovered pride. "For now." We were all a bit aghast. He chuckled fondly. "She is so young and beautiful, she will see. But for now—"

Annamaria said flatly, "Di Bello is sixty-five."

Chef started, "But her beauty is—"

"Thanks to the knife."

Sofia muttered, *"La strega."*

I was about to return to the distraction of the murder, when it was Annamaria who changed the mood, surprisingly. She rose energetically and swept a happy—if a bit forced—glance around our table. In fifteen seconds she had assigned tasks to her loved ones and set the tone by whistling what actually seemed to be "Funiculì, Funiculà" as she cleared plates. In all things but her private life, the woman knew when to move on. In that sense, at least, she resembled Chef himself.

The walk into Cortona took me half an hour, and, dressed in what my mother would call an "off-season coat," which always sounded faintly sordid or unworthy, I found my way to Via Ghibellina and the Hotel Italia. For now, I would let the unspoken pact among the villa's residents go unprobed, and I would see how the day unfolded. It felt wonderful to leave the grounds alone, away from the intrigues and dramas and crime scene—and a staggering amount of work wherever I turned—and let whatever Tuscany was just wash over me.

While I waited for Ember in the hotel lobby, I wondered what I would do when I returned to the States. Maybe sometime that day I should eyeball my résumé, reach out to my usual food industry network peeps, even—even—call home. No, maybe not that. But somehow, as Ember emerged from the elevator and caught sight of me, I realized in my heart I wanted to stay at the Villa Orlandini until I solved Bu's murder. It mattered.

Chef Claudio Orlandini may have been my culinary hero for over ten years now, ever since I decided the kitchen was my favorite room in any abode, the holy place where I wanted to define a life's work, but he was too unworkable to make a reality out of the purpose of my hire. It suddenly seemed likely that I had accepted the cooking school design project as a way of making a pilgrimage.

I hope you don't leave, Nell. I know you want to.

And then there was the friendship with Pete. Was staying through the solution to Bu's death a compromise? I'd be leaving anyway, I told myself, if I stayed through the six months to a year it would take to get the Villa Orlandini Cooking School built, opened, and attracting the sort of attention internationally that it deserved—and that I craved to provide. But there was an end, even, to that, Pete. I'd just be kicking another Nell Valenti tin can down the road.

I was here through seeing Bu get justice.

And it took me by surprise how much that meant to me.

Ember stopped right in front of me, dressed in a bright green tunic and black pants, with ropes of black beads around her neck. Her toenails were green. Her hair was gelled into a tamer style than "electrocution," and I could swear I saw the merest hint of gray roots. In her earlobe gauges she had cleverly put flesh-toned disks that drew no attention to themselves. The Ember of yesterday would have gone for shock value. Today she looked like a film-maker with some chops.

She thumbed her phone into action. "Have you seen it?" she breathed. She passed me the phone, where the *Guard-ian* headline blared: **Noted Filmmaker Slain.** Underneath ran: **Buford Kaplan, 41, Netflix documentarian, was found murdered at the Villa Orlandini in Cortona, Italy. Working at present on Continental cooking school start-ups, Kaplan was filming a dinner party hosted by world-renowned chef Claudio Orlandini when he met his death. On-site was Or-nella Valenti, up-and-coming American cooking school de-signer, and luminaries included—"**

There were two photos, one of Noted Filmmaker Buford Kaplan back in the day when he was a bit slimmer, dressed in a tux, alone on the red carpet. The camera had caught him with an expression I knew well, the one I saw when-ever Bu was hankering to call someone out. The other photo was an unflattering study in human chaos, snapped by someone after Bu's body was discovered and the local cop Serafina had arrived. It was good of absolutely nobody, but certainly made the point of how unguarded we all were in those terrible moments.

In the background was Contessa, who was caught ready to topple over; next to her were Sofia, goggle-eyed at the excitement, and Pete, who looked like he was trying to or-ganize everything; and there, too, in the background, were

Macy, Annamaria, and Rosa in a tangle of flesh. But in the foreground, ah, the foreground, in a photo that could easily have been captioned **Number One Suspect in the Poor Sap's Murder**, what with folded arms, cruel eyes, and a smirk, was . . . me. The paper had captioned the second photo, **Present at the Murder Party**.

I closed my eyes. "Who took this picture?"

"Pretty sure it was the chamber of commerce guy, with his phone. There would have been plenty of buyers."

While Ember and I rode up in the elevator to the fourth floor, where the breakfast buffet was set up on the terrace, she filled me in on my personal nightmare—"Looks like the murder's turning up on all the major media outlets!"—and added dryly, "Not sure this is the brand you want for the Orlandini Cooking School." My mouth felt slack, and as I stepped out onto the terrazzo, I gripped the door frame with both hands. As I trembled my way into a wrought-iron chair, she chirped: "Fix you a plate, Nell?"

"Sure." How I can slur one syllable, I don't know, but that's what I did.

Ember seemed peppy, and the woman had to be a dozen years older than I was. "What do you want?"

"Everything."

"So . . . everything."

"If it's an egg, I want it. If it's a pancake, I want it." I stared straight ahead. "Oatmeal, yes. Fruit, yes. Muffin, bagel, Danish, yes, yes, and yes."

"I got the picture. Be right back." Suddenly, she whirled, digging into a pocket. "Bu's phone." She pressed it into my hand. "I forgot it in my camera bag. He always stashed it there when he wanted to be free of what he called 'the damn thing.'"

I turned it over in my hand, my heart pounding at the possibilities. "Why give it to me instead of the cops?"

Ember looked at me, wide-eyed. "I like you better than I like them."

Maybe, when it came right down to it, that reason explained a lot throughout human history. I felt touched. "So," I said slowly, "he didn't have it on him when he was killed?"

"Nope. But he was sure bothering Treni with it at dinner that night."

"Really?"

"You didn't see him?"

"No."

"Looked like old photos." She gave a robust laugh. "And Treni looked like a bone from his *osso buco* was stuck in his gullet."

"What happened?"

She waved it away. "Finally, I took the phone away from him and dropped it in my camera bag." She started toward the buffet. "His passcode's 283342, which spells Buddha." While she was gone, I tapped Bu's phone and saw an old college yearbook photo pop up as his background. It was a shot of the student staff of a literary magazine called the *Vane*. A typical line-up of tall kids in the back, one of whom was Bu, big even then, only with a haystack of brown hair. But there in the front row, posing awkwardly with flexed fingers, startled eyes, and a sweater vest, was, impossibly, Ernesto Treni, international food critic. Only back then his name was Ernie Traynor. Aside from this geeky photo from twenty-five years ago, I wondered what Bu had on Ernesto. Later, I'd do a quick Google search.

For now, what with "the Murder Party" photo soaring through cyberspace, I would eat myself into a stupor, a place where this kind of colossal mischance either doesn't happen or maybe just doesn't hurt. *All the major media outlets.* I felt wronged. And Ember was right: not the Or-

landini brand we were going for. I could see the course
schedule now: *Enjoy unlocking the mysteries of* il risotto *at
this medieval villa where dark desires loom and the final
course is murder!* I groaned.

The school hadn't even been built yet, and already we
were having an image problem. Were the Orlandinis going
to be hopelessly linked with violent death—like the Bor-
gias? To be fair, Bu was bashed, which could have happened anywhere. Bludgeoning is not a particularly, oh,
culinary crime, which made me feel somewhat better. Had
it been poison, we never would have recovered. In the public mind, poison is linked forevermore with food and drink.

Damage control.

I knew the term, but not how to go about it in this in-
stance. What was best for me—depart for New Jersey with
roadrunner speed—might not be best for Chef and Pete and
Annamaria. So my brilliant decision to stay on hand long
enough to solve the murder was now extended to include
however long it then took to restore normalcy and reputation to the Orlandinis. If that included going ahead with my
timetable for the cooking school, it meant I was tied down
for at least half a year.

Then I weighed the two. Hasty retreat, good for me. Extended stay to trowel normalcy all over the villa, good for
the Orlandinis. I wondered if I could just give them a short
list of tips on my way to the train station. Maybe. But—
here Ember set the Everest of food in front of me—the
unavoidable truth was that poor Bu had been killed by
someone at the villa, guest or staff, and was I really proposing to fling myself into a dark tangle I didn't understand?

"A literal food pyramid," she pointed out. "I thought
you'd appreciate it." Blueberry pancakes were on the bottom, topped by cheese omelets, topped by cream cheese

pastries, topped by a glaze of runny oatmeal. I nearly wept with pleasure. On Ember's own plate was one hard-boiled egg, one strip of bacon, and half an English muffin. "So," she asked with some bounce in her voice, "what do you need to know?"

We both dug in. As I chewed a ripe half strawberry ruminatively, I concentrated on Bu. "When and why did Bu break down, Ember? What had he been working on?"

Her eyebrows drew together, and she pointed her knife at me. "May not have had anything to do with work, though, right?"

I considered. "Right," I said slowly, "but can you speak to his private life?"

Ember snorted. "Not at all. Either Bu was pretty closed about that stuff, or—which is what I really suspect— nothing much was going on."

"Okay, work, then. Tell me what you can."

She glided an open jam pot under her nose, then knifed some of the red jelly over her English muffin. "Remember," she said, "we weren't working together a lot during that time—"

"Whatever you know, or what you've read or heard. I can always verify." Then I added: "I just need a picture." And then, of course, what flashed before my eyes was the *Guardian*'s shot of Nell Valenti, killer at large, impresario of murder. I saturated the foundational pancake with maple syrup and hacked off a large, goopy slice.

Ember sat back as a waiter refilled her coffee cup. Even after he left, she continued to stare thoughtfully into the brew. "I don't think he broke down from overwork."

I couldn't help a smile. "No, that wouldn't be Bu."

"No, seriously. The breakdown came as the pressures of—well—no-work piled up, I think. From what I heard, he was up to his ears in possible projects, mudslides of research, that sort of thing."

"Any money troubles?"

She scoffed. "Also not Bu. I have a good nose for dough depletion issues, believe me. I grew up in the poorest county in Ohio, so I know."

I nodded, not about to tell her my money problems were all of my own making, considering the empire I had rejected, and I was proud of them. All my dumpster-diving own. But I was managing. Ember went on to tell me about the leads Bu was following a couple of years ago, before he did *Sotto Terra* and before he sold the idea of European cooking school start-ups to Netflix.

Up until that time, Anthony Bourdain had a lock on globe-trotting to lesser-known food cultures, so Bu pitched the cooking school slant. How, during the welter of unformed ideas period, he managed not to blow out sooner, said Ember, she didn't know. In some of the net-emptying he was doing back then, he seemed to reel between a professional high ("This is great stuff, huge stuff") and disgust and alarm ("What's the world coming to?"). Killers, it seemed to me, can surface out of either of those extremes.

In Bu's case, which was it?

"Whenever we caught up by phone during that time, he was real scatterbrained. Too many choices. He couldn't settle." She nibbled her bacon strip and narrowed her eyes at me. "He couldn't prioritize. And he couldn't stop. He kept digging and digging. I think he kept hoping all the possible stories would"—she searched for the word—"meld into one great überexposé of foul deeds."

He had fallen into a few stories that obsessed him. The hackability of the U.S. ballistic missile defense system. The rise of C.R.O.P., an agroterrorist association that was bombing Monsanto sites. The DOA's introduction of parasitic microorganisms into developing nations' food supplies. The uncovering of an international shadow group of aristocrats called Praeclarum that invisibly funded Hitler's rise. "So what happened?"

"I think a few brain cells blew out, finally."

"He broke down."

Nodding, she looked thoughtful. "He needed a major reboot, I told him. The problem was, he was sweating his career." All the talented filmmakers, younger than Buford, all the new cyber-corridors of film production companies he didn't know how to navigate, all the din, the volume, the excellence, the mediocrity. It was Scramble City.

It was so clear to me. "He burned out."

Ember nodded tightly. "He disappeared for a while, popping up on Instagram with selfies from a tent in Yosemite, an airboat in the Everglades, a sad front porch in Albany."

"Nothing worked?"

"Not until the Prajna Center."

"And he came up with a softball project like start-up cooking schools in Europe." Compared to some of the other ideas that had gripped him, Bu seemed to have focused on the cooking schools as a way back out of the rabbit hole that had turned out to be a little too deep and a little too Mad Tea Party. I was teasing the red peppers out of the omelet layer in my stack. "What happened to the big ideas, Ember?"

"What do you mean?"

"The hacking, the Nazi backers. The others."

"Ah." She nodded, taking a big breath. "I couldn't say. It was interesting, though; he could never quite focus on one. Or so it seemed. I had some bad moments wondering if he was trying to edge me out."

"Was he?"

"I just don't know, Nell, and we were plenty busy with the start-ups, so I didn't think about the other projects at all. Maybe he'd let a couple of the ideas go. Maybe he had front-burnered something that in his off hours he was still digging around in."

"Would it surprise you?"

"No," said Ember, fingering one of her earlobe disks. "It wouldn't. Maybe six months at the Prajna Center helped him prioritize. Have you gone through the files?"

"Once. I need to go back through them."

Ember's eyes took in the beautiful view from the terrazzo of the Hotel Italia, a panorama of the Valdichiana plain as far as the eye could see. How green and brown and red and cream was my valley, all the colors of a history that had nothing at all to do with Dr. Val Valenti's studio at Chelsea Piers, nothing at all to do with my old apartment in Weehawken, New Jersey, where the clang of the radiators sounded like steeple bells.

My phone trilled.

When it turned out to be Pete, I think I trilled a little, too. "Nell? Are you coming back soon?"

There was something urgent in his voice. "Yes, why?"

A small silence. Then: "We heard from Joe Batta. The *medico legale* put the time of Buford's death between eight and eight thirty that night."

I had to think quickly. "So, Chef—"

"Is out of it, Nell. From what we can tell, thanks to your list, he took off at eight forty-five, so when he ran across Bu by the fountain—"

I said softly, "Kah-plon *morto*."

"Just as he said."

"Oh, Pete, I'm so relieved. Annamaria must be—"

"Hold on a minute, Nell." Pete's voice dropped. "That's not all."

"What do you mean?" My heart picked up speed.

"Joe Batta says they got an anonymous call."

I sat back, Ember's eyes on me quizzically. "Okay . . ."

"Apparently he wants to talk to you about your assault on Bu earlier in the day." Someone had ratted me out, after all. Why couldn't I have just left it alone? Somewhere in the Kitchen Cabinet's sworn defense of me, there was a gaping hole. Each of those faces crossed my mind. Who? Who was it? I was scared, and at that moment I felt sure I wasn't up to my secret adversary. "Nell?" His voice came closer. "Nell?"

"I'm here." I barely heard myself.

"You have to come back," said Pete. "Now."

"When's the commissario coming to the villa?"

A beat. "He's already here."

15

Heading back to the villa on side streets, I was buzzed by a lunatic on a black Vespa that sounded like a giant hornet. As I jumped out of the way, I stepped in a puddle and windmilled my arms to keep from falling. The driver half rose from his seat and jerked his head around. He hollered, waved, and rounded a corner at a dangerous angle. An elderly woman dressed in a voluminous white blouse and calf-length brown skirt shook a fist at the kid. I had a champion.

Then she clomped over to me in sensible shoes, her short gray hair brushed back from a face as lined as a roadmap. She clutched a net shopping bag as though it held some newfound Etruscan treasure and not Metamucil with a picture of an orange segment—*"Gusto arancia!"* The one-sided conversation that ensued was full-out Italian indignation on my behalf.

We trudged along together, and I could only murmur and nod. I don't think in the two blocks we kept company that she realized I didn't know what she was saying. But I think she offered up a *malocchio* against the motorized miscreant, and we were both satisfied. So when she turned into a narrow doorway painted a glossy gold, I got off what sounded like a perfect *"Arrivederci,"* and she pointed in the direction of the cursed Vespa, made a hideous face with puffed-out cheeks, cackled, and disappeared. I believe she had just described the precise effects of the evil eye the Vespa driver could be expecting, something along the lines of the Phantom of the Opera. Next time maybe I'd see him coming.

A gaggle of rubbernecking tourists passed us, their lanyards flopping against their chests. The balding guide was narrating something about La Bella Cortona while walking backward. As I stepped into the road that led quickly to the Villa Orlandini, the sun was nearly overhead. For some reason, it made me optimistic, like I could just snap my fingers at the commissario. But when I turned into the villa grounds, I stopped in my tracks, gazing down the drive to the courtyard.

In addition to the little Ape, still whimpering from its mad dash to Rome, and the ocean green T-Bird that looked too cool altogether to worry, there was the white van for Rosa and Sofia's convent—plus two dark blue SUVs emblazoned CARABINIERI below the red stripes. I have to admit, the sight of them flattened my spirits. They looked substantial and official, and I was worried. It helped to tell myself we were all on the same page, working to find out the truth about Bu's murder. I didn't do it. I didn't know who did it. I didn't know why he was killed. Who can match that for sheer ignorance? I was counting on standing out in the field.

As soon as I reached the courtyard, Annamaria came dashing out of the common room door, followed by Pete, who approached as though the ship was in no immediate danger. Although my *Italian for Idiots* book did not actually have a chapter on How to Talk When You Are Questioned by the Police, somehow I managed to field Pete's and Annamaria's differing points of view on the subject. My nighttime weeping pal wrung her hands, her expression a study in advanced taxidermy, and she hoarsely commanded me, "Tell him nothing, nothing."

Pete countered neutrally, "Tell him everything."

"Give him crackpot ideas."

"Stick to the facts."

"All will be lost."

"Just answer the questions."

"In the name of the Holy Mother—"

"We'll be fine."

"Do you want me to have to kill myself?"

"Not just yet."

For some reason, my advisory committee made me smile, and I realized I would be just fine. I had nothing to fear. "Where is Chef?" I put to them as we all headed toward the entrance to the main building of the villa.

"Pop is showing Joe Batta my olive grove."

"Oh," I said, interested, "that sounds friendly."

Pete held open the door, and we let Annamaria pass inside. "They've known each other since boyhood—"

"Great!"

"—when they were rivals."

Hoist the red flags. "At what?"

"Girls, bocce, how far they could spit, pee, that sort of thing." He sounded offhand.

Annamaria started to turn away, but then she whirled and closed the space between us. *"Ricorda,"* she whispered tensely, *"tutto dipende da te."* It all depends on me? Me?

How did that happen? What kind of world could it possibly be for all to depend on me? This is what happens when you stop paying attention for a moment while responsibility gets tossed around the circle like a hot potato.

No. I refused. "Annamaria." I set my hands on her tight shoulders. "I am responsible for the cooking school—for now—" I couldn't look at Pete. "But that's all." I don't know whether she caught my drift, but voices from the dining room, heading toward us, made her turn woodenly and head like a sleepwalker toward the kitchen. We watched her go. Without turning to him, I asked Pete, "I thought Chef was in the clear."

"He is."

"Then why—"

"It was an anonymous call to the cops, Nell."

"I know that."

"They were protecting you," he said slowly, "to protect me."

"What are you talking about?"

"I know you believe Pop, Annamaria, Macy, all of them, had some kind of pact going to keep that incident secret to protect you, but—"

"How else can you explain it?"

"Do you remember what else happened in the kitchen that day?"

"With Bu?" He nodded. "He was trash-talking everybody in the room. He was vile. I kicked him in the pants, and he went sprawling. Then he whined."

"Then what?"

I thought hard. "Well, after that, you—"

"Go on."

What had he done? What had he said? *I will take care of you personally.* "You threatened him, Pete."

"I did."

A beat. "They were protecting you, not me at all. I was just the first line of defense."

"You were the second line, only you didn't know it. Pop, Annamaria, Macy, Rosa, Sofia, Giada, Lisa, and Laura were the first line. They were the firewall."

"Giada, Lisa, and Laura weren't even there."

"Believe me, Rosa and Sofia didn't waste any time filling the sisters in on what happened."

"It was you all along." He nodded. I felt strangely wistful. Reality checks do that to you. "And now somebody broke ranks . . ."

"And Annamaria doesn't know who. But I'm the indispensable Pierfranco. I keep Pop at a simmer. I handle the business of the villa. I do errands nicely. I pick up cooking school designers at train stations. I grow particularly nice olives that may bring added value to the villa. Most importantly"—he took a deep breath—"I'm the next generation of Orlandinis."

"No," I said, "most importantly—she just loves you."

"Well, I guess there's that, too."

And Annamaria Bari, I was coming to see, had tremendous powers of concentration. She really had no interest in who killed Buford Kaplan on the grounds of the Villa Orlandini. All that mattered to her was that it wasn't one of the two Orlandinis she loved. Now someone from the kitchen that day had broken fealty. Not for a minute would Annamaria wonder about all the implications of this betrayal— why implicate Nell Valenti? Why at this point in the police investigation? Was Pete Orlandini the real target? Was the anonymous caller the real killer of Bu Kaplan? If not, did the caller have new information that needed outing indirectly, without putting him- or herself under scrutiny? All

Annamaria would absorb was that someone—someone, hardly matters who—had endangered Chef and Pierfranco.

With my heart pounding, I followed Pete into the common room.

*B*uongiorno, *Signorina Valenti,*" said Commissario Joe Batta, with a little bow of his head. We sat. With a broad smile and a quick look around, Chef clapped his hands once, as if to say *Let the party commence.* He, Pete, and the commissario appeared to discuss the upcoming olive harvest with great relish, with Joe Batta making some off-color comment about olives the size of *testicoli.* Rumbles of laughter ensued. Pete slid me a wan look.

The commissario was wearing what I can only describe as the outfit of an undertaker from the wrong side of town. The black suit was thin and shiny, the loafers had social-climbing tassels, and the necktie was 1980s skinny, black, with a pattern of what I first took to be dice but turned out to be human skulls, as if they had been shaken out of a jar. From the somber look on Joe Batta's long face, the necktie struck me like gallows humor. No other creature on Earth has the concentrated interest of a cobra, except Joe Batta of the *carabinieri.*

Behind him was a tall, expressionless woman dressed in a bold street-length wraparound dress in a red and white floral design. A red kerchief covered her hair; white-framed sunglasses covered her eyes. Red leather slides and a straw document case completed the look. With his tanned head half turning toward her, he introduced the woman as Nina, his *traduttore.* Giving him the benefit of the doubt, I decided he had brought along his translator.

As Chef headed toward the kitchen as though this was a perfectly normal day—no Dalia, but murder and olives the size of *testicoli*—Pete motioned us to have a seat. I appreciated the wink he shot me as he headed out of the common room, and through the windows overlooking the courtyard, I watched him stride along the cloister walk, off to the grove. I felt helpless, hapless, and hopeless.

When I looked back at Joe Batta and Nina the translator, I found Joe shifting his neck back and forth as he regarded me. It struck me that we think of ourselves in these instances as the mongoose when in point of fact we're just the field mouse du jour. Nina did not remove her sunglasses, Joe Batta slowly unwrapped a hard candy, and I folded my hands in my lap.

Marshaling his thoughts by staring at the ceiling, Joe Batta popped the candy into his sizable mouth and worked it around with his tongue like it was the percussion section in a jazz band. When I couldn't stand the suspense one minute more, I jumped in and nervously asked him whether the murder weapon had provided good information. At which Joe Batta frowned, shaking his head while making negative noises, blaming the porousness of brick. Then it was his turn, and he began quizzing me about my finding of the body, which I thought we had already covered late the night of the murder. I had the feeling he was warming up. Nina's nearly disembodied voice was deep and pleasant, and I had to guard against getting lulled.

Into what, I couldn't say—indiscretion? inaccuracy? blabbing? During the first hour we covered my hiring as a cooking school designer for the Orlandinis, and my last job at the Prajna Center in the Berkshires, in the Commonwealth of Massachusetts, in the USA, where I had met Buford Kaplan and we had begun a *storia d'amore*.

At that one, Nina translated with an infinitesimal smile, "Loff affair."

I quibbled. "Those were the commissario's words," I said reasonably, just wanting to set the record straight. "I wouldn't call it that." I flashed a smile bigger than hers. She passed on this observation to Joe Batta, who seemed unsatisfied somehow. They asked, with heads tilted at exactly the same angle, if I could be more precise, *per favore*? As I studied these two, I knew I had to choose my words carefully. Was everything in Italy an affair of the heart? And if not, is that nevertheless how they understood every relationship that ended up in bed?

How best to be more precise in describing my six-month relationship with the man I knew as Bu? "An error of sex" was closest to the truth, but there was no way to get around how the commissario would interpret that description as just an alternative motive for murder. Love affair, error of sex—either could lead to a good bashing by a crumbling fountain in Tuscany. "A fling without joy" was an alternative that was honest and pathetic, something anybody could grasp. Hardly worth lifting the brick. No-fault boredom and second thoughts.

I settled for that. To Nina I said, "A fling without joy."

A shrewd look told me she knew whereof I spoke. She turned to Joe Batta. The concept I was pretty sure got translated to him as "Bed with nothing, pht."

He went on to probe sharply whether I knew when I took the job at the villa that Signor Buford would be coming to film for Netflix. I did not. But it unsettled me that he sounded like he equated Bu's work with something along the lines of Cecil B. DeMille's. After covering broad areas such as on what kind of terms Bu and I parted, he asked what exactly I had in mind when I assaulted the great filmmaker in the kitchen of the Villa Orlandini—to hear him tell it, tantamount to assassins setting upon Thomas Becket in Canterbury Cathedral—and whether I had a history of violence in my personal relationships.

That did it. At that moment, I knew much depended on my response to this—this—calumny, a word I had never used with reference either to myself or, for that matter, to anything at all—and I glanced out the windows to cool off and prepare my answer.

A car was appearing in the drive, slowly approaching the courtyard.

Let wonderment win the day, I told myself. Raising my hands and maintaining complete composure, I offered my best defense. "Commissario," said I, crossing my hands on my chest, "I assure you I am a very peaceable person. I escort spiders out of my apartment." Was that my best evidence? Nina's mouth twitched as she translated that. He seemed unconvinced. I went on, "When my purse got snatched, I figured the snatcher needed it more than I did. I get along with everybody—which, granted, may be something I should work on—but my relationships are all peaceful, uneventful, perhaps even a little humdrum—" He was nodding understandingly when I made the mistake of zeroing in on the boxy beige Fiat that was hanging back, not quite pulling all the way in to the courtyard.

And suddenly I recognized it. I recognized how that Fiat had been dogging my steps ever since I had arrived. It had been the first car I saw when I alighted at the Cortona train station three days ago, when I mistook the young guy in sunglasses for my ride to the villa. It had mingled with the delivery vans and tradesmen's pickups in the packed courtyard the day of the lightning-swift reno of the worst spots of the villa before the dinner party. It was pulled over with a flat tire as Pete and I had passed it *en route* to the contessa's. And now, here it was again.

I could hardly see straight.

But maybe that was a good thing.

"Hold on a minute, Commissario," I muttered as I jumped to my feet and dashed toward the back entrance to this main building.

"*Signorina!*" Joe Batta called after me.

Outside and quick on my feet, I ran stealthily alongside the chapel, sticking for cover behind the thick, gnarly wisterias overarching the drive, until I came up behind the boxy beige Fiat and wrenched open the door on the driver's side. "Get out of the car!" I said to the same dude who had watched me from afar at the train station. The driver, still wearing sunglasses, stammered at me—in what I pretty much recognized as my native tongue.

When he didn't make a move, I insisted. "Get out of the car!" He lifted both hands in a *back off* kind of gesture, which only made me madder. "Who are you?" I hissed. "Why are you following me?" I watched my hands reach out like the creature rising up out of the black lagoon, and the next thing I knew, I had grabbed him by the collar. I tugged the way I did when I was trying to get a sleeping bag out of its sack.

"Whoa, Ms. Valenti," he said in a low voice. "You may want to walk it back. In fact, if I were you, I'd play along." With just his pinkie he straightened out his sunglasses. "Your cop pal is watching. Call me Hal."

"Hal?" I slid my eyes to the left. Not even twenty feet away stood Commissario Joe Batta, his arms folded, scowling—trying to reconcile the statement of the impresario at the Murder Party that she airlifts spiders to safety with behavior that leaves much to be desired when it comes to human males.

Undone.

I could see it all clearly.

Leaving the villa, leaving Cortona, leaving Italy, might not even be a choice.

"I work for your father," he whispered, flipping a PI license at me. I stepped back from the fracas in the Fiat to take a breath. "Just follow my lead." Then he blustered: "Nell, darling!" Sliding out of the Fiat, he held out his arms. "Rough and tumble as ever!"

I exploded with joy. "Hal!" With that, we laughed, hugged, patted, squeezed, and air-kissed any number of cheeks. I widened my eyes as far as I could just short of mania. "What are you doing here?"

He spun better than Rumpelstiltskin. "Val's been worried about that daughter of his, and I said I'd keep an eye out for her while she got settled."

"Nice of you! Saves him having to hire a PI. Val hates that. Calls them—let me see—oh, yes, dung beetles—"

Hal's eyes glittered. "Oh, I'm sure."

"—and sometimes maggots."

"That Val." The driver shook his head from side to side, fondly.

"But I'm so glad you found the time to stop by for a little visit. I've got company right now, but care to join me for a drink in town later? The Hotel Italia?"

His eyebrows rippled. "Say, five?"

A movement off to the left pulled my gaze. Bored, Joe Batta was turning on his heel and heading back inside. "Five it is," I said, adding, "Hal," and for good measure, "Jeepers!"

"Oh, c'mere, you," said the driver, and we clapped arms around each other all over again. In the clinch, under his breath, he asked, "For real?"

"Check the weather report for Hell."

"Gotcha."

We sprang apart, holding hands like Fred and Ginger in the outstretched way they do before all the footwork begins, and I said merrily, "I'll have to call Val sometime."

Hal swung a leg into the Fiat. "Ta, then, Nellie Belle."

"Hal," I said stiffly, pushing the driver's door shut. I had more important things on my mind than Hal the private dick my father had hired to report to him on how I was doing.

"See you around," he mouthed at me as he reversed, turning the steering wheel hard to the right. When he caught me in the act of deflating, he shrugged ruefully. Then he straightened out the wheel, adding out of the side of his mouth, "Best money I've made all year."

I watched him shift into first. "You sure you're working for my father?"

"That whole dung beetle thing?"

I kicked his tire. "Nah." I felt morose. "I made that up."

"Jeepers." He winked at me. Then: "One more week," he told me, and slowly headed out.

And I walked on rubber legs back into the common room, where the commissario and his *traduttore* sat waiting. Never had I ever felt quite so much like a common housefly. Nina the snappy dresser thumbed the voice memo app on her phone, then nodded at the cadaverous commissario. He folded his long fingers into something kind of prayerful, and spoke just two words: *"La cucina."* Nina, I noted, didn't even see fit to translate. With their heads high, and only their jaws working at the hard candies, they waited. I resigned myself to a complete description—going easy on seasonings of dismay or hysteria—of the kicking of the often odious Bu in the kitchen on the day of what turned out to be his murder.

Actually, I was able to keep it fairly simple, because, it

occurred to me with some astonishment, it was. Buford Kaplan began trash-talking everyone in the room—"I guess it's his filmmaking foreplay," I offered to them, and Nina translated with a meaningful look at the commissario, as if to say, *What do you say we try it sometime?*—and I just couldn't let it stand. Not for any single one of them there in the kitchen with me. But, most of all, it was Chef. It was Annamaria. It was Pete. When I ended the story with a final, "He owed them respect," I have to say I never sounded more Sicilian, and as I dramatized the statement by clapping the back of my left hand into the palm of my right, my eyelids felt heavy with dire purposes.

The two across from me sat up a little straighter.

Joe Batta cleared his throat. I think he had swallowed the hard candy prematurely.

"Any other questions, Commissario?" I asked blandly. "About the kitchen?" For me, the really interesting question was the one about the anonymous caller to the cops, not where poor Buford had shoved his files, so to speak. Who, after two days of silence on the matter, had needed to—as kids across time and space always say—tell on me? Why now, suddenly? Why, especially, since I was the second line of defense against leaving the wonderful Pete wide open to closer scrutiny by the *carabinieri*? Why bring the kitchen incident to the officials' attention . . . at all? At all.

"Two more," said the commissario. Nina was suddenly all business as he ticked off the first on his long index finger. "What happened after the kicking of Signor Kah-plon in the pants?"

I nodded and told him I supplemented it with a tongue-lashing.

"The content of which was—?"

I lifted my chin and said pleasantly, "I called him a jack-

ass and told him to get out." Some things really do bear repeating. The words felt better on my tongue than any number
of sweets. Joe Batta, on the other hand, seemed surprised
that calling Bu a jackass and telling him to get out was what
I termed a tongue-lashing, as if it lacked heft somehow.
"And," he asked, rotating a loose fist in the unresisting air,
"that's it?"

"Rosa came in to let us know the guests were arriving."

"Ah."

"So we all headed out to the courtyard to welcome them."
Not only was it plausible, it was true—minus the Pete part. I
willed the commissario to accept it as is and move on. But if
he pressed about any other remarks or kickings from others
on the scene, I would have to elaborate. If I was the second
line of defense between the *carabinieri* and Pete Orlandini,
beloved by the principals, then I would try with all my might
to do the job. Perhaps a little nudging in another direction
would help. "What is your other question, Commissario?"

Not a question, translated the mysterious and floral Nina,
but it is the commissario's official request that if you locate
files and work notes of Boo-fort Kah-plon, you contact the
office directly. I nodded, adding *"Capisco."* As for his other
question—here, both of their faces grew long and rather
embarrassed—it was this: What would Signorina Valenti
like the office of the *medico legale* to do with the body of
the deceased?

16

And so it came to pass that Buford Kaplan was buried in Tuscany, because as it turned out, neither of the remaining two stateside Kaplans wanted to take charge of arrangements to, well, repatriate him. When the office of the *medico legale* contacted the family, the conversations proved to be brief and unsatisfactory. The cousin was appalled, asserting she hardly knew "Bunton," as she put it. The aged great-aunt was in the memory care unit of a skilled nursing facility and was having trouble keeping the news of her nephew Bu separate from the fate of Archduke Ferdinand.

So, it was down to me, for reasons that made no sense to me—for example, *You're all we've got, and besides you're the ex-girlfriend.* How exactly this encumbered me with the mortal remains of the murder victim, I was at a loss to say. But I, Nell, was the beleaguered only child of Dr. Val and Ardis Valenti, and I had learned at their knees how best to work with reasons that make no sense.

As they left, Joe Batta—through Nina—informed me

that the murder investigation was continuing "apace," and that I should be so kind as to let them know the day and time of the memorial service because he wished to attend. The irony did not escape me that if I thought Bu's body was enough of a burden in life, now it was a true deadweight, and to boot, I had to plan a send-off. I was unsure I would ever be done with poor Bu. However, I made the commissario promise no mortal remains would make their way to this doorstep until the ground was ready to receive them.

Joe Batta actually queried, in English, "No viewing?"

This word, he knows. "No, Signor Commissario"—I came close to adding, *You jackass, now get out!*—"no viewing." The two of them were shaping expressions meant to convey that I was either falling short or sinning big. I smiled reassuringly and said, "It's how Buford would have wanted it."

I waved them goodbye in the courtyard, as two more *carabinieri* appeared from elsewhere—Macy's barn? the dormitory?—whereupon there followed a lively comparing of notes, and then all four of the detectives drove off. As I waved them goodbye, I was left wondering about a few things. Who knew either first- or secondhand about the kitchen kicking that day and placed an anonymous call to the cops? Where were Bu's belongings, and exactly what kind of red wine would pair best with my going through them slowly? Despite what Pete thought, what possible connection could there be between Bu's filmmaking and Pete's olive growing that led first to the partial poisoning of the grove, and then to Bu's murder?

On that last question, the one answer that wouldn't leave me alone was frightening in its implications. Bu Kaplan could have been killed on villa grounds as a way of dooming the villa, the Orlandinis, even the cooking school. A way of guaranteeing failure, loss of reputation, fear in the community, negative press that just won't quit—if this was what we were dealing with, then there was something chillingly impersonal about it, and I felt afraid.

I narrowed my eyes in the direction of the meadows between Pete's olive grove and the woods where the estimable Stella dug up *tartufi*. A nice final resting place for poor Bu, I thought. But then I sensed it was so isolated, so singular, that I would gaze wistfully down in that direction during the rains, during the nights, during festivities that only underscored Bu's grave as a kind of one-off, what with no other graves nearby. It would always look like it was set apart due to plague or meanness, and that didn't feel right to me. And that scenario worked only if I stayed on at the villa.

If, as I planned, once the murder itself was solved, I left Tuscany for home, the new scenarios seemed even colder and more awful. For then there was absolutely nobody who would gaze down at the pathetic single grave during the heavy rains and so on, no one who—after a very short time, most likely—would even remember the dead man's name. Oh, Bu, it was all so sad and impossible.

But he hadn't meant it to be.

Ember made some calls, trying to get Bu into the ground at either the Duomo or the Basilica in Cortona, but these we thought were really his "reach" cemeteries, since he wasn't bringing anything to the table in the way of Catholicism. We were right. It was Annamaria who solved the problem of the burial and told us she had made arrangements with the Abbess of her sisters' religious order of Poor Veronicans, who would in turn make arrangements with the office of the *medico legale* to have Bu's mortal remains boxed and shipped to them. Part of the mission of the Poor Veronicans was assertiveness in the face of others' difficulties, which often translated into a kind of freewheeling hospitality and consecrated ground open to all. We were invited to the cemetery within the walls of the Veronican abbey grounds at ten o'clock the next morning, at which point the rest, as the Abbess put it, was on us.

I didn't know quite what to expect, but the setting was even lovelier than any spot on the grounds of the Villa Orlandini. Rosa, Sofia, Macy, Annamaria, Chef, Ember, and I rode to the abbey in the white van that had disgorged a bunch of energetic Veronicans the morning of the fateful dinner party. Pete went on ahead in the T-Bird by about twenty minutes, telling me he saw an opportunity to check out the garden shed now that the Abbess had come across with a spare key. Annamaria led the way through the rusty iron gate that breached an eight-foot-high stone wall that stretched out of sight in either direction. Passing through, we found ourselves in the cemetery, where we were joined by her sisters Laura, Lisa, and Giada. Everyone spread out, making our separate ways among the graves, hands in pockets, heading toward a newer section.

It was an odd day, even aside from the fact that Bu was being buried. Clouds clumped and evaporated, cooling a sun that seemed unsure of itself. A breeze picked up. "North wind," said Pete as he jogged up alongside us. "Change in the weather." Chef nodded solemnly, clasping his hands in front of himself, as if it was a change in the weather that had brought us all together that day, and not the burial of the murdered Bu. Maybe a change in the weather meant more in his daily life than a very public death and disaster on the grounds of his beloved villa.

As we neared the open grave and the coffin that sat alongside, Pete shot me a little nod. He had found a stockpile of banned aldicarb. I noticed that Commissario Joe

Batta had joined the little group, his sharp, mournful eyes pinning each of us in turn. Bu had been delivered—the Orlandinis were picking up the tab for the plain pine box—and all we had to do was be respectful. We fanned out around the box and the hole in the ground, and it crossed my mind how rituals can be a kind of default behavior when we don't know what else to do.

I watched Annamaria's sisters cluster together, Ember pat the coffin a couple of times, and Pete and Chef in their dark suits stand at attention on either side of the coffin, like pallbearers. Macy and Annamaria stood comfortably close to each other, the way I had first seen them on the day I arrived, hanging out in the villa courtyard, enjoying the fine weather. Skirts and shirttails rippled. Jackets were buttoned up, caps slung over heads, feet shuffled. We exchanged looks.

When the silence lengthened, it became clear that nobody was in charge, nobody was turning up to walk us through this makeshift funeral, so I stepped forward. It was, as the invisible Abbess had said, "on us." I recited "Fern Hill," my favorite poem, from memory, even though I was pretty sure only Ember and Pete understood the words, and when I got to the lines about the owls making off with the farm, I started to bawl. Chef passed me a handkerchief. I wiped my nose and made it through the rest of the poem, pretty much muffing the image of the sea singing in its chains. By the time I stopped, I caught the looks of horror on the other faces.

This recital was followed by Ember, who unfolded a printout and read Bu's filmography from IMDb out loud. Appreciative murmurs ensued. I couldn't help rolling my eyes just a little bit. Out of the side of her mouth, Ember whispered, "Know your audience." At that moment, Rosa sounded a sour note on a pitch pipe, and the gaggle of sisters made a few exploratory hums. Then they sang Billy Joel's "Just the Way You Are" phonetically.

"Salmo Ventitré," blared Rosa, as if she was announcing the next WWE match. As it turned out, she was ordering up Psalm 23, and we all got behind it quite gamely. "The Lord is my shepherd," declared everyone standing around the pine box, "I shall not want." It was good up to that point in nicely coordinated Italian and English, and then the order of things the shepherd does got very murky.

Does he lead us beside still waters first, followed by making us lie down in green pastures, or vice versa? Does the comforting rod and staff come before the set table, or after? And somehow the anointeth my head with oil got mixed in with the restoreth my soul, which was way too soon, but you can see how that can happen. By the end of it, Chef was arguing with Rosa, and Annamaria was glaring at the coffin.

Finally, Bu was lowered. We were all feeling subdued by the time what I had come to think of as the white Veronica van dropped us back off in the courtyard of the villa. The commissario pulled in right behind us, swinging to the left to park next to the Ape. As she alighted, Annamaria announced that a funeral lunch would be set up *pronto in la cappella.* Back home, that usually signified cold cuts, dill pickles, and chips. Pete met me at the van. "Beautiful poem," he said. I shrugged. "No, really. I'd never heard it before."

I inhaled, feeling devoid of any feeble explanations. "Thanks," I said softly.

"There goes Giada." He gave my arm a squeeze. "I want to catch her before we eat."

"Want me to come, too?"

"It would only mortify her. I just want the truth."

I watched as Pete fell in alongside Giada Bari, who was stepping stiffly across the courtyard, leaning away from anyone who came too close. Pete spoke quietly to her, and made a graceful gesture with his hand, for her to come with him. From where I sat with my forehead against the cool window, she had a Mary, Queen of Scots look as she followed Pete, her wrists crossed in front of her as though they were manacled. How she managed to look both featherlight and rock-heavy at the same time was mildly interesting. They headed toward the Silver Wind olive grove.

When Joe Batta came over to me, I wondered how he had finagled an invitation to the funeral lunch. *Will no one rid me of this troublesome cop?*

"Signorina," he intoned.

"Yes?"

"We search Signor Kaplan's belongings." He seemed pleased he knew the word "belongings."

"Yes?" I was sounding less steady by the minute.

He folded his hands the way Dr. Val Valenti did when he was about to confront a lying teenager in the studio audience. "Do you neglect to include Signor Kaplan's files?"

"Files?"

"I see nothing of business."

"No?"

He pushed out his lips, reflectively. "Perhaps you . . . overlook?"

"Perhaps I did." I favored Joe Batta with my most helpful smile. "I'll check around the villa." I had just reduced this sprawling five-hundred-year-old establishment to my one-bedroom apartment in Weehawken.

Suddenly his eyes got hooded. "And especially"—he drawled—"your room."

"My room?"

"Where the *signor* was staying."

Was he really trying this on? "No," I informed him, my cheeks burning, "where the *signor* was not staying."

"As you say."

It was an awkward little troop that overheard the conversation, shifting from foot to foot there in the courtyard. Chef, Macy, Rosa, Sofia. Suddenly all eyes had settled on me with spontaneous, shared dismay that if the silence continued one second more, who knows what kind of files I'd hide—or poem I'd recite. Then they started to move away from me. Chef headed at a good pace toward the kitchen entrance, promising a frittata to die for, which was not a great way to put it, although it lured Joe Batta, who followed. Rosa legged it toward the dormitory, with no explanation, and Sofia gabbled something about olives and disappeared in the opposite direction. When I looked around for Pete and Giada, they, too, had vanished. Even Macy abandoned me, murmuring something about much as she'd like to join us, she had some urgent chores—

Standing by the SUV, Ember called after her. "Tending some crops?"

"Not today," said Macy with a grin, waving. "Anyway, we've just got a small garden patch," she called back to us as she lightly dashed toward her barn room. Whatever else she said was lost in the enveloping air.

Ember touched my sleeve. "Tomorrow morning, I'm on my way out of town."

"Out of town? Where are you going? They're letting you leave?"

She reared back with a whoop of a laugh. "You think I'm the number one suspect? And here I thought we were friends."

"Just envy, that's all." The wind moved across the court-yard, swirling dead petals, crumpled tissues, and a take-out coffee cup in its path. Somewhere a door was slammed shut by it. But Bu was out of the weather for good, buried behind a locked garden wall for all time.

"Apparently, my alibi has been verified, thanks to your very thorough notes"—here, Ember gave me a soft little salute—"so after a chocolate croissant and a large dark roast coffee in the morning, I'm heading for Albarracín to film that final segment of the series."

"You got the green light."

"I did. But—" She paused. "You should know, the pro-ducers are trying to substitute Chef Chantelle Lemieux's start-up in Cannes."

I digested it. "Taking Villa Orlandini out of the picture altogether?"

She nodded once. "How do you feel about that?"

In truth, I didn't know. Would there be other opportuni-ties? Better opportunities? I have to admit, I was feeling . . . passed over. We'd had a day of demented scrambling to pull the worst spots of the villa into some semblance of respect-ability in order to host a "pre-launch dinner party" for dig-nitaries in a position to influence the success of the future cooking school. We had pulled off an elegant, envelope-busting dinner despite Chef's sudden disappearance right in the middle of it.

We had experienced a violent death, then weathered the work of the *carabinieri*, Annamaria's hurt and anger, Chef's sheepish return, and mud. And what I realized in that mo-ment of review was that these were extraordinary people I was working with, people who would more than step up, who would see what needed to be done—or at least endured—and put their shoulders into it. Nobody quit, nobody shirked, nobody dominated. I couldn't have hand-picked a better team to start up the cooking school at the Villa Orlandini.

Was I talking myself into staying?

I felt a little frisson of excitement that had nothing to do with the north wind.

"How do I feel about that?" I felt a glint in my eye. "Tell those producers we have a contract, Ember, and we're holding them to it."

After a moment, she said quietly, "Good girl." Then: "I'll tell them."

I folded my arms, which kept me a little bit warmer. "What can you do for us, Ember?"

She inhaled, then coughed. "Look, I have to go to Albarracín. Two, three days, tops. I'll see what I've got in the way of establishing shots from the other night, Nell. There isn't much, but I can come back." I watched as her eyes narrowed, and when she spoke, as we stood in a rumpus of windblown dust around our ankles, it was like an incantation. "I'm getting a new slant. You think setting up a cooking school is a slam dunk? Orlandini's will be the Against All Odds segment. We'll take the murder head-on, Nell. The loss of human life, the investigation that tramples routine as it goes about its necessary job, the missed deadlines, the deep distractions, the bad PR." At that, with a wide smile, she grabbed both my arms. "But at the end of the day, exceptional food. The product of what transcends."

I think I gasped. "Do you really think you can do it?"

"I think . . . I already have. I'll even shoot Chef Chantelle's start-up. Shorter segments, less like the 'Sixty Minutes' of food, if you know what I mean. I'll pace it for millennials. The rest of us"—she turned to go—"will just have to keep up. Practice your lines, Nell."

"What lines?"

She sketched the vision in the air. "I picture you, decked out in full chef's gear, with your arms crossed, in front of the expanded commercial Orlandini kitchen, saying into the camera"—she narrowed her eyes—"'Cooking well is the best revenge.'" With that, Ember Weston sprang over to the car and called over her shoulder, "Oh, I asked the Netflix producers how Cortona got added. They said they heard about the Orlandini start-up from our very own Ernesto Treni. *Ciao.*"

My quick Google search of the "Ernie Traynor" from the old photo I found on Bu's phone had yielded a couple of interesting documents. One, from about fifteen years ago, was a piece on the rise of college plagiarism cases, citing in one example the expulsion of Ernie Traynor for a pattern of stealing obscure restaurant reviews and using them in essay courses. From what I could tell, it was literary magazine colleague Buford Kaplan who went to the university's honor board about Ernie. Another document noted an award for journalistic integrity presented to Ernesto Treni just two years ago. I could imagine Bu's malevolent joy when Ernesto turned up at Chef's swank dinner the other night—and then mocking him throughout the antipasto course with these memories.

I watched Ember drive off, then turned into the wind. "Nella! *Ciao,* Nella," came a sweet soprano voice from behind me. I turned. Rosa, now wearing a black bib apron, was jumping from foot to foot back in the cloister, waving her arms like she was trying to get the attention of a rescue plane. "Nella! *Vieni dentro! Tutto è pronto.*"

"*Dieci minuti,* Rosa, *grazie.*"

Ten minutes. First, I had a call to make. And for that, I strolled toward the olive grove, held up my phone, and took stock of my present state. Something felt different as I pressed the number for the private landline my parents still used.

Old Nell, the Nell of yesterday, would have felt like a purple clump of anger and defensiveness. And Old Nell would not have been wrong. I couldn't join the Valenti "empire" because I wouldn't have been able to perpetuate that television image of the beloved Dr. Val as a down-home, folksy—if you'd call someone from Jersey City, New Jersey, "folksy"—sage dispensing practical love, sex, parenting, and workplace wisdom. At least not the parenting part. How many times had I listened to him jocularly warn off helicopter and snowplow parents? This from a man who anonymously bought all the team equipment so I could be given a spot on the girls' ice hockey team. The school newspaper published an editorial cartoon of the Nell Valenti Glorious Ten-Carat Ice Rink with my father drawn as Dr. Val Zamboni, a path-clearing machine. I was embarrassed for weeks, and the only stand I could take was to quit the team. Another low point from my school days was when my father became the only Angel-level benefactor (to the tune of five grand) of my high school musical so I could be one of the Hot Box Girls in *Guys and Dolls* when in fact all I could do was shuffle ball change.

He filmed two episodes of his weekday cable TV sniff-fest at Fordham in my sophomore year, which pumped up alumni contributions. He threw a gala for the International Culinary Center when in my first year there after Fordham I mused over coffee with my parents that I'd like to go into cooking school design, but ICC had no program along those lines. Then. Yet. Soon rectified. I learned then that keeping my trap shut about hopes and dreams was essential to happiness. But it really seemed a shame.

When I railed against him, he really didn't get it. "Sugar

Pie Honey Bunch, we just like to support you." And he would go on his number-one-ranked show and offer sensible advice about letting your child fail, all the while with that folksy manner, Jersey-style. Who could possibly guess the big disconnect between advice like "No kid ever died from falling on his ass" and "Just what'll it cost to get my daughter on the team, in the play, or at the college?"

Bottom line, instead of failing on my own, and earning it, I failed anyway in other ways because it couldn't be helped. I lost friends, dates, a certain amount of respect for my parents, and a certain amount of respect for myself—because I could never trust any success. True? Or paid for? Real? Or eased? When I hit the workforce, finally, and made it clear to them that I was resisting the tractor beam pulling me inexorably into the Dr. Val empire, I thought he had gotten the message and backed off. This job four thousand miles away from Mom and Dad seemed to be just the right amount of buffer zone, protecting my independence and rendering Dad ineffective. Until yesterday. His tactics had changed. So, then, would my own, if I could pull it off.

I pressed the number for the private landline, knowing my ID would flash on the phone. After a couple of rings, he picked up. "Nell?" came the voice known so well to millions of television viewers. Before waiting for an answer, he called to my mother, "Honey, guess who's on the line!"

She actually answered something that sounded like "The *Missouri Review*?"

"Dad," I said, taking a deep breath, "I met Hal."

"Oh."

I smiled to myself. My father has always expressed a deep dislike for the word "Oh." In fact, he went off on the inoffensive little "oh" for a whole segment between commercials on his show, opining how namby-pamby it was.

How unhelpful and inadequate it was. How it simply shot the conversation back to the other person without the speaker's having gotten in something along the lines of a more expressive point. How all you're doing when you utter "oh" is buying time, instead of spending time to make a strong, clear point.

And now, here he was, Dr. Val Valenti, saying something namby-pamby, because for possibly the first time in my life, I had taken him by surprise. No, more than that. I wasn't yelling at him, or crying out of anger and frustration. I had reduced my father to buying time instead of spending time, and it felt overdue. "Dad," I went on kindly, "I know you're feeling anxious about me."

"For the love of God, Nell," his words tumbled out, "first that hotbed of Buddhism—if that isn't a front for something, I don't know what. And now this, this, this hotbed of pasta fazool—you up and run off to—this is Italy, Italy, Nell, they've been killing people for centuries and now there you are looking like a maniac on the front page of the top papers, top, Nell, in the Western world, oh dear God, oh what are you thinking, oh when in the name of everything that's holy in Jersey City are you coming the hell on home?" He threw in a "Billie Jean" for good measure, like everything was reasonably peachy.

"Dad," I tried again, "I know you're feeling anxious about me." I heard him sucking in breath like he was about to erupt again, so I cut him off. "Dad, you will just have to take my word for it, but I'm fine."

"Oh, yes? Oh, yes?" The poor man sounded like he was hyperventilating.

To the soundtrack of his huffing on the other end of the line, I went on to describe in just how many ways I was fine. A world-class chef, wonderful coworkers, classy accommodations (here I left out the porcupine), excellent food and wine, cute neighborhood dog, archaeologists, aristocrats—and a project that's a staggering challenge—

"Then there's the little matter of a murder—"

"Yes," I agreed with no blare of defensiveness, "but the detectives will get to the bottom of it. Light will be cast, Dad." It was one of his signature TV promises about psychotherapy. *Light will be cast!*

"Good Golly, Miss Molly."

"It's a little bit rack and ruin around here, to tell you the truth, but it's like Mount Olympus going to seed, the potential is just that great." Standing at the window, I noticed Pete come into view from the olive grove, heading with Giada for the funeral luncheon. "I will get a world-class cooking school up and running here."

"Nell, I just don't know how—"

And suddenly I saw it. "I'm asking you to trust me." This put him sweetly on the spot. Either he had to cope with the fact that he didn't—which was pure Val Valenti neurosis—or he had to agree to a trust he had somehow never managed to reach inside himself and haul up to the surface ever since I was twelve and asking to go out sailing with a friend in her Sunfish, just the two of us. "Oh . . . kay," he said slowly, seeing his own predicament.

"I promise I'll call if I need help."

"Oh . . . kay." Dr. Val Valenti wasn't buying any of it, but had no alternative.

A bright idea. "Would you and Mom like to come to the opening?"

He blustered, "Sure!"

"I'll add you to the guest list." And now—unless they came up with a whopper—they'd be obligated to come to Italy, where they've been killing people for centuries, whatever that means. Maybe I could start a pool here at the villa as to just what kind of excuse for not coming to the opening would be offered up by my father for my consumption.

Maybe he'd have finally decided to have that face-lift. Or maybe his astrologer begged him not to travel that entire month of whenever the opening was happening. Or maybe they'd managed to book His Holiness the Fourteenth Dalai Lama on the show but that was the only date in the whole year His Holiness could do it, he was just that jammed.

When I inquired, my father told me my mother was thriving, tenacious as ever, even finagled an agreement for the show to be aired in Singapore. Singapore! Then, almost as an afterthought, I said, "Oh, and Dad, Hal tells me you're into him for another week."

I could hear him squirm. "Well, I suppose I could cancel—"

"Let him stay on. We all understand each other now. Tell Hal I'll try not to let it get too exciting."

Dad gave me his best fake laugh, the one he musters when he's uncomfortable but senses it's meant to be a light moment. Then he dropped back to serious: "Ornella, tell me again that light will be cast."

"Light, Dad," I waxed, "will be positively thrown."

We hung up.

17

I didn't for a minute believe any of this hard-won new ground would last, but I was pleased I didn't respond with angry blubbering to the fact that my parents were having me followed by a PI named Hal. And I had accomplished some new Nell behavior without pondering other people—I had approached Dr. Val Valenti in a different way, and not because it had anything to do with him, but because I was a nearly thirty-year-old professional woman to everyone here at the villa, and I was acting . . . my age. I felt myself smiling as I approached the Abbess's room, where I could run a brush through my hair and refresh my lipstick.

Within three feet of the patio planter, I knew something was wrong.

The red door was standing wide open.

I stepped silently inside, careful not to touch the door frame, and set down my tote bag. The early-afternoon sunlight hit the room slantwise. I took the center of the room and turned slowly, scouting for any major changes. The room hadn't been tossed, which only eliminated some of the more obvious possibilities—someone working quickly, someone looking for something very specific, someone out simply to disturb me—but there are times when the obvious is welcome. This was one of those times. The only apparent changes I saw were baseboard dust behind the spot where the piano had stood, an old postcard from Monte Carlo that had slipped under the Victrola, and an indentation on the carpet where the birdcage had originally stood before its move to and from the common room.

Had someone searched the room of a woman dead several years? What was he looking for? Why wait that long? Could it have been quite so difficult to get into this room in all that time? Hard to believe. But if I couldn't buy it that Pete's mother was the target of a break-in, then that left only one other possibility, and my knees felt shaky.

I was the target.

If there's one thing growing up in New Jersey teaches you it's that nobody scoffs like us. We invented the art of verbal contempt. We are responsible for sentences that begin with "What." *What, you think you're so important? What, you can't call your mother?* Standing weak-kneed in the Abbess's room, I said to myself, *What, you got so much to hide?* It seemed a key question. It fueled me with just enough disdain that I could narrow my eyes at the place, looking for smaller clues, tinier reasons for a sneak thief coming improbably after me, Nell Valenti. It filled me with a sense of an upper hand in the moment. I knew all my tells. Which was a whole lot more than anybody coming onto the scene. I was new to Chef, Pete, Annamaria, Macy, Rosa, and the others.

I went first into the bathroom, here again careful not to touch anything, careful just to look. I always leave my toothbrush overhanging the edge of a basin, just by the head, so the bristles don't marinate in anything on the sink and can dry out. Here, it was just the way I left it. I opened the medicine cabinet. I always turn any pill bottles I open daily so the fronts face the back of the shelf until, groggy from sleep, I take the pill. Then I turn the bottle to face front: my signal for *pill taken*. At night, before bed, I turn it to face the back again. When I arrived at the Villa Orlandini I was on antibiotics for suspected Lyme disease, having just discovered a tick clinging to my ankle at the Prajna Center, and I don't mean Bu. Inside the medicine cabinet that afternoon, the bottle was still facing forward.

This was the sort of thing I was looking for, four thousand miles from New Jersey, steeled by my Jersey paranoia and scoffing. And there was nothing. Nothing out of place, nothing moved, nothing taken, nothing left behind. My underwear looked undisturbed, which was nothing new. Shirts, pajamas, jeans, skirts, socks, shoes. And then I spied the new shoulder bag I had bought from the paranoid traveler's shop back home. I approached it like bricks were strapped to my shoes, there, where I was pretty sure I myself had left it on the lower shelf of the nightstand. Was the strap hanging a little farther over the lip of the shelf than I had left it? How would I ever know?

I sat down on the bed and set the shoulder bag on my lap.

Now my fingers felt numb. An improvement, I thought, over the trembling.

After a moment, I opened the bag, which still smelled new. I took a moment to admire its cockeyed newness. There was something I had come to appreciate about any bag with two dozen slots, zippered pouches, pockets, holders, and thingamajigs—they are meant to hold very specific items. And when the bag is new—like when my Instant Pot was new—I follow directions closely, syncing with the manufacturer's intentions. It only seems right.

After enough homage has been paid (usually no more than a month's worth) I settle into experimenting with my own Valenti ways of doing things. This, I admit, can have drawbacks, such as the incident of the singed eyebrows from the quick release valve of the Instant Pot, but generally I prefer my own ways. But this theft-proof shoulder bag was brand-new. Everything had its place. Homage was alive and well inside the reinforced leather maw.

I thumbed through my wallet, which was still in the main compartment. The Visa, ATM, debit, Costco, NYPL, and Starbucks cards were all in their usual places. If anyone had taken them out of their slots, it had happened one at a time. Receipts and cash—euros and US dollars—in theirs. Hairbrush, little Clinique makeup case, unopened bags of airline pretzels, all kept the wallet company in the main compartment.

But I slid out my own manila folder I had started to keep on the Orlandini job—pretty thin, considering how little I knew about a project I had been persuaded to take for half a year at the very least, sight unseen. And when I opened the folder, a little the worse for transatlantic wear, I discovered the first wrong thing.

The pages were still loose, all right. But now they were out of order.

For about half a minute I sat there just nodding at them.

I always organize in reverse chronological order, most recent memos, letters, contracts on top, and work backward. I do this without exception, and I was less likely to muff this order than I was to screw up the pill bottles or the toothbrush. All I had in the first file of my Villa Orlandini Cooking School project were two sheets of notes I had made in flight, a printed itinerary for the trip to Tuscany, a scant couple of emails I had exchanged with the lawyer who had hired me, and the letter of hire the lawyer had signed and sent when I insisted.

There were also a few pages I had torn from trade magazines featuring photos of the villa and the great Chef himself, plus a few more distant snapshots of other family and friends. One of these saved magazine pages was slightly smaller than the others—*La Cena*, the great Italian high-end trade magazine, was one-eighth of an inch smaller, in both length and width, than the others. I had set this page smack-dab in the middle of the others, and now it was tidily sitting on top of them.

Someone had looked through my Orlandini file. Done, someone had neatened up the photos torn from the magazines. Not a professional, I thought. Or possibly just someone tripped up by his or her own systems for doing things. Did the Orlandini job have more to do with Bu's murder than I thought? Slowly I closed the file, and as I was setting it back inside the main compartment of my new shoulder bag, I noticed another change. My passports had been switched. Easy to do: both are blue, both the same size. Canada and the United States.

My mother, Ardis Wentworth Valenti, is Canadian. I carry both passports, just in case, although I can never say what that case might be. In my new shoulder bag, there were side-by-side netted slots for travel documents, maybe a cheap and small datebook, maybe your smartphone. I was traveling to Tuscany on my US passport, and because I'm a leftie, I reach first for things on the left side of a desk, a kitchen counter, a shoulder bag. That passport had been in the left slot, the Canadian on the right.

Now they were switched.

What had the snoop or thief or worse been looking for? What had been learned? That my name was Ornella Valenti, that I had a street address in Weehawken, New Jersey, that my thirtieth birthday was coming up in October, that my height was average and my eyes and hair were brown? That I was exactly who I said I was? In two countries, no less? I had to think hard about what this trespasser had hoped to discover. What had I given up that wasn't already public knowledge? Was I at some kind of risk I couldn't even know?

Was someone at the Villa Orlandini threatened by me?

When I took on the job to turn the cooking school at the Orlandini villa into a world-class destination, I had upped my game. The money, the setting, the reputation of Chef—all had been a draw I couldn't decline. It would mean my whole future career. Now I was here, now I was perceived as a threat, and more than I had ever bargained for was at stake.

I set my shoulder bag back on the lower shelf of the nightstand. Then I phoned Pete. When I heard his *"Pronto,"* I steadied my voice. "Someone broke into my room." I gazed straight ahead at the window, where I sat just out of range of the Tuscan sunlight.

A beat. "Are you all right?"

Just as I was about to tell him I was fine, just as I was about to go into detail about what the thief had disturbed among all my things, I was slammed by the truth. The thief hadn't been snooping me out—it was Bu's file. Bu's work file, the very same documents Joe Batta had collared me in the courtyard and accused me of keeping from the authorities. "Call you back," I blurted, ending the call to Pete. How had I missed it? I shoved the mattress aside, and when the blue file folder failed to edge into sight, I went weak in the knees. The thief had found it. What could I have been thinking? Under the mattress, Nell? Really?

My hands went limp at my sides.

All Bu's papers about past projects, current projects.

I went back to my tote bag, where I set it by the door, then drew out the one item I had pulled from his folders.

Future Projects.

The only file that the thief hadn't found.

Somewhere among those future projects might be the solution to Bu's murder.

And I wasn't at all sure I'd like the answer.

P ete caught up with me over the buffet Annamaria had set out, melon slices and frittatas with *pancetta*—basically, Italian for bacon—and parmigiano-reggiano cheese. Giada slunk off to the common room with a swirl of what looked like Scotch. Nobody paid any attention.

"Everything all right?" I asked him.

"Giada and I were just discussing some work she'll be doing for me in the olive grove."

I took a leap. "Penance for the poison?"

He slid me a quick look. "Oh, yes," he said softly. "She'll have to work it off."

"Why'd she do it?"

He looked at the clouds shifting and rolling. "From what I can tell, Giada believes Annamaria works too hard, and that I should forget this stupid olive business, as she puts it, and help her sister more, ease her burden, that sort of thing."

"Any truth to that?"

"What do you think?"

I thought about it. "In the short time I've been here, I'd

say Annamaria Bari wants you to be happy and—how to put it?"

"Wants the kitchen to be her sole kingdom with Chef."

We walked in silence. "Do the others know about Giada?"

"No. Only you."

"Thanks. We'll keep it that way." A sudden thought. "Is Giada the underbaked one?"

"Actually, no. She's the bossy one."

"Then who—?"

He waved it off. "Each of them thinks all the others are underbaked." He helped himself to a wedge of frittata. "Tell me about the break-in."

I felt a chill. "I think it was a fast job. The thief checked out some of my things, but nothing was disturbed."

"Taken?"

I gave him a rueful smile. "Bu's files, which, like a teenager hiding her diary, I stuck under my mattress."

He hummed. "No one will look for it there."

"Well, there's a saving grace."

"Namely?"

"I had put Bu's Future Projects file in my tote."

"So—" he said slowly.

"It wasn't under the mattress with the others. It wasn't there for the taking."

A beat. "But the thief might miss it."

I gazed at Chef, who was presiding over the lunch table. "Just not too soon, I hope."

"And"—Pete leveled his fork at me—"we don't know if the key to Bu's murder lies in any of his future projects."

"True."

He looked at me earnestly. "In fact, I'd say chances are just as good the solution lies in the files the thief got."

"And will now destroy." There goes the evidence . . .

"There's a Sangiovese I'd like you to try. Come."

We skirted the table, where Chef was apparently re-counting some ancient story about Annamaria and himself, much to her feline delight. As Pete poured the light-bodied red wine into a crystal glass, I changed the subject. "I just got off the phone with my father. He's seen the newspapers."

"The Murder Party?"

"Oh, yes."

Pete seemed thoughtful. "And he wants you to come home."

"From the place where people have been killing people for centuries. Yes."

"So different from America." He stopped walking, and turned to face me. "What did you tell him?"

"I told him how full of potential the villa is. I told him how wonderful my coworkers are. How this project will be my masterpiece."

After a long moment, he spoke. "You're staying." It was edged with a little bit of wonder. I nodded, wordlessly. Thrusting his hands in his pockets, he scrutinized me. "Did you number me among the wonderful coworkers?"

"Not by name. But you were definitely in the mix."

Guiding me by the elbow, he directed me toward the kitchen, where I could fill him in privately on my discovery of a motive for Ernesto Treni. The college yearbook shot of a Bu Kaplan with a head of hair and the international food critic formerly known as Ernie, plus the scoop on the charges of plagiarism of restaurant reviews—neatly leveled by the hairy Bu—that led to expulsion.

"So . . . some on-the-spot blackmail?"

"Oh, not even, I'm betting," I told Pete.

"Treni's published in *La Cena*, top food trade magazine, right? Bu outed him once—what's going to stop him from doing it again, now that Treni's at the top of his career?"

"It's a motive," I agreed.

"And a good one." He lifted his wineglass. "In an hour, you'll get to grill him in the comfort of the moss room."

"What?"

"Pop just got a call from Treni, who's coming by to clear up some delicate points about his review before he submits it."

"Good." My voice sounded unconvinced, even to me.

"What's up, Nell? Remember, Bu Kaplan left the table during *primo* to meet someone," Pete reminded me.

Sipping my wine, I stepped closer to him. "I've been thinking. Bu sat next to Treni at dinner, and according to Ember, he'd been passing his phone back and forth, messing with the poor guy right through the crostini and the *tartufi*. Why would Bu have to leave to have a meeting with him?"

Pete saw the point. We agreed to ruminate. Following the buffet, everyone scattered. Pete had to go into Cortona to the bank. Chef casually mentioned he'd swing by the Bocciofila in Cortona to see if anything was underway on the bocce green. Annamaria set about cleaning up the funeral luncheon. Giada professed an urgent need to water olive trees. Rosa put together a plate to take to Macy wherever she might be working.

As for me, I collected Bu's phone, put the incriminating college group photo on the screen, and waited in the cool shadows of the cloister for a bright blue Fiat Panda. When it arrived, I had a bad moment, realizing I might well be confronting a killer all by my lonesome. Was zeal running away with me? Pete knew Treni was coming—couldn't he have chosen a better time to go to the bank? As Ernesto Treni stepped out of the Panda, hitched his pants, and blinked around the courtyard appreciatively, I walked over to him. To my surprise, he seemed delighted to see me, presenting me with a bottle of what he was extolling as a *meraviglioso* red wine. This I accepted with a grim smile—fleetingly I wondered how he could have broken into my room, what with living at a distance from the villa—and then I held up between us the evidence on Bu's phone.

"Ah," he said, peering. And then, when he realized what it was, repeated, "Ah."

In one breath I had thanked the food critic for the wine and pointed out he had a motive for murder. The word "infelicitous" came to mind. My head started to ache.

The Italian accent dropped away like water weight. "How much do you know?"

In the empty courtyard, I contemplated trying to get away with something along the lines of what a fun, cool, old-timey picture I had found of him and his dear old pal Buford. But if Treni was going to throttle me, let it be in service to truth. "Enough," I equivocated. The courtyard was still empty.

"Boy oh boy," said Ernie Traynor. "Bu could never let me forget. Yeah, I got kicked out of school, but I ended up with a great gig here, right? Could have missed it, who knows, if I had stayed in college, so Bu Kaplan did me a favor. No biggie." I felt myself deflate as the international food critic, master of beautiful cats, giver of *meraviglioso* wine, tour guide to the hungry and unfamous, leaned toward me with a delighted secret. "But sometimes you just gotta let the bully think he wins." Hitching his pants up yet again, Ernesto gazed around the empty courtyard. "Saves time, saves brains, saves skin. Take it from me," he said, wrapping it up. "Swell gig you got here, kiddo. Now, point me toward Chef."

I did better than that.

I escorted my former number one suspect into the main

building, and when he headed toward Chef's voice, coming
from the common room, I cruised into the kitchen. There I
helped myself to a mugful of Sofia's dark roast coffee and
hazelnut biscotti and headed back to the Abbess's room,
bent against the wind, to spend the rest of the afternoon
thumbing through Bu's file on future projects. With any
luck, I'd find some tidbits of information that might give me
some insight into why he was killed. I only hoped the tidbits didn't point in more than one direction. I honestly
didn't think I was up to comparative finger pointing.

Letting myself into the room I could call mine while I
lived at the villa, I shivered from the air temperature, which
was starting to drop. I set the coffee and biscotti on the
nightstand, stacked bed pillows, kicked off shoes, and settled myself against the headboard of Caterina Orlandini's
bed. The Future Projects folder was a bit of a catchall for
proposals being shopped and negotiations under way for a
new contract. Here I found Bu's notes about an international shadow group of aristocrats called Praeclarum that
had financed Hitler's rise, a kind of United Nations of fas-
cist money men. At the top of this sheet, Bu had scrawled,
Popping the top off the can of worms! The folder was rich
with paper clips, newspaper clippings, staples, and spread-
sheets. Another sheet had a few provocative ideas scribbled
by Bu.

*Who are the descendants, and what do they have to con-
tribute to the understanding of grandpa's goose-stepping
sympathies?* There was one other Post-it note stuck to the
spreadsheet, under the category of Italian aristocrats be-
longing to Praeclarum. *Great timing, pin the aristo at the
Orlandini dinner party on start-up project.*

Had Bu the filmmaker pulled it off, that afternoon in the
courtyard? I heard his voice clearly as the contessa pushed

by him, her face averted. The sly Bu, with that teasing tone: *Still calling yourself Contessa?* As I stood in my beautiful room, wishing for more insight, I ran my finger down the list of names of Italians who had secretly funneled funds to the coffers of the Nazi Party in Germany. When I didn't find a Ciano, I felt stymied. Had to be here, I grumbled, and looked again. I Googled modern Italian nobility and discovered that under the 1948 Constitution of the Italian Republic, titles of nobility are no longer recognized. *Still calling yourself Contessa?* Is that what Bu meant? And wouldn't it be a dangerous vanity for the contessa to do so if the layers peeled on the Praeclarum onion could lead to her dead husband?

Why couldn't I find the name Ciano?

And weren't my dates off? Any husband of the contessa would have been born at the tail end of the war, so the Praeclarum member would have to have been the father-in-law. Were the contessa and her now dead husband caught up in preserving the great family secret? And was filmmaker Bu Kaplan a sudden threat to the illusion of respectability that they had been burdened for decades to preserve?

I stood up, stretching my back and pulling my sweater more tightly around me. I bent over the gas heater and decided to raise the question of getting some heat at dinner that evening. I wandered the room, letting the sweet smell of suspicion settle in around me. But was I being premature, lured by what looked like a great fit to the solution of Bu's murder? Putting off what felt like my next moves, I splashed water on my face, ran a wet comb through my hair, and flossed. Elapsed time: 2.75 minutes.

I couldn't even decide what to order for breakfast, let alone identify a killer, in that amount of time. Sighing, I stuck my hand inside the birdcage and let my fingers sift the light, colorful feathers collected by Pete's mom. I could identify two of the feathers—from a warbler and a woodpecker—but I felt tugged toward spending all the hours between now and bedtime on my Mac, attempting to nail down the source of all the others. Therein, Nell, damnation lay.

*S*uddenly my phone shrilled at me.
    It was Pete.

I barely got out the *"Pronto"* when he said quietly, "I've got the contessa here."

My eyes widened. "The contessa!" This was unexpected. When we saw her a day ago, she clearly couldn't wait to get away from Cortona. Being caught up in a murder inquiry had rather cooled her ardor, I thought. But now, here she was.

I heard him exhale. "And," he went on, "she says she wants to confess. You'd better come over."

After I murmured I'd be right there, I shrugged into a fleece jacket, which I topped with a fleece coat, then I snagged a pair of gloves and headed out of the room. But as I turned in the direction of Pete's cottage, I felt a wave of nausea. It didn't feel entirely good, closing in on the contessa, but why? Maybe now I understood that murder has two faces. I knew the first: Bu's. Now I was sharing air and space with the second in that act, that of the killer—at whose hands a life was violently ended. Joe Batta would want proof, but as I approached Pete's door, hearing the contessa's hysterical voice, I found myself thinking of proof in a different way. After all, even an overriding normalcy is finally no proof against being pushed past your breaking point.

Pete opened the door, and stepped aside for me to enter. "Did you call Joe Batta?" I said under my breath as I passed him.

"Not yet. There's time for that."

From where she stood in an open mink coat in the middle of the living room, the contessa settled on me with wide, terrified eyes. "Is it all over?" I was nearly inaudible. "What was she going on about when I showed up?"

A brief smile. "Pretty much the weather."

"She sounded hysterical." I added, "I figured she had reached the violent part of her narrative."

"No," said Pete reflectively, "she reached the part of the narrative where the wind blew her hair into what you'd find on a pathetic old boozer."

We exchanged a look. I turned to the woman. *"Buona sera, Contessa."* It seemed innocuous enough, but she stared at me as her lips quivered like a blancmange. But the contessa's response to my foray into "Chapter One: Italian Greetings" was something shrill along the lines of "You call this, this a good evening?" Then she swept her forearms up into the classic gesture of overwrought Italians everywhere that pretty much expresses fatalism. My own forearm responded with what I figured for a graceful gesture toward a sofa. "Please sit down, Contessa, *per favore*," said I, adding, "Take a load off."

The mink was oversized and gingerly approaching rattiness, but she sat, and the coat surrounded her, like a mealtime offering in a cage of the nasty critters, who swarmed. On the contessa's expensively dark Ava Gardner head was a mink pillbox hat set at an angle. Her expression as she looked at me was like fanning the pages of a comical flip book. She glowered, melted, charmed, ignored, seduced, and turned from me. It was impossible to arrange my face into anything that met her chaos of looks. I stared.

What followed, Pete translated as she went, was that the contessa couldn't take any more, no more, *niente—il commissario* won't leave her alone, and he's coming back tomorrow to find all new coals to rake her over. She has no one, no one—one set of red fingernails raked at her sunken cheek—and she didn't know what else to do and came to us for help.

Pete slid a lacquer tray before us, a glass of red wine for me and two shot glasses topped with a dark amber Scotch for them. Pete and I clinked, and Contessa Aurora Ciano reproved us as though a toast was in bad taste. As if she was here to confess to an impetuous murder—I gave her the legal benefit of a doubt on the spur-of-the-moment quality of the act—and we were failing a taste test of another sort. She may never invite us to another soirée, but then, she might not, anyway, what with circumstances now out of her control.

I sipped.

Pete knocked back.

The contessa clung to the glass with two hands. For a brief moment, I had the feeling she was wishing it into cyanide. Pete and I waited. After a short time, weighed down by her mink, which, from her twitching shoulders, seemed to be more problematic than her crime, she began. I expected a twenty-minute discourse on the events leading up to the braining of Bu, some tardy reflection on loss of self-control, some commentary on what transpired out there with the big man by the broken fountain in those fateful minutes in the dark, some final accounting of the colossal human error of it all.

That would be classic confession. Big error, big picture. But when she began, the Italian tumbled out at such an alarming rate Pete could hardly translate. "Mussolini . . . family name . . . splendid palazzo . . . a sack of gold . . ." And then it was over. Nowhere did her confession appear to cover Nazi fund-raisers or the spur-of-the-moment braining of Bu. I sat back, wondering.

Pete leaned forward, wondering.

The contessa kept looking back and forth from Pete to me, wondering.

We were a study in perplexity. Finally, Pete rattled off a few quick questions to her in Italian. *"Sì, sì, sì,"* she told him with an elegant shrug and one of those Italian frowns that's meant to convey *I cannot be held responsible for the whole world.* "Ask her," I said to Pete, "what she knows about Praeclarum." He did.

The contessa's face twisted in an effort of memory. *"Sì,* Praeclarum," she said easily. She wanted to know if we were talking about the nail salon near the Villa Borghese in Rome? We told her no. The ancient baths near the Colosseum? We told her no. She snapped her fingers, sure of her ground. Praeclarum, *sì,* that—how you say?—shelter house for the farmers' market near the Tiber. When it became clear she really didn't know anything about a shadow group of Nazi-loving Italian aristocrats, we just nodded, smiled, and had another drink. After a moment, I looked at Pete, and asked, "So what did she confess to? With luck, murder?"

He eyed his Scotch, then cleared up a couple of points with the contessa, who was reapplying her lipstick. To me he explained, "In nineteen thirty-eight, Matteo Pamphili, who later became the contessa's father-in-law, bought a title from the Mussolini home shopping network." Her in-laws loved it, her husband loved it, and although the shoppiness of it bothered the contessa, it eased her way in becoming a great socialite. And fine parties, she says, ease pain."

"Then who is Ciano?" I asked.

"It's her maiden name. She kept the title but got rid of the in-laws' name."

"Ah." I saw all. "And then along came Buford Kaplan." *Still calling yourself Contessa?* At the mention of his name, Contessa bit her freshly colored lips, edging her front teeth with bright red. Somehow, I pondered, swanning around with a fake, marketplace sort of nobility didn't seem anywhere nearly as terrible. "Pete," I said to him, "ask her about Bu's murder."

Setting down his shot glass, he clasped his hands, leaning toward the woman on the edge of her chair. In soft Italian, he asked her about Signor Buford Kaplan, clicking his tongue as though imitating a cartoon coconut falling on somebody's head.

Now it was Contessa's turn to curl away from us, scowling. It was so clear she was demanding *What are you suggesting?* I didn't need a translator. She pulled herself up straight—the plush and slightly ratty mink straightened along with her—and everything she could square or toss—her head, her shoulders, for starters—occurred. She positively glowed. I must admit, righteous indignation was like a spa day for her. She even ventured into English, "I need support; I don't need lawyer." And with the classic Italian upraised hand twirling like a benediction, she added haughtily, "If I need lawyer, I don't come"—she appraised Pete—"to you."

Contessa stood, smoothing the dress under the billowing fur, continuing in Italian while I struggled to keep up. She admitted she had lied to the police. Actually, she had met the buffoon Kaplan several years ago while he moved in party circles in Rome, turning over the soil for some film he was making, and he found out her secret, yes, and oh, how she fretted he would expose her . . . but—here she said something in a universal language along the lines of "pht," her curled fingers popping open like a burst bubble—nothing came of it, but she fretted, because he had the knowledge, *capisce?*

"At the bottom of the day," she said philosophically, drifting back into her native tongue, the buffoon Kaplan teased, the contessa fretted. Then the contessa licked her lips and gazed frankly at Pete and me. "It was"—she looked dreamily past us, and finally went on in English—"what we did." The teasing, the fretting. An Italian worldview.

I tried summing it up, just to see if I understood her point. "The past was over."

"Over?" She mused, then shook her head. "It goes . . . its own way."

"But—" I tried.

"Because," said the contessa softly, "it should." At the look on my face, she swirled the last of her Scotch. "Ah, all you *americani*," she added with a fond laugh, "you cling to air."

18

In my presence, Pete gave the contessa enough reassurance to prop her up through another possible grilling by the tomb effigy named Joe Batta and to ease her drive back to a bed at La Chiesina just outside of town. He invited her to stay for dinner—Annamaria's homemade spinach pasta with Chef's *pomodoro* sauce—but she declined, citing the need for beauty sleep. In the lamplight by Pete's front door, I saw fine lines in the contessa's tired face. Without happiness, droop wins. And with happiness, droop still wins, but I figure you don't care.

I found as we saw the contessa to her BMW that I felt just a little bit fond of her. For one brief moment she set aside her hard-won (well-paid) identity as a big shot Roman socialite, and I could see how hard she worked to be the gracious and beautiful Contessa Aurora Ciano. It mattered to her. Maybe even to others. She leaned in for her cheek to receive Pete's light kiss. To me, she extended a hand. I didn't agree with her about the past—not when it included murder—but we could still be friends. It was easier now that I could eliminate her as a suspect.

In the dusk, we headed silently toward the entrance into the main building, and I tugged my fleece tight around me. Then I pulled up short. Someone was turning on the sconces inside *la cappella*, and one by one the soft light suffused the stained glass. It was lovely. Pete held open the door, and I shivered coming in from the cold. Chef hurtled toward us, dressed in a pink polo shirt and gray pants, and launched into a rushing stream of high-spirited Italian I couldn't follow. Two words bubbled up, though, and I caught something that bordered on joyful about the difference between *soffritto* and *battuto*—did the Bella Nella know? Ah, a test. Pete seemed unconcerned. Sofia was lighting the final sconce, and she flashed me a shy smile.

"*Soffritto,*" I declared with a heartiness that I hope matched Chef's, who was motionless in a kind of demented anticipation of what I had to say. "Onions," I said, ticking off on my fingers, "celery, and carrots, all finely chopped, and sautéed until"—ah, he was giving me the side-eye now, expecting me to muff the important point—"al dente." Chef was so delighted you would think I had scored a bocce goal for the team. He hollered the translation: "To the bite!"

Now sure of myself, I added as a bonus that *soffritto* is the base of a good tomato sauce. "And"—I held up a hand—"let's not even talk about tomatoes," I said with the kind of smugness that looks like I know what I'm talking about, actually hoping he wouldn't go on to ask about tomatoes. Truly, in Italian cooking, a can of worms—which is pretty much how true Italian chefs would actually describe what's generally available in supermarkets.

I sat down in my usual seat and watched Chef leap to the other side of the table. "*E adesso—*" he said command-

ingly to the still empty room, except for Pete, *"il battuto?"*
And therein lay the challenge. Did my job suddenly depend
on my answer? Did Chef consider the difference between
soffritto and *battuto* something esoteric—or what every
Italian schoolkid knew? Well, if that was the case, the
schoolkids had it over me.

Hoping not to give away my total lack of knowledge on
this point, I thought quickly. Onions, celery, carrots. It
made sense to me that the elusive *battuto* must include
something else, but was it a substitution . . . or an addition?
As I opened my napkin, aired it with deliberate slowness
and a Mona Lisa smile, and set it on my lap, I built suspense. What had my Nonna Valenti used in her tomato
sauce base? And then I saw it in all its bulbous, distinctive,
flavorful wonder: *aglio!*

"As any Italian schoolkid knows, Chef, *battuto* is—shall
we say—*soffritto* with the addition of garlic."

Pete leaned in close. "Teacher's pet."

Chef, jubilant he had not hired a nincompoop, uncorked
the evening's Montepulciano, chattering on about the *pomodoro* sauce he had made for dinner. As Macy, Annamaria, Rosa, and Sofia entered the chapel dining room,
they bore plates with steam rising from the plated pasta.
The ceremony of fine dining. Macy set down a plate in
front of me, and I inhaled the heady aroma of real Roma
tomatoes and garlic sautéed just to the bite, before browning. Chef was watching me. With a sure smile, I mouthed
"battuto" at him. He blew me a kiss. Around here, it didn't
take much. Happy, I fingered the centerpiece, a long and
narrow glass vase with pebbles and olives—some still on
their pretty gray-green stems—intermingled.

Over dinner—and nothing in the known world beats
homemade pasta, so I inclined my head at Annamaria, who

acknowledged the praise—the conversation was lively. Hard to recall that the day had begun with a burial. Hard to recall a north wind was bringing change. Pete and Macy discussed the beginning of the olive harvest and whether they needed to line up more hands—at this, both of them glanced at Rosa and Sofia.

Rosa divulged the five sisters, not including the non-singing Annamaria, were undertaking their greatest Joel challenge to date, namely his "Scenes from an Italian Restaurant"—*"Molto complicato,"* she breathed, and Sofia breathed, *"Veramente"*—and Annamaria clapped. They will help Pierfranco on their breaks. I asked everyone how to turn on the gas heater in the Abbess's room, since I figured I'd be freezing by midnight at this rate, and Pete explained how to do it—but, at least three of them cautioned, be sure to keep the window open, otherwise a very nasty end of *la Bella* Nella. Chef asked in a general way whether Contessa had killed Signor Buford Kaplan, and it sounded like he'd be fine either way, yes or no.

It was my Sam Spade moment, so I sat back and crossed my legs. "No, she did not." From the furrowed brows all around, I was guessing this was a surprise. So I hurried on. "I'm working my way through Signor Kaplan's work file on potential film projects—"

"Oo," said Sofia, biting her lip.

Some excited suggestions for box office mega-hits were floated. "Dalia di Bello."

"That witch."

"Maybe Billy Joel do Garibaldi."

"Maybe Billy Joel do Santo Francesco."

These fantasies were followed by starstruck moans. Rapping my knife against my glass, I overrode them. "—and I am down to Signor Kaplan's material on killings at a

Monsanto facility in Missouri." At words like "Monsanto,"
"Missouri," and "facility," they lost interest and a whole lot
of garlic bread got passed around. "Monsanto," I repeated,
louder, "corporate . . . seeds." At Pete's frozen smile, I realized I was coming up short on Monsanto. I widened my
eyes at the audience I had suddenly lost. "Killings." That
should get them. "Two! Two killings. *Molto grande, molto
importante*," I insisted, and nattered on in English for another minute about agroterrorists.

No dice.

Then Annamaria saved the day conversationally and
purred that according to today's online edition of *Il Tempo*,
Dalia di Bello and Rodolfo Impreza are cruising to Santorini. In the photo they are both wearing thongs.

"Thongs?" Rosa lifted her shoulders as she buttered her
slice of garlic bread. *"Due di loro,"* she said sanguinely,
"too old." She punctuated the comment with a shudder.

"Certo," agreed Sofia, wrinkling her nose.

Annamaria didn't have so much as a word to add.

Chef sat in stony silence for all of fifteen seconds, no
doubt recalling his humiliation.

But I noticed he could only take it out on Santorini.
Making the kind of quick little spitting noise that is usually
in this country followed by an oratorical *malocchio*, Chef
muttered, "Santorini," as though the whitewashed Greek
isle in the glorious Aegean was responsible for all his trouble with di Bello, and Santorini was welcome to it.

Hands got folded—not mine; I was forking pasta into
my mouth—in a brief contemplation of the wickedness of
goddesses everywhere. Suddenly Chef's sun came back out
as everyone else's was setting west of Cortona, and he
beamed at me. *"Battuto,"* he said with a soft smile, then
pointed to his eyes and then to me, three or four times, as

if to say he had his eyes on me. At that moment *a tavola,* as the sisters broke into song about engineer boots, leather jackets, and tight blue jeans, it seemed like a good thing.

W hen Chef suggested *caffè* in the common room, the idea apparently entailed some secret meaning everyone was privy to except me. While I sat on the edge of the Cassina sofa and I waited to see what—besides coffee and dessert—would happen, Annamaria dished up some *panna cotta* topped with Kahlua and raspberries, and Rosa, Macy, and Sofia disappeared. During that time, Chef did some pretty fine one-man charades—the Orlandini version was to act out a movie in just three charades—and I found his *Titanic* particularly astonishing, what with the King of the World move, a peppy bump and grind, and drowning.

Pete built a fire in the fireplace, crouching quietly on the hearth as he stacked the tinder and kindling. Me, I settled back into the sofa, ready for whatever the others brought back. These turned out to be an accordion (Rosa), a harmonica (Macy), and a hand drum (Sofia). This crowd, I realized, would find the Bella Nella comes up short in the parlor entertainment department. I might beg off for that night, but I'd have to rummage around up my sleeve to produce something. Still, I came pretty close to enchanted with the little trio, when Rosa squeezed her way into our hearts with "Come Back to Sorrento." Sofia hung back, striking the hand drum with soft, rhythmic pats, and Macy seemed content with well-placed tremolos.

Finally, I begged off, the first to leave, citing fatigue and the need to finish going through the dead man's files. At their unanimous disappointment, I made my offer. "Find me a pair of size nine tap shoes," I announced, "and I'll give you a little Shim Sham." This was so incredibly well-received that my heart started pounding as I worried that they might actually be able to come up with the damn shoes. They let me go in a stream of murmured *buona notte*s, and I walked back to the Abbess's room alone with just the crescent moon in the chilly night.

For the first order of business, I turned on the gas heater according to Pete's easy instructions, and I pushed the front window half-open, propping it in place with the dowel. Getting into my black Victoria's Secret pajamas, the only pair I own, I stared down with no gusto at the pile of spread-out files and folders on the bed. I had the time, I had the opportunity, but the events of the day had caught up with me. It began with Bu, it continued with Bu, and it could—and probably should—end with Bu, right here alone in my room, but I was beat.

I glanced at the list of his future film projects, having eliminated all but one—and not too shabby for a start in the morning. To justify my procrastination, I opened the final folder and thumbed through photos and clippings. Two guards knifed to death, Monsanto seed labs in Missouri two years prior, three homemade bombs detonated, suspected underground organization called Committee to Restore Overfarmed Prairies, "C.R.O.P.," FBI manhunt, no arrests—all nearly two years ago to the day. Promising to bring fresh eyes and gray cells to Bu's potential project in the morning, I moved the whole stack to the desk.

The teeth got a haphazard brushing, and in the very little light from the rising moon, I made my way in the near dark to the bed, wondering how long it would take the gas heater cranked up pretty high, to warm the room. Sometimes, for me, there's no peace in darkness, but that night it was different. Settling under the comforter, I felt invisible, and it was a kind of peace. The burial, the files, the contessa, the murder, Pete and more Pete—a deep disturbance of a day here in my Tuscan life, but what was good drifted off, and what was bad was banished.

And I was content.

Looking back, I could say I felt no dread—and I should have.

But my mind went to the day of the murder, the chaos in the courtyard throughout the day, the arrival of Bu and Ember in their red Range Rover. Something kept tugging at me, just out of reach, and as I punched my pillow into a wad under my head, I reexamined Bu's interactions as dinner guests arrived. Back to the contessa. *Still calling yourself Contessa?* he had teased the poor woman. And he had acknowledged Treni with something—maybe *Always good to see you*? His opening salvo at his old, plagiarizing pal Ernie Traynor. But what was it with Macy Garner? About her Bu had stepped farther into a mysterious zone. I remembered thinking it was odd. Here I turned on my side, settling down in the room's warmer air, thanks to the gas heater I had cranked to the max. He had called something to the reluctant Macy, something about her being on the edge of crops. Or crops being on the edge. What does it even mean? I stilled my mind, inviting the memory. Car doors slamming, Chef bounding around, Contessa skulking, Bu moving toward Macy Garner, ten feet away.

And then I heard it. Bu hadn't entirely said in plain talk what it was he was telling Macy. He hadn't said *edge*; he had said she was on a *knife's edge*. And as clear as if poor old Bu was whispering into her hair at the end of pillow talk, he hadn't said *crops*, plural, to Macy. He had said *crop*, and I recalled wondering in that moment whether he somehow associated Macy Garner, who had come to the villa through Global Farm Friends, with a single crop. Like the Ocean Spray farmers who just grow cranberries. Not crops. Crop.

It was a very good thing I was already lying down, when I made the connection. Crop. C.R.O.P. There in the dark of the Abbess's room, my lips soundlessly formed the words. Committee to Restore Overfarmed—And for one frightening moment I saw glittering objects in the ashes of Macy's bonfire. A can, some coins, mangled eyeglasses . . . and a buckle. With green threads that had missed the flames. A buckle from the straps of an apron. A green apron. Lying motionless, I remembered Annamaria handing Macy Garner a green apron when it was all hands on deck in the kitchen that night.

The truth hit me hard: She got Bu's blood on it.

And she stashed the bloodstained apron until she could burn it up in the brush bonfire. Later, she—

It was then, from the bed no more than six feet from the open window, I heard the tiny sounds outside the Abbess's room. Soft footfalls on pebbles. My ears strained. And very slowly, a shadow began to cross right in front of my window, opened to vent the gas heater. Lying on my side as still as death, I watched one shadowy hand take hold of the window, push it imperceptibly wider by no more than an inch, while the other hand noiselessly slid the dowel from its spot as a prop. Very slowly, the window was closed all the way, and what someone assumed was a sleeping Nell would gradually be overcome with carbon monoxide . . .

When I found I was gripping my phone under the covers, I texted Pete with fingers that felt wooden. **SOS bring gun.** And as the shadow glided past the window, I slipped quickly from bed, hardly knowing what I had in mind, and drew open the front door, headed to the right, and let go of all caution. In two bounds that could have landed me a spot on the Olympic long jump team, I flew at the back of the killer, launching us in a furious headlong tangle toward the ground.

Her head took the brunt of the big cerulean blue pot of geraniums, which effectively ended her struggle. But in my blind uncertainty of what exactly was happening, I couldn't let go of her short hair, and I kept shrieking and ramming her senseless head against the ground. While I sprawled all over her, wishing I were bigger, tougher, meaner, I heard shouts, and a light crisscrossed the area, then shone full in my tearstained face. There was Pete, brandishing the gun, telling me to stop. "Point it at Macy, at Macy, Pete," I cried. "She killed Bu," I could barely squeak out.

"Nell, move off her."

"She'll get away."

"No, she won't. Move off her, Nell."

More feet running, more Italian I didn't understand. It was Annamaria. I rolled off Macy and pushed my fists into my eyes—so much I didn't want to take in anymore. "She closed the window on me," I managed. "Don't touch it." One of them entered the room and turned on all the lights, turned off the heater and left the door standing open. One of them called the cops. Next to me, Macy Garner stirred, but didn't come around, and I scrambled away from her. Pete sat beside me, and my head drooped against his collarbone. The cool night air felt good, finally, against my skin, and as soon as I could, I lifted my face to the little bit of Tuscan moon that had shown me the killer. The little bit of Tuscan moon that, in a world that suddenly felt like an unfamiliar place, was right where it should be. All I felt was grateful, and I squeezed my eyes shut.

Pete spoke into my hair. "Piece of gum?"

"Gum?" He might as well have been talking about algo-
rithms.

"Your text." When I gave a nod, he went on. "You said
SOS. Bring gum."

"Oh, no, oh, no—"

"I took a chance," he said. "I brought both."

Joe Batta was looking sterner than usual when he clapped
handcuffs on Macy Garner, or Garnet Mayes, which was her
C.R.O.P. nom de guerre. Chef, who had thrown on his bocce
clothes in the alarm of the night, stepped toward the young
woman who had lived and worked at Villa Orlandini for a
year and a half and was now gripped by the commissario.
"Perché, Messy?" said Chef. He turned his palms upward
to her. And in that moment I understood that he liked Macy.
She helped Pete with Silver Wind olives, she appreciated the
villa, the grounds, the town, the countryside, the culture—
not at all an ugly American. She fit. Got his jokes. Lived in
the barn. Drove him to Bocciofila. Carted wine. Mowed
grass. An easy addition to the life at Villa Orlandini. *Perché, Messy?*

"He recognized me," she huffed, hardly able to get it out
through stiff lips. "And"—Macy Garner lifted her chin,
reddened eyes scanning the villa as quickly as she could,
missing nothing, not the old stone archways, the darkened
stained glass of the old chapel, the people—"I never wanted
to leave."

Chef nodded, understanding, but held up his hands now
in amazement. "But the women's prison is in Lombardy,
Messy." Apparently a region equivalent with some circle of
Hell, and Chef's dark eyes were huge with the horror of it.
"Is not the same." He gestured sweepingly toward trees and
sky and Annamaria and dirt.

Then, lighting the way with the flashlight on my phone,

I led Joe Batta to the place well behind the barn, where the bonfire had reduced brush and a green bib apron to ashes. In silence we crouched, and I pointed the narrow circle of light to the buckle. He nodded slowly, drew it out of the ashes with a pen, and pushed it into an evidence bag. As we headed back to the courtyard, Joe Batta was whistling.

Reaching the others, he gave Macy's arm a tug, and she turned away, but not before I caught her forlorn look. "Sorry," she mouthed at me, without meeting my eyes. I have to say, *Sorry* didn't cover her attempted murder of me, her breaking into my room to check out whether I was on her trail, and I said nothing in return. As the *carabinieri* escorted her to the waiting SUV, nightjars called from tree to tree, and I noticed the wind had been reduced to weak little breezes around our feet. Sofia darted forward, yelling a question in anxious Italian at Macy. It had something to do with *spinaci* and *aglio,* spinach and garlic, how to take care of them, as if the entire world depended on it.

With a rumbling laugh, as Joe Batta pressed on her shoulder, guiding her into the car, Macy Garner flopped a weak hand in our direction. "How do I know?" she said with a laugh, then shouted, "I don't know a spade from a shovel." She was still laughing when the car door closed and muffled the sound. In another minute, it pulled away and they were gone.

All of us stood there until there wasn't so much as a tail-light left to follow. I worried we would say inadequate things out of a sadness right then that felt like a flood. I didn't want Chef to mutter anything about bocce in the morning. I didn't want Annamaria to say anything about *caffè* and biscotti in the kitchen. I didn't want Rosa and Sofia to say anything about how maybe bossy old Giada might know the answer about the spinach and garlic. I

didn't want Pete to offer even his wonderful company
to me.

As for me, I felt like one of those swales I remember
from trips to Long Beach Island as a kid, shifting sand gul-
lies shaped by the incoming tide, emptied by the outgoing
tide. All I felt was empty. From the others I heard only
murmurs of *buona notte*—with a squeeze of my arm from
Pete—as we all just went our separate ways, just our rasp-
ing footsteps fading, but marking our freedom, our chance
at another day ahead in the goodness of Tuscany.

*A*t sunrise I was first in the kitchen at the villa. I was
making the buttermilk blueberry scone recipe I had
learned at the International Culinary Center, and I had already French pressed a full carafe of dark roast. I hit the
music app on my phone and was listening to Sarah Vaughan
sing George Gershwin from my playlist when the kitchen
door opened and Annamaria came in. Without a word, it
struck us both at the same time we were wearing white
blouses and gray pants. "Like girlfriends," said Annamaria.

"Like girlfriends in seventh grade," I said.

"Or the convent," she quipped.

Something more was needed, so I brushed off my flour-
coated hands on a dish towel and crossed to her for a tentative hug. At that, she kept nodding, then finished up with a
soft, *"Sta bene,* Nell."

Nell. Not Nella. An imperceptible difference, but I heard
it, and I smiled.

She moved to peer into the bowl with the last of the
scone dough. Then she opened the oven to check on the
ones baking. "Come," declared Annamaria, turning on her
heel and leading the way back out into the hall and to the

room next door. She pulled a lanyard out from under her white collar, over her head, and selected a key, which did the trick in the lock. "The old—how you say—vestry," she explained, proud of her English.

We stepped inside this surprisingly spacious room adjacent to the kitchen. I found myself eyeing floor tile that matched the tile in the old chapel, now the sublime dining room at Villa Orlandini. Here in the vestry the walls were stone blocks, and two long narrow windows coated with centuries of grime faced the back of the property. The only furnishings were large, warped wooden chests with brass fittings where priestly vestments and ritual objects had been held. The wall adjoining the kitchen held a tall and roomy archway that had clearly been boarded up years ago.

"You break through?" suggested Annamaria. "Make more kitchen?"

I saw it. "For the school!" My first thought was about the enormity of the job. My second thought, though, was about the enormity of the job and the sensational, functional beauty of what could be the finished job. I could see it, and I grabbed Annamaria's hands. I was delighted it had been her idea. My own imagination over the last few days hadn't played with any design possibilities.

Back in the working part of the kitchen, I plated my scones and set them out on the worktable, while Annamaria set out cups, cream, sugar, spoons. Soon all had converged, hunched on their stools like schoolchildren dreading the day's lesson on the nitrogen cycle. Chef, Rosa, Sofia, surprisingly Giada, and Annamaria. The fact that Macy was missing didn't escape anyone, I could tell, and we sat silently for a few pensive moments, pulling apart my rich and flavorful scones. The scent of the lemon zest filled the room alight with what felt like new sun. Only Pierfranco was missing. Chef sat up importantly, declaring that today begins the olive harvest, which calls his beloved son to the grove. Also, he helps Vincenzo, whose joints are no good today. Later he takes Stella to discover more *tartufi* while the season—here, Chef leaped at a new word, "abounds!"

Since Pete pretty much knew the story already, I had everyone's attention as I described how, for me, investigating the murder of Signor Kaplan—here they exchanged looks; "Her lover," Sofia mouthed—certain information and moments came together to point me finally in the direction of (I paused dramatically) the true killer.

The afternoon Signor Kaplan and his very fine assistant (here Chef toggled his head, representing another point of view) arrived, and—with my forefinger raised—you may remember hearing Signor confront Macy Garner with covert meaning known only to the two of them. In using the word "crop" he was actually letting Macy Garner know that he knew about the Committee to Restore Overfarmed Prairies—C.R.O.P.—and her murder of two Monsanto guards.

Sofia and Rosa went pale, warbling about all the kitchen knives at the villa! What temptation! I continued, intoning how that moment sealed Signor Kaplan's fate. I actually put it that way—"sealed Signor Kaplan's fate." Trite, but I was coming up short, even full of scone and a good night's sleep, teetering on the brink of sorrow about it all again. This time it was my turn to square my shoulders, breathing in some much-needed strength, and I went on, reviewing the suspicious observations I had from my visit to Macy Garner in her barn room, and then outside in the garden.

"To grow garlic, all you need is a clove, not an entire bulb. And"—I nearly bellowed what seemed to be my final piece of damning evidence—"I found out that asparagus takes two"—here I held up two fingers dramatically—"years to grow, not one, so if Macy promised Annamaria asparagus in the spring, well, they are both going to be out of luck." Winding down, I shot a world-weary glance at the ceiling. Many signs, many clues—I exhaled on the last word—much truth. It was Macy Garner, I went on to say, who made the anonymous call to the cops, to put suspicion on me. Or Pete. She didn't care. She just needed to deflect it from herself. Modestly, I sucked in air and looked at the crumbs on my plate, and told them quietly my investigation was at an end. At the furrowed brows aimed at me, I brushed together my hands, and told them, *"Finito!"*

They clapped.

Chef whistled.

If only my father could see this reception, I thought.

Then everyone broke into separate little conversations. Brilliant, someone said, shooting me a worshipful look I waved away. One of them said, *What a detective.* Someone else muttered, *Better than a baker.* There was generalized agreement on something, and as they popped up in a rustle of skirts and cotton pants, the sun breached the windowsill, and cleaning up commenced to some random snatches of Billy Joel.

My boss, Chef Claudio Orlandini, pulled me into a great hug, followed by kisses on both cheeks, followed by a fond few pats on my head. "Bella Nella" finished off his praise. Then: "Shoo, shoo, shoo, go help Pierfranco. He'll be bringing up heavy baskets, capisce?"

I certainly capisced.

In a hurry, I made my way outside, standing in the cloister, feeling the warmth of the coming day, and shielded my eyes in the direction of the grove. Past the Abbess's room, past Pete's cottage, all the way down through the sloping grounds. Beyond even the Silver Wind grove, where I could barely make out Pete heading my way, the worthy Stella prancing alongside, his arms full of a bushel basket. Beyond him were the waves of Tuscan fields spreading all the way to a beckoning horizon. Overhead the sky was a modest blue that looked like it might very well come to swagger a little bit as the day wore on, sporting thin clouds like calligraphy.

I felt myself smiling as I darted back through the courtyard and wrenched open the door to the Ape that had brought me to the villa that first day, the vehicle that was at my disposal for as long as I was here. I turned the key, stepped on the clutch, shifted into reverse, and sputtered backward, surprised at myself. Out of the corner of my eye, I saw Chef step out of the main building, taking in the sight with his capable hands on his hips.

"Come on, sweet thing," I coaxed Baby Blue, driving right across the cloister walk as I steered toward the grove. One of us was humming, but I couldn't say which, and together the Ape and I bumped over the rough spots, making a new way that had nothing to do with driveways and paved paths. We passed the Abbess's room, passed the cottage, and met a laughing Pete emerging from the grove. With a skeptical look at me, Stella sat quickly. I swung the Ape around so it would already be heading back up the hill whenever we had finished the task, turned it off, and pulled up the brake.

"How do you like her?" asked Pete, grinning at me, rubbing sweat off his forehead with his forearm.

"Stella?" The tawny truffle-hunting dog and I gave each other the side-eye. "I like her. Very able. Very sweet." I leaned down and extended my hand. Stella's head inched only as close as dignity would permit. Then she fixed me with a look that said, *Still no treat? When will you ever learn?*

"Actually," said Pete, "I meant the Ape."

Again I said, "I like her. Very able. Very sweet."

"Ah," he said knowingly, "you know the truth quickly."

I temporized. "Not always." I gave him a shy look.

Then, without a word, our four hands lifted the laden basket filled with ripe Moraiolo olives up and into the flatbed of the Ape, while Stella supervised. Taking a few steps back, we looked at the result. The can-do farm truck I had doubted seemed to gleam in the increasing sunlight. In the back, the basket had all the colors of hard work and Tuscan flavors, blue-black olives and a scattering of silver leaves, and carrying it to Pete's oil producers gave the Ape real work. "They look like they belong together," I laughed. Without a cloud in the sky, Pete and I both suddenly fell silent, sliding each other a long look. In that moment, without saying a thing, we knew we weren't talking about farm trucks and olives.

Peperoni al Forno Ripieni di Ricotta

Baked Peppers Stuffed with Ricotta

*In memory of my cousin Lisa Fein Lang, who
shared this recipe with me*

(SERVES 12 AS A SIDE DISH)
PREPARATION TIME: 15 MINUTES
COOK TIME: 40 MINUTES

INGREDIENTS FOR THE PEPPERS

6 bell peppers—red, yellow, and green
3 cups ricotta cheese
2 eggs
⅓ cup Pecorino cheese, grated (Pecorino is sheep's milk
    cheese, a Tuscan gem)
1 tablespoon minced garlic
1 tablespoon fresh oregano or marjoram, chopped
Salt and freshly ground pepper, to taste

INGREDIENTS FOR THE DRESSING

1 tablespoon minced garlic
3 tablespoons red wine vinegar
1 tablespoon tomato paste

½ cup Moraiolo olive oil (typically Tuscan, with notes of
   artichokes and herbs, but any good extra virgin olive
   oil will do)
Chiffonade of fresh basil
Kalamata olives

DIRECTIONS

Preheat oven to 350°F.

Cut peppers in half through the stem end and take out
the seeds. In a small bowl, mix ricotta, eggs, Pecorino, garlic, oregano or marjoram, salt, and pepper. Stuff the mix-
ture into the pepper halves. Place on a lightly oiled baking
dish and bake about 40 minutes. Remove from the oven and
cool. Then refrigerate overnight.

For the dressing, whisk the garlic, vinegar, tomato paste,
and olive oil in a small bowl.

When ready to serve, cut the pepper halves in half and
place them on a serving dish. Drizzle with the dressing, and
scatter basil and olives over all.

Tips

*To make a chiffonade, stack the basil leaves, roll them up, then
slice them crosswise into ribbons.*

*When shopping for bell peppers, turn them over and count the
bumps. Peppers with four bumps are sweeter!*

Acknowledgments

It takes a village to raise a book. I'm grateful to the following for their help: young filmmaker Yonah Sadeh, for expertise on equipment and lingo; my cousin Andrea Ferrari Nasi, for Italian phrases and idioms; Maurizio Montalto, for the Italian police work; beloved brainstormers Casey Daniels, Emilie Richards, and Serena Miller, for digging into this story—twice!—with me; outstanding editor Miranda Hill, for her close reading and collegiality; my agent, John Talbot, for finding just the right home for this series; the Loretta Paganini School of Cooking, for providing tasty times in an Italian kitchen; and my husband Michael, for everything else. I couldn't have a better village.

Ready to find
your next great read?

Let us help.

Visit prh.com/nextread

Penguin
Random
House